PARTHIAN SHOT

PARTHIAN

Loyd Little

SHOT

The Viking Press ☆ New York

Library of Congress Cataloging in Publication Data
Little, Loyd, 1940–
    Parthian shot.
    I. Title.
PZ4.L7784Par [PS3562.17829]   813'.5'4   74-30250
ISBN 0-670-54063-3
Printed in U.S.A.

To Lê Thành Lân,
the men of Special Forces Detachment A-6,
IV Corps,
and to my wife, Drena.

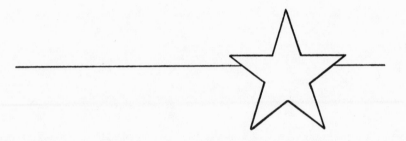

Parthian Shot: The Parthian horsemen were accustomed to baffle the enemy by their rapid manœuvres, and to discharge their missiles backward while in real or pretended flight; hence used allusively in *Parthian fight, shaft, shot, glance,* etc.

— Oxford English Dictionary

One American historian has argued that the Parthians were merely inept horsemen and clumsy archers.

The truth lies somewhere in between, as it always does.

PARTHIAN SHOT

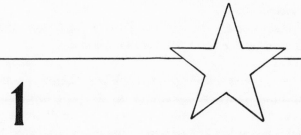

1

Four miles high in the Thangiha Ri mountains of south China, two of the great rivers of the world begin. On the northern slope of a mountain so remote that it has no name, a trickle from a glacier becomes a stream and the stream becomes the great Yangtze, flowing through China to Shanghai and the Yellow Sea.

On the eastern slope, a few miles away, the glacier gives birth to another river, which the Chinese call the Lan-ts'ang. Gathering strength from its tributaries, the Dze-chu, the Pam, and the Seng, the river plunges off the eastern edge of the Himalayas and slices through mile-deep canyons, so treacherous that the Kublai Khan lost a quarter of a million men trying to cross them. The river falls out of China fast and the chill is long gone from the water by the time it separates Laos from Burma and from Thailand.

The river is now called the Mekong. It twists and loops through Cambodia and finally spreads its fingers over Vietnam's delta. The river moves more slowly here, sluggishly across the flat land, perhaps weary after its twenty-six-hundred-mile journey.

Fifteen hundred miles north of the Thangiha Ri lies the Gobi

Desert, and during June and July the sun heats the sand to 130 degrees Fahrenheit every day. The air becomes an enormous geyser of heat, almost sirocco, rushing to the sky. So great is its movement that far to the south, out over the South China Sea, the winds turn inland, drawn by that inferno and dragging water from the ocean across Southeastern Asia.

By late July the rains come every afternoon in South Vietnam. And the Mekong, swollen and cupreous, spills over its banks into the rice fields.

Nineteen sixty-four was the Year of the Dragon and during that summer the rains fell more than usual.

THE FIRST clue that Top was back from Danang was noise in Nan Phuc. It was still pok time, so everyone was asleep except a few kids. I was sunbathing on the sandbags around my machine-gun bunker, daydreaming of a long-legged blonde in a blue bikini who had just asked me to rub suntan lotion on her back. I was sliding my hand down her back, far down, and I knew she was wondering if I was going to slip my fingers beneath her bikini bottom, when I heard the kids.

I sat up and shielded my eyes against a sun that was smothering us with 90-degree heat that felt like 110 with the high humidity we had. Sweat rolled down my body like rainwater. A passel of ankle-biters were surrounding someone —it must be Top. Downtown Nan Phuc, such as it was, existed three hundred yards away and beyond our concrete bunkers, barbed wire, punji stakes, electrically triggered gasoline drums, antipersonnel mines, and moat.

Top had been gone eleven days and we were anxious for some word. We were also anxious to get Second Lieutenant James Wheaty off our backs. Wheaty had driven us nearly crazy with his constant indecisions and, worse, his worrying about his indecisions.

As I hopped off the sandbags and shrugged on my camouflaged shirt, I wondered how Top had gotten back.

He'd probably caught a ride up the Bassac. Nan Phuc, a village of some five hundred people, huddled on the bank of the Bassac River, a branch of the mighty Mekong during the dry season. During the monsoons, which had begun a month ago, all the rivers in the delta lost their identities to the floods.

I felt better with the water rising. Viet Cong activity had increased in the last few months, and I liked the idea of being in a sampan surrounded by acres of water instead of tripping the light fantastic on a jungle trail no wider than a coffin.

Top had gone to Danang, headquarters for the Eighth Special Forces Group, to find out why our six-man team had not been relieved. It was now October 2, 1964, and our six-month tour had ended September 18.

It wasn't as if the Army had told us to wait; they hadn't told us anything. To complicate things even more, two days before we were to be relieved we blew a beat frequency oscillator on our AN/GRC 109 radio and couldn't reach the C-team. We tried going through Vietnamese radio channels but got nowhere.

I didn't particularly mind. The pay was good and I liked Nan Phuc. With only nine months left in the Army, the idea of picking up cigarette butts at Fort Bragg and standing inspections on Saturday mornings was less than enchanting. Besides, there had been persistent rumors that the Army was upping our tours in Vietnam to a full year. Maybe that was what had happened.

The pencil pushers in Saigon called our operation here a Civilian Irregular Defense Group (CIDG). If that doesn't ring a bell, how about New Life Hamlet, or Popular Forces, or Maze Hamlet, or Mobile Action Cadre, or Strategic Hamlet? There seemed to be a theory that the best way to improve our pacification plan was to change its name from time to time.

Our mission in Nan Phuc was, to quote from Special Forces Letter of Instruction-9 (Revised), ". . . a phased and combined military-civilian counterinsurgency effort designed to destroy the Viet Cong infrastructure and create a secure environment and establish firm governmental control over the population by locally recruiting a strike force which would not only provide a military vehicle but give an exploitable entree to the populace."

Which meant we were here to recruit some of the local boys, train them, and let them defend themselves.

What it really meant was that the government of South Vietnam had been unable to do the job. So they asked us to do it. Actually, they asked the Central Intelligence Agency for help and the CIA told us to do it. At least, it had started out that way. But three months ago the CIA had lost a vicious political dogfight for control of Special Forces in Vietnam and now we took our orders from the regular Army. That is, until we lost touch with the Army.

Special Forces teams had come here two years ago, and today Nan Phuc had five companies of men, a warehouse of guns and ammunition, and a damned good dispensary. We and the Viet Cong had been toe to toe a half dozen times in the past six months, and we had held our own almost every time. In a guerrilla war that's nearly as good as winning. The worst licking we had taken was in a day-long attack at Hiep Phung when the Cong showed up with an old PT boat, mounted underneath a fifty-caliber machine gun. Six CIDG were killed and another twenty-one wounded. The VC were still using the Bassac for infiltration and opium smuggling, but we were hurting them.

I rubbed my sleeve across my bald head to sop up the sweat. You might as well know now: I had been getting bald since I was eighteen, five years ago. In truth, there was no more "getting" to it. My head had achieved the true splendor of complete genetic alopecia—hereditary baldness. All the males on my father's side were bald by the time they were twenty-one. Maybe that was why I joined Special Forces—the green beret covered more than sins of commission.

4

I grabbed my carbine and went into the team house to get a beer and roust Lieutenant Wheaty. There was just me (I'm Staff Sergeant Phil Warren) and Wheaty in camp. SSG Leroy Santee, our black supply sergeant, who, I found out later, thought he was Oriental, was on a patrol and should be back tonight. Sergeant Lance Cranston, our brilliant but strange communications man, was in Nan Phuc, shooting pool with the constabulary. Nan Phuc needed a policeman like it needed more rain. But Vietnam's former prime minister, Ngo Dinh Diem, in a futile effort to establish rapport with the common folk, had appointed the son of the village chief as Nan Phuc's official police captain two years ago. Since then our man in khaki had not heard a single word (except for his monthly salary of three thousand piasters, about twenty dollars) from the government. He had no idea what a police captain did, so he bought a felt-covered pool table and set it up in his living room. It was the only pool table in the delta, maybe in all South Vietnam. Cranston, who was from New York, spent most of his free time shooting pool there. Our sixth team member was First Sergeant Matthew Hood, who handled intelligence and who was being spooklike somewhere.

I hollered at Wheaty and opened a Ba Muoi Ba beer. Ba Muoi Ba (it literally means thirty-three) was the cheapest and, therefore, most famous Vietnamese beer, well known for its delicate bouquet—a bouquet achieved by careful aging for a good forty-five minutes—and for its taste, which was an understatement of its nickname, Tiger Piss.

As Wheaty came into the team room, Top walked through the door, dropped his duffel bag, and said, "Hello, shitheads."

Master Sergeant Wiley O'Hara was back. He opened a beer, threw his beret on the table, and sat down heavily. It was good to see that worn, leathery, lined face again.

"Goddamn, it's great to be here. There's a bunch of crazy people out there," said Top.

"We're glad you're back, too," said Wheaty. "It's been nearly two weeks."

"I almost didn't make it," said Top, swallowing beer noisily. "Somebody took some potshots at us."

"On the Bassac?" I asked. We traveled the river every few weeks, usually down the fifteen miles to Chau An. Although it wasn't much bigger than Nan Phuc, some hard-to-get supplies could be bought there. Only once before had someone sniped at us.

"Yes, but south of Chau An, about sixty miles. I caught a ride with a fisherman from Can Tho yesterday morning." Can Tho was the largest city in the delta and straddled the Bassac 135 miles beyond Chau An. "I don't know if the VC saw me or if they knew I'd be in that boat or if they've taken to shooting at fishermen now. It came from the far shore and sounded like an old Enfield." Top paused and lit a cigarette. "The river is really rising fast. I was going to take a sicylo up from Chau An, but the word was that the path was already impassable. I caught a ride with another fisherman."

Irrigation canals sliced through the riverbank every half mile or so to let water into the paddies. During the dry season, a sicylo—a three-wheeled bicycle for hire which could carry the driver and two other people—would be carried across the ditch by the driver and his passengers. During the floods only a single plank, at best, spanned them.

"Well?" asked Wheaty, beating me by only a second.

"Well, what?" returned Top.

"What did they say in Danang? When are we going home?"

"That's a long story, Lieutenant. But as near as I can tell, the six of us are back at Fort Bragg."

"Come on, Top. Quit kidding," said Wheaty, grinning.

"That's exactly what I told the captain, the major, and the colonel, and damned if they almost didn't convince me we're not here any more." Top swung his feet up on the kitchen table. "I got to Danang last Thursday and you wouldn't recognize it any more. They got an Air Force commando unit up there, Vietnamese Special Forces, a bunch of legs, mama-sans selling everything from San Miguels to their daughters, and we're extending the airstrip to handle jets. I'd almost forgotten how much fucking red tape the Army has. I started with a captain who said operational control of A-teams was now being handled by a major, who just arrived from the States. After a day of waiting around with my finger up my ass I finally saw the major, who told me Team A-376 had been withdrawn on September fifteenth and had been processed out and shipped home on a C-140 two days later. In fact, he showed me a set of orders assigning us to the Third Special Forces Group at Bragg. Which is bad, 'cause I was hoping we'd get in the Fifth. You know the Fifth commander is old Rusty Edwards, a goddamned good soldier—"

"Wait a minute," shouted Wheaty. "We didn't get shipped anywhere! We're—"

"Don't get your shit hot, Lieutenant, I'm coming to that," said Top. "So I showed him my ID card and our original orders, and he said, 'Yes, it seems a little unusual. Maybe you'd better talk with the colonel.' So I sat on my duff for another day before I finally got to see Colonel Preston. He was that CO at Ranger School who thought he might make general before he retired if he got into Special Forces. He was a straight-leg, non-Airborne type and couldn't do the PT at jump school so they changed the rules, saying that all colonels who were married and over fifty-five years old and had four kids and were from East Jesus, South Dakota, didn't have to do but half the PT. Anyway, I went in to see him and gave him our situation. He thought it over and called the major in."

Top dropped his feet off the table.

" 'Tell me, Major,' " Top said in a gruff imitation of the colonel. " 'This man says his team is still out there in . . . ah . . . at a camp.'

" 'No, sir,' " said Top, mincing his words effetely, mocking the major. " 'This man is a member of Detachment A-376, which was officially returned to Bragg on seventeen September.'

" 'What about their team replacement?' the colonel asked.

" 'The team was not replaced. As you may recall, sir, our TO&E called for a demonstration team at headquarters. Since A-376 was a half team anyway, we decided to use that manpower to augment the team on special assignment here.' The major left and Preston leaned back and said something like, 'This would look bad if, in fact, your team were still here.' " Top shook his head in amazement.

"He said he had no provision for interfering with a team assigned to the Third Special Forces, and then he started talking about the Agency. He allowed as how he understood how the Agency worked and that he wouldn't interfere with our orders. And that, anyway, we were officially back at Bragg. I said, 'Well, fuck me, Colonel. I ain't seen the Agency in over three months and I ain't at Bragg.' He mumbled something about how he understood it all and that he would check into it and let us know. It was the craziest thing I ever saw," said Top.

"And that's it?" asked Wheaty unbelievingly.

"Preston's top dog. I waited around three days and didn't hear anything. I found out he went to Saigon to meet some senator and wasn't expected back for a week. I figured I'd get my ass back to camp. He'll find the mistake in a couple days and let us know."

"I don't believe it," I said. "That is ridiculous." Unfortunately, it was believable.

"What do we do now?" asked Wheaty.

"Shit, sir, you're the officer," Top said, smiling.

That stopped Wheaty for a moment. While he seemed flattered at Top's reference to his theoretical station in life, he looked terrified about the possibility of making a decision.

Wheaty stood up and retied his boots. He moved around a lot when he was trying to appear calm and collected.

Wheaty finally said, in his artificial-bass officer's voice, "Men, we'll have a team meeting tonight and see where we stand." He said it while watching Top to see whether or not O'Hara thought it was a good idea. As usual, Top ignored him.

Wheaty never failed to astound me. I think he was incapable of looking at himself from the outside. When he was trying to be an officer, he dropped his voice about two octaves. Apparently he thought this showed leadership. But obviously no one had ever explained to Wheaty that his artificial bass voice sounded absurd; his voice cracked into his normal tenor every few words, making him sound like a teenager. Wheaty also said "men" a lot, because in OCS they'd taught him that it made officers closer to enlisted men. At twenty-one, he was the youngest man on the team. Fresh from OCS and jump school, he joined Special Forces because he heard promotions were faster. They were. What baffled him was that he was still a second lieutenant. He was the executive officer, a first lieutenant's slot. If a second looey got the job, he was usually promoted within a month or two. Except for Wheaty. It only reinforced his belief that he was going to be kicked out of the Army when they discovered he was a tenor.

We all became aware that a gentle beating on the tin roof was getting louder. I glanced at my watch: 1530 hours. The rains were late today. Top said he was going to change clothes, and Wheaty trailed him out, asking if he had gotten any pussy in Danang. I missed the answer.

Me and my beer went outside to watch the rains. I rather enjoyed them now. Everything and everyone would stop for the rest of the afternoon. I leaned against the sandbags surrounding the team house and stared at the rain splattering in puddles that wouldn't dry up for four more months. So the

9

Army has lost us. Situation Normal, All Fucked Up. But they must know what they're doing. This is only temporary. Maybe.

I thought for a few minutes about Top. He had closely cropped graying hair, and his face was square and filled with scars and wrinkles. He had those outdoorsy, hard good looks that many old soldiers and sailors get. When I joined the team a year ago, I figured him to be about forty-five years old. I was stunned to learn he was thirty-four.

As the team medic, the first thing I knew about these men was their medical histories.

O'Hara, Wiley Thomas. Rank: master sergeant. Height: five feet ten and a half inches. The same as me, although he was built a little heavier. Weight: 185 pounds. Childhood diseases: the usual. Tonsils still intact. Emergency appendectomy at age sixteen. Two false front teeth from a fight in 1953. Suspected chronic bronchitis. Top was a heavy smoker. Two to three packs a day. Suspected peptic ulcer. Treated and cured of malaria, plasmodium falciparum, June–September, 1963. Scars: seven-inch scar on upper right arm from a knife fight in Columbus, Georgia, in 1955. Small scar on right forehead from beer bottle, Fort Jackson, 1957. Scars on the front and back of left thigh, shrapnel, Korea, 1952. Normal heartbeat 73 per minute. Normal temperature 97.7. Normal blood pressure 120/80. No known allergic reactions.

That was how I first knew Top. Dozens of long hours on guard duty with him and I knew him differently.

He was born in Laslo, Mississippi, an upstate, backwoods town of about two thousand people. The closed society. I recalled Top's words from late one night, "My father was a truck driver and a hard drinker who believed in keeping a woman barefoot and pregnant. I was one of the mean kids in town, spoiling for a fight, never turning down a dare, always the first to try something new. Shit, Warren, you wouldn't believe that town. It was a rough, mean, nigger-hating town.

Me and my brother used to hang around black bottom to watch the coons fight on Saturday night. Why, the first man I ever saw killed, I was twelve. There were these two niggers, fighting like hell over a nickel. One finally went inside and got a shotgun, came out and blew a hole in the other's chest from three feet away. It was a twelve-gauge shotgun, too. The sheriff kept on pushing a stick down through that hole." Top stopped a moment and then went on, "For two weeks after that my mother had to sleep with me. It ain't hard to kill a person. It's only hard the first time. After that, nothing."

O'Hara had joined the Army the day he was seventeen. From what he told me, I gathered he didn't change much. He kept getting into trouble for fighting and drinking and eventually was assigned to the 256th Tank Battalion at Fort Benning.

"The 256th had a nickname: 'The Baby Rapers.' The outfit was made up of drunks, bums, and guys gone crazy from a world all shot to hell in World War Two," Top said.

O'Hara and The Baby Rapers went to Korea in 1952 and carried their tanks with them. Top never talked about that. The only time I ever saw him in Class A's was the day John F. Kennedy came to Bragg and Top wore a Silver Star, with cluster, a Purple Heart, and two rows of lesser hero medals.

Top talked hard and was hard, but there was a gentle side to him and he was embarrassed any time it showed. Once on a medical patrol I found him talking with a six-year-old girl, and his eyes were as soft as any mother's. After scooting her off, he said something about how she'd have nice legs in a couple of years. I had the feeling that he had not begun to question his life and attitudes until the last several years.

I knew from Hood, who had been with Top in Vietnam once before, that O'Hara had been married three times. Hood described his last wife, Beth, as "the good one." She had seen through O'Hara and had been able to calm him down, keep him off the bottle. She was the cousin of the supply officer at

Bragg, and O'Hara met her one morning on base. Top told me, "The first words I ever said to her were, 'Hey, babe, let's you and me go somewhere and fuck.' She said, 'I don't even want to associate with the likes of you.' I said, 'Okay, if that's the way you feel.' " O'Hara said he called her up the next day and apologized. They had been married five years and had two children when she died of cancer of the uterus. The children now lived with her brother and sister-in-law in Columbia, South Carolina.

Top, a loner by personality and now by circumstance, drifted into Special Forces in the late 1950s. He was in Laos with the CIA in 1959, trying to beef up the Laotian army. But it was on his first trip to Vietnam that the real trouble came.

He was the top sergeant on a full twelve-man team at the now-famous camp of Hop Tac in the giant rain forest that stretched from Cambodia to within thirty miles of Saigon. It was a favorite Viet Cong staging area. Top and Hood (who was his intelligence sergeant) were both on a supply run to Saigon the night the VC hit. It was the first time the Cong seriously tried to overrun a Special Forces camp, and one of the last times. First came the mortar attack at 0300 hours, and then at dawn, with the sun at their backs, they came. According to what O'Hara could piece together from the nearby villagers, the VC came in wave after wave, climbing over the bodies of the dead and wounded. They finally broke in, killed what few Vietnamese were left, and took the four Americans who were still alive. They left behind seventy-three dead CIDG, six dead Americans, and more than two hundred of their own. And when you figure the VC carry off as many of their own dead as possible, it was a costly victory indeed.

Top and Hood were back in the camp twelve hours after they heard the news. But it was Top who went a little crazy. He took off alone and roamed around that rain forest for two months, hunting those four men. A Special Forces team finally found him, nearly dead from malaria and leeches and

12

starvation, and sent him back to the States. The four have never been found, and Top blames himself for it. Even now, whenever there was a rumor of American prisoners in the area, he gets a strange look in his eyes.

Walls of rain chased each other across our compound. Steam rose from the barracks roofs. Not a soul was to be seen. A Company was in camp for training, but everyone was inside sleeping or playing cards now. We rotated the companies— four weeks in the field and one week in camp for R&R and training. Officially, these men were called an "anti-guerrilla strike force," and we called them strikers. They were paid directly by us. Regular Vietnamese army troops were called Arvins (ARVN—Army, Republic of Vietnam), and they were paid indirectly by the U.S.

So we were stranded in the delta. I didn't know how willing the good Lord was, but the creeks sure were rising. I flipped my cigarette toward a puddle and went inside for a late-afternoon nap in the rain.

2

THE ENTIRE team was back for supper. We were having pork ribs, fresh grapefruit, tomatoes, potatoes, and rice pudding. Lon's cooking, for the most part, was delicious. He was a middle-aged, thin, tired-looking Chinese whom Top had met on his previous tour in Vietnam. We never figured out how Top found Lon. He simply appeared, carrying his pots and pans, during our third week here. The only food he persistently destroyed was rice pudding, which was odd since he was Chinese. Lon had convinced himself that all Americans loved rice pudding, and that conviction was never swayed by the fact that nobody, not even Scourge, the dog, would eat his rice pudding. It tasted like finely chopped, burnt popcorn and sour cream. Foul.

When local vegetables were out of season, Lon bought USOM food on the black market in Chau An. I found it absurdly humorous that the United States Overseas Mission, one of the vast bureaucratic arms of AID, spent millions shipping food to the poor souls of South Vietnam only to have it bought by an expatriate Chinese and eaten by Americans.

I gathered from the conversation that Top had filled in the rest of the team on his trip to Danang. Nobody seemed worried. But then I had yet to see any of these men worried. A strange collection of men. Each different, each independent, and each rebellious for personal reasons. I wasn't sure I understood them at all. Hood said little, but that was typical. He rarely talked, and those deep-set dark eyes hid more than they revealed.

Santee was saying, "We ought to sell the camp—guns, dogs, and everything—at auction one day—one of those where you sell it piece by piece and then take a bid on everything—"

Top grumbled, "Hogjaw, maybe you got a little Jew blood in you, too?"

Cranston said, "What do you mean, sell our camp? That's uncool, man. What if the Cong buy it?" Cranston adjusted his black-rimmed glasses. "Far fucking out, man." Cranston always talked like that. He was born ten years too late. He should have been in the beat generation.

Santee said, "Sure, we give the village chief three per cent to set it up, give the camp commander three per cent since he might not be high bidder. If we sold the camp for five million piasters, that'd be about seventy-five thousand dollars, minus six per cent and split six ways—"

"Cut the crap," said O'Hara. "The lieutenant's got something to say."

"Men," said Wheaty in that awful bass voice, "I believe Sergeant O'Hara told you what Colonel Preston said in Danang. Obviously there is some kind of mistake. Top brought back a tube for the radio, and tomorrow I will try to raise the C-team and straighten this mess out." Wheaty's voice broke high suddenly and he coughed and went on. "Until we get further clarification, there isn't much we can do except carry on with our respective missions."

There was little anyone added of consequence. Santee was

fantasizing. Cranston was unconcerned. Top was eyeing everyone in his own secret way to check out our reactions. I looked for a place to hide my rice pudding. Hood said nothing.

After supper Santee joined me on my favorite sandbag and we watched Scourge trying to mount our other dog, Susie. Susie was the bane of Scourge's life. She came in heat every week or two, it seemed, and she let every mongrel within five miles fuck her, except Scourge.

Santee said, "What do you think about all this?"

"Maybe she just doesn't like him," I said.

"Not the dogs. Our being stuck here."

"I don't know. Preston clearly can't distinguish between his ass and a sixty-millimeter mortar. He's probably already discovered the mistake. The Army'll pay us, eventually. All this hostile-fire pay, cost-of-living allowance, specialty pay, and clothes allowance adds up. As long as we're here, we're getting about double stateside pay. I'm in no great hurry to get home."

"That's the way I figure it," Santee said. "I'm pulling down more here than I ever made in my life before. And a few little things on the side help out."

Santee was our supply sergeant, and he had that legendary ability of all supply sergeants to get anything. For example, there was our fifty-caliber machine gun. Our camp was two kilometers from the Cambodian border on the western side. It was the closest Cambodia came to our camp, and if the VC ever attacked, it might be from that direction. Our back was to the Bassac; Nan Phuc was to the north; and to the south stretched miles of rice fields. Two months ago we asked our C-team, the regional Special Forces operational and logistical headquarters, for a fifty caliber. The C-team informed us a fifty was not on the Army's Table of Organization and Equipment for an A-team. We said, yeah, we know about that, but we need one to cover two clicks of open ground from us to Cambodia. We used the slang for kilometer, "click."

Besides, our intelligence suggested the VC had heavy mortars and maybe a recoilless. The C-team said, "Sorry about that." The irony was that if we had asked the CIA four months ago, they would have said, "How many do you want?" When we arrived in Vietnam, the CIA didn't hand us a TO&E, they asked us what we needed to get the job done. Cranston carried a sten gun; Top had a twelve-gauge shotgun and a Thompson; and Santee was fond of the M-3 submachine gun. I carried a carbine. It was such a fine little gun—you could break it apart underwater and five minutes later it would be working again.

Anyway, Top sent Santee to Saigon with orders to get a fifty. Nine days later a fishing boat docked in Nan Phuc and two fishermen helped Santee off-load a nearly new Browning. We had her sandbagged on a platform twenty feet tall and facing Cambodia. She'd chop down trees a half mile away.

Santee never said where he got the gun, but he hinted it had to do with an elderly Chinese druggist in the Cholon district of Saigon.

Santee stood just shy of six feet, but his leanness exaggerated his height. He carried himself easily and was relaxed. A big, jutting jaw gave him the nickname "Hogjaw." It wasn't a real nickname, only one that Top had started and the team had picked up. You looked at Santee and knew that when he grew old and lost his teeth, his mouth would have that shrunken, caved-in appearance. His kinky black hair was cut closely, and his skin was dark walnut.

He was allergic to penicillin, and I had insisted that that be stamped on his dog tags before we left Bragg. At thirty-one, he still had both his appendix and tonsils. He broke his left leg below the knee when he was playing football in junior high school. Left-handed. Blood type AB positive, the same as Cranston's. Normal heartbeat 65, and blood pressure 110/80. He was in excellent health.

Top was right, in his own crude way—Santee was the

capitalist of the team. Back at Bragg he had peddled old parachutes, shirts "with three free initials on the pocket," and Knapp Shoes, whatever the hell they were. Several weeks ago Santee had persuaded two aging women in Nan Phuc to make Viet Cong flags. He reasoned that with more Americans coming to Vietnam, VC flags would soon be favorite souvenirs. The hard part had been convincing the women they should make Viet Cong flags. Santee had set up a complicated courier system of fishermen who smuggled the flags south.

Santee rarely talked about his childhood. I knew he was from Augusta, Georgia. His father had been a garbage collector at Fort Gordon, and Santee dropped out of school in the tenth grade to go to work. There were seven children in the family. "I must have hauled away a million empty beer and whiskey bottles from that base," said Santee one night. "I promised myself that someday I'd be rich enough to drive my father around the base in the biggest, longest, most expensive car I could buy." That dream would never come true. A week after he told me that, the Army radioed us that his father had died suddenly of a heart attack. Later Top told me Santee had doubled the $150 monthly allotment to his mother. Three hundred dollars out of a staff sergeant's take-home pay of $512 was no small amount.

Top and Santee maintained an odd relationship. Top told his nigger jokes in front of Santee, as well as behind him. Whatever else, Top was honest. Things like, "Of course, you got big feet, Hogjaw, all niggers got big feet. It comes from going barefoot in Africa." Top and Santee would both crack up laughing. It was as if both men were playing the last act of the Old South. Each man to his own role. Top was the cornpone, grit racist, and Santee was the happy nigger dancing in the cotton fields. And it was as if they both knew it and were somehow deeply trapped in the mysticism of it all. It was weird.

We chatted a few minutes more and Santee wandered off to

inspect the latest batch of VC flags. Scourge gave up when Susie finally nipped him sharply on the nose. The sun was setting behind the tree line that marked the border. Between here and there the rice fields were filling up with water, and in a few weeks there would be a giant lake from the Bassac to Cambodia. We would be surrounded by water until next year.

I had a beer, checked the guard roster, and, finding I didn't have guard tonight, went to bed.

The next morning I pumped water. For six hours a day, twice a week, I ran our urlator, a miniature water-treatment plant, pumping three thousand gallons of water into our storage tank. We siphoned the water straight from the moat and pushed it through five separate purification processes. It emerged cloudy but safe.

From my perch on the water tank, forty feet up in the air, I noticed a lot of activity with the strikers. At 1030 hours a platoon left camp in full battle gear. When I came down for lunch, Top explained what happened. "The Cong got the village chief on Tan Dao last night. They came in sometime before dawn. He's missing, maybe dead. His wife was knocked around and she doesn't remember much. They left some propaganda and a puddle of blood."

There was silence around the table. This was the closest to our camp the Viet Cong had struck. Tan Dao was a small island in the Bassac a mile downriver from Nan Phuc. I had taken a medical patrol there only four days ago.

Top went on, "This time the Cong fucked up badly. The village chief was a cousin of Major Choi's, and he is pissed. He sent a platoon up the river to Phu Duc. He thinks they came across the border there."

I couldn't believe the VC were so dumb as to kidnap the cousin of Major Lam Than Choi, our camp commander. They should have learned their lesson by now. These people were Hoa Hao (pronounced "wah how") and already hated the Viet Cong for deep-seated reasons. The Hoa Hao was a

Buddhist sect, which numbered about one million people, mostly in southwestern Vietnam. The sect was begun in 1939 by Huynh Phu So, a native of Tan Chau, forty miles east of us.

The story went that So was a frail, sickly youth until age twenty, when he traveled to Nhuc Phui, one of the Seven Mountains near Chau An. There he was miraculously cured and began traveling the countryside preaching a reformed Buddhism, later known as Phat Gio Hoa Hao, or simply Hoa Hao. He emphasized the individual's direct relationship with Buddha, as opposed to the passive, accept-whatever-happens form of Buddhism throughout most of South Vietnam.

The religion proved immensely successful, so much so that by 1941 the French became terrified that the Hoa Hao might align themselves with the Japanese. In an attempt to prevent this, the French threw So into a mental institution. This made the Hoa Hao so furious that they turned to the Japanese, who trained and armed a tough Hoa Hao force of 35,000 men.

In the meantime France fell to Germany and Japan occupied Vietnam. The Japanese lived up to their bargain and freed So. But Japan suddenly became occupied in the Pacific and the Hoa Hao became terrorists, roaming the countryside, imposing taxes, and taking land. After the war the Viet Minh tried to persuade the Hoa Hao to come over to their side. Having little luck, the Viet Minh, with no more forethought than the French, killed Huynh Phu So. Near his home they cut off his arms, legs, and head and stuck them, still bleeding, on bamboo stakes.

Thus began the Hoa Hao's deep, abiding hate for the Viet Minh. Once the Hoa Hao captured a full company of Viet Minh. They tied them together in bundles and drowned them in the Bassac.

In the early 1950s the Hoa Hao joined the French against the Viet Minh. In retrospect, it's clear the Hoa Hao played a careful game of acquiring French arms without French strings attached. (Yes, we had thought about this many times.) Armed now with the weapons of the French and the Japanese, the Hoa Hao became nearly omnipotent in a hundred-square-mile area from Can Tho to the Cambodian border. They controlled traffic, smuggled opium, and imposed taxes at will. But as a benevolent dictatorship. The armies of the Hoa Hao were mainly directed at keeping out the Viet Minh, the border bandits, and the French Legionnaires.

After the French were defeated in 1954, Prime Minister Ngo Dinh Diem decided to regain control of the six provinces the Hoa Hao now controlled. Diem, in 1957, promised amnesty to all Hoa Hao soldiers and recognition of their religion if the Hoa Hao armies would come to Saigon and turn in their guns. Three of the four Hoa Hao generals believed Diem. They were ambushed fifteen miles outside Saigon by four divisions of the South Vietnamese Army and mercilessly cut down. Ba Cut, the Hoa Hao religious and military leader at that time, was quickly beheaded by Diem.

The fourth general was Truong Kim Cu, and he began operating a small guerrilla force in the Nan Phuc district—where we were—against both the Viet Cong and the government of South Vietnam. Militarily, his movement never amounted to much—too few men and guns.

Cu had under him at that time a young sergeant named Lam Than Choi. Cu was later killed by the VC and Choi was now our camp commander. Some of the guerrillas who were with Cu were now our strikers, and they remembered for those who didn't. Three years ago the Vietnamese Army had tried to send to Nan Phuc their own Special Forces team (Luc Lung Duc Biet or LLDB). The morning after they arrived, twelve headless bodies were floating down the Bassac on bamboo rafts. That was when the Green Berets had been called.

We got along damn well with the Hoa Hao. Top and Hood,

of course, had been in Vietnam before. Plus, we didn't hassle the Hoa Hao about the government. The Hoa Hao weren't allowed to vote in national elections, and no doubt our disdain for Saigon showed.

There was some sense of identity between us and the Hoa Hao. The men who volunteered for Special Forces, for jump school, for Vietnam duty, and for A-team assignments were not run-of-the-mill soldiers. Each was escaping the regular Army standardization for some reason. And the regular Army attitude toward Green Berets, in spite of clever public relations, was one of suspicion and dislike. It was easier for us to sympathize with the problems of the Hoa Hao than the problems of the latest coup winner in Saigon.

The heat that afternoon was terrific, and I couldn't sleep during pok time. I found Cranston shooting pool in the police chief's home and talked him into waterskiing. We had considered it several times, and today seemed as good a time as any. A month ago Santee and Major Choi had motored into camp in a fifteen-foot fiberglass boat, powered by an eighty-horsepower Evinrude. They never told where they got the boat.

We made the skis out of ordinary two-by-six planks, with a pair of Bata boots nailed to them. It was 1330 hours, and we wanted to hit the water before the afternoon rains. I thought briefly about the Viet Cong, but, after all, it was daylight. Cranston, me, and two strikers, who suggested politely we had a fever of the brain, rigged a parachute cord for a ski line and motored out to the middle of the Bassac. The water was high, only a few feet shy of the bank tops. I stripped to my jockey shorts, laced the skis on, and jumped in. I made it up the first time but forgot the skis had no curved tips. I leaned forward crossing the wake and somersaulted three times. That broke the strikers up. I got up again and was soon skiing like a pro. I had to lean back more than normal.

For the first time, I saw a crowd of villagers on the shore, excitedly laughing and pointing at us. They probably had never seen anyone ski before, and I waved as we sped by.

Cranston headed upriver, and we were about two miles from Nan Phuc when it happened. The two strikers were pointing at the shore a hundred yards to my right. I looked but saw nothing. Then my stomach lurched ice-cold as I heard a *crack!* over my head. Somebody was shooting at us.

Cranston opened the motor up, and the strikers flattened out and began firing at a grove of banana trees. I squatted on the skis and zigzagged back and forth to make less of a target. Splashes between me and the boat told me somebody out there didn't like me.

Are you running with me, Jesus? What a way to go, I thought. "Dear Mr. and Mrs. Warren: We regret to inform you that your son, SSG Phil Warren, was killed by hostile fire as he was waterskiing in his jockey shorts on the Bassac River."

The trouble was that we were speeding away from camp and closer to lion country. Cranston signaled a turn. My knees were shaking, and not solely because of the skiing. One striker stood up and motioned with my carbine, which I had left in the boat. He was asking if I wanted my gun. I nodded yes, before I remembered I was moving at thirty miles an hour, one inch above the water, on a pair of two-by-sixes. He threw the gun. I said a silent prayer and somehow grabbed it without losing my balance.

Cranston steered as close to the near shore as possible to keep away from the snipers. Two whaps over my head told me we were back in range. I sat on my ankles, switched the ski rope to my left hand, and rested the carbine across my left forearm. I pushed the safety off and fired short bursts of two and three. Cranston and both strikers were firing, too. We must have singed some tail feathers, because the shooting dried up to an occasional burst. Finally we were by and coming into Nan Phuc again.

I slung the carbine and Cranston wheeled in a sharp curve toward the shore. The gunfire must have been audible here—either that or word of the waterskiing had spread—because at least three-fourths of Nan Phuc's population were standing there. I dropped the rope a hundred feet out and coasted to a beautiful stop in waist-deep water. The crowd cheered heartily.

After Cranston docked, we located one hole in the boat, up high on the stern. We walked to camp, slightly shaken and dreading what Top would say.

"Waterfuckingskiing!" screamed Top. He was standing at the gate with his hands on his hips. "You stupid fuckheads. If you ain't got any better sense than to go waterskiing the day after a platoon of Viet Cong snuck down the river, you both deserve to get your asses shot off."

Top chewed our ass all the way back to the team house. The camp had heard the shooting and the villagers had told them one of the Americans was running on the water.

"Do you know what a war zone is?" asked Top. "Do you know where you are?" We both felt so worthless. "The next time I see your ass on a pair of skis, the skis will be halfway up it."

Cranston and I slunk off to change clothes.

I had a busy sick call that afternoon and didn't know about the answer from the C-team until supper. Wheaty handed me the decoded message:

SUBJECT: Inquiry from Toad [that was Wheaty's code name] about reassignment stateside.
CLASSIFICATION: Top Secret.
MESSAGE: Weeping Willow [Colonel Preston's code name] reports all personnel in Det. A-376 shipped to Fort Bragg 091764. Willow suggests we disregard future messages from the alleged Det. A-376. Possible impersonation by Viet Cong. END MESSAGE

P.S. The VC have closed the Bassac just north of Can Tho to all river traffic.

"That's ridiculous," I said.

"It's the dumbest goddamned thing I ever saw," muttered Top.

Santee asked, "How come they sent that if they thought we were Viet Cong?"

"It wasn't official," answered Cranston. "The radio operator at Can Tho and I were in Signal School together and we know each other's work. You can tell who's sending if you work with them long enough. It's just like handwriting. He added a 'Sorry about that' at the end of the message. I guess he thought we should know what they said."

Lon took away our plates and gave us a bowl filled with something that looked like broiled glue. I sniffed. It was either broiled glue or rice pudding.

Top went into the kitchen and said something to Lon. I hoped he was finally telling him, in a nice way, that his rice pudding was hopeless. A moment later Lon left.

Top sat down. "We're going to have a team meeting. Nothing goes beyond this room. We about got us a problem."

"Why don't we simply tell Lon his pudding is no good?" I asked.

"Not that problem, shithead. Us and the Army. You all read the message and you know the situation. You also know about the VC raid on Tan Dao last night and about Cranston and Warren getting shot at while they grab-assed around on the river today." Top lit a cigarette. "Now as I see it, we've more or less been left sucking hind tit. Headquarters thinks we've all been shipped to the States. The C-team can't or won't acknowledge we're here. We need to figure out our next step."

"What about helicopters?" asked Wheaty.

Hood answered. "There's little chance of that, unless we can get radio clearance. Anyway, there are less than a half dozen choppers in the entire delta—and they belong to generals and province chiefs."

"What about walking out?" I asked.

"Fat chance," said Top. "The rains this year are heavier than ever, and flooding is worse toward Can Tho, which is where we'd have to walk to. And you all saw the radio message—the VC are in control of the Bassac. I doubt we could get a boat through now."

"Besides," added Hood, "what if we left and the next day headquarters sent a chopper in? I have a feeling we'd be in a world of trouble for walking out on a camp."

Top tapped the table with a finger. "I ain't never had good sense, so if you all want to bust out, I'm crazy enough to try it. But whatever we do, we do it together. If you all want to go, we'll go. If you want to stay, we all stay."

Top looked around the table. "Hood, give us all a little briefing on the latest VC situation."

Hood got up, rummaged around a shelf in the corner, and spread out our area map. Locks of curly black hair fell over his forehead as he bent. I looked at his face and thought what a shame his family couldn't afford doctors when he was a teenager. Hood must have had an awful case of acne—his face was a pitted mass of scars. Not scars really, but dozens of tiny pinpoints of puckered flesh. That terrible skin combined with those hooded eyes could be very disquieting.

He said, "The 183rd has closed the Bassac twelve miles this side of Can Tho. No South Vietnamese Navy boats have gotten through in the last two days, and the villagers report heavy taxation on civilian boats. We think there may be two 105s mounted on each side of the river. We got the 485th based in Prek Tonlea and operational down the border to across from the Seven Mountains. They've been building up for over three months. Scattered activity along the border. Even though we've given them grief on the Bassac, they could be planning an attack within four to five months here at Nan Phuc or at the Seven Mountains."

Names like the 485th and 183rd didn't mean the Viet Cong had that many regiments. They gave them high numbers to confuse us further. At least, we didn't think there were 484 other regiments.

Cranston asked, "What's with Major Choi? I mean, does he mind our being here? What are his plans?"

"I'll be honest with you," said Top. "I think these bandits are organizing their own army again. While I was talking to Choi, he got a call over the radio from Long Xuyen, and whoever he was talking to called him General Choi, and right away Choi said something so fast I missed it. I'll bet you the wart on my ass the Hoa Hao have a couple ammo dumps hidden around here somewhere. Waiting."

Top put his cigarette out. "Choi said this afternoon we could stay on until we find out what's happening. We can borrow money from him if we need it. He said he'd like us to stay and help him and the Hoa Hao, although he's willing to give us an armed escort as far as Chau An if we think we can make it the rest of the way." Top waited for comments. None came.

"Here's what I recommend: Choi's going to try Vietnamese channels tomorrow. Our best bet is to stay here awhile longer and see what happens. About the only place we'd get, trying to walk out, would be a POW camp. What do you say?"

We agreed.

"Then it's settled." Top glanced at me and Cranston. "Unless the bathing beauties want to ski out."

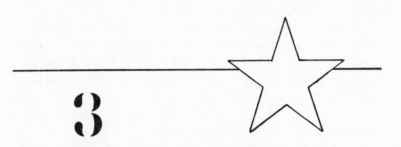

3

TWO DAYS later the IV Corps Commander answered Choi's inquiry: According to MAAG (the Military Assistance and Advisory Group was the joint command for the U.S. military in Vietnam), team A-376 had been withdrawn in mid-September. I think none of us really expected the Vietnamese Army to unravel the knot. It could only be a matter of time before somebody missed us.

Our schedule remained as it had been: company training in the morning, two-and-a-half-hour pok time at noon, and in the late afternoon more training or, in my case, medical patrols. Only in Nan Phuc was I able to keep sufficiently accurate records to give effective treatments. At first I gave the full amount of medicine with careful instructions to take so much every so many hours until it was gone. Only to discover later that my patient had taken it all at once because if one was good, a dozen were a dozen times better; or had thrown it all away because it didn't look strong enough to chase away evil spirits; or had sold it.

I had made only one serious mistake so far. Nine weeks ago, on the island of Tan Dao, where the VC had kidnaped the still-missing village chief, I had diagnosed a smallpox epidemic. I found it first on a six-year-old girl. She had red crops of lesions, swollen lymph nodes, and a slight fever. Then I found the same thing on four more children. That night Cranston radioed the C-team. At noon the next day a big Chinook landed and dropped off Group Surgeon Colonel Brian Dusk, two other doctors, and three medics, who unloaded iced bins of serum. I took the doctors to Tan Dao, while the medics began inoculations in Nan Phuc.

The colonel examined my six-year-old girl. Dusk pointed out significantly, it seemed to me, that the girl had no lesions on her face, hands, or feet and that the fever was gone. The doctors examined the other children.

Then Dusk said to me, "Sergeant Warren, what you have here and what you have brought me six hundred miles for is a mild epidemic of varicella, commonly called chicken pox. The treatment is washing the lesions, APC's for fever, and isolating the patient from other people and from any so-called medics in the area."

I was crushed. "At least," I joked, "a lot of Hoa Hao now have smallpox vaccinations."

Dusk didn't laugh.

On Saturday, a week after Top returned to camp, he, Wheaty, and I took a two-day patrol into Cambodia to check out reports of a Viet Cong build-up. Choi approved. Top said we might as well take advantage of the fact that we weren't here. A month ago we had asked the C-team for permission to take a reconnaissance patrol into Cambodia. To look around, no fighting. The C-team said, "MAAG forbids the crossing of internationally recognized borders by United States military personnel or indigenous military personnel under their command, because of the possible far-reaching political implications." A sorry way to run a war.

At 2000 hours, as twilight thickened into dark, we slipped out the front gate. With us were Frenchy, a middle-aged Vietnamese and one of Choi's top bodyguards, and four hand-picked strikers. As always, Frenchy carried a thirty-caliber machine gun. It weighed fifteen pounds and the eight hundred rounds of linked ammo crisscrossing his chest added another ten pounds.

His name was Thich Su Buoi, but he had acquired the nickname Frenchy years ago because he spoke some French. He was five feet four and much broader than the average Vietnamese. He was twelve years old when he joined the Hoa Hao army during Japan's invasion of Indochina. Frenchy was one of the few Hoa Hao I knew who seemed honestly fond of the French. He was convinced, he said, that the Japanese could never have been driven out of Vietnam without the help of the French. More important, his older brother had been released from a Japanese POW camp by the French. Frenchy told me one day in confidence that we Americans were probably Frenchmen returning to save his country. And if not French, then here under French orders. He further suspected, he said, that the Viet Cong were Japanese agents. Old enemies may be the best enemies. They're always there when you need them.

We wore black pajamas and the conical bamboo hats of the farmers. The night was sticky hot as we skirted Nan Phuc and crossed the paddies. Because of the water, we walked single file on the banks of the irrigation ditches, which, from the air, gave the land that blocked, maze appearance. The lanterns of Nan Phuc faded away behind us.

We reached B Company's headquarters without incident a little before 2200 hours. Captain Minh, the company commander, invited us into his hut for a cup of tea. Minh was fat, prosperous, and, at thirty-two, the youngest of our company commanders.

We sat cross-legged on the slatted floor. A teen-aged boy served steaming hot tea in small, handleless cups. "Any activity tonight?" Top asked Minh.

"The Viet Cong are very still tonight. There was some shooting a few miles north last night. We do not know what it was. There is much movement in Cambodia. The VC have moved the civilians back three kilometers from the border. Heavy taxation. Are you crossing the Chlong tonight?"

The Chlong River, which flowed by fifty feet away, was the border between South Vietnam and Cambodia for eight miles in both directions.

"Yes. We will need two sampans," said Top, unfolding a plastic-covered map.

"Maybe you should cross tomorrow," said Minh, shaking his head. "It is very bad to cross at night. Many VC may be around."

The captain's words were not so much a statement of fact as the caution of a man who has lived with the lions a long time and wants to live longer.

"Show us where the Cambodian outposts are and any places where the VC are setting up night ambushes," said Top.

Minh drew X's on the map. The outposts were ostensibly manned by the Cambodians, but the Viet Cong often staffed them at night. We discussed the crossing for another half hour.

We left with a final warning from Minh and moved north on a small, worn path along the river bank. The Chlong was a black valley through the bamboo thickets flanking our trail. The moon wouldn't be up for several more hours. Behind us, eight of Minh's men carried the sampans.

After an hour Top stopped. "We'll cross here. Frenchy and I will go in the first sampan. I'll whistle bobwhite if it's okay. Don't mess around on the river. If we're hit give us covering fire and we'll try to get back. Any time we get split up or lost, rendezvous will be here at 2000 hours tomorrow night. Lieutenant, call B Company and tell them we're crossing now. We'll maintain radio silence in Cambodia. Questions?"

Minh's soldiers spread out silently in the bamboo to cover us.

Top, Frenchy, and two CIDGs slipped into their sampan and began paddling. The river was seventy-five meters wide.

"You think we'll run into any VC?" Wheaty whispered.

"I doubt it. They can't watch every section of the river," I said.

Top's sampan reached mid-river and disappeared into the darkness of the far bank. The only noises were a few night birds and the water rustling along.

"I wouldn't mind a little action," said Wheaty with a low laugh. "We might pick up a few medals. Maybe a bronze star or even higher."

Always planning, always scheming. That was our Wheaty. He had a smooth, almost pretty face, blue eyes, and dark, dirty-blond hair. Top kidded him mercilessly about shaving only twice a week. Wheaty stood five feet ten and weighed 175 pounds. His normal heartbeat was 60 per minute; his blood pressure was 110/80, and he was in good health. Wheaty had been troubled with diarrhea for the first month we were here. His only scar was a ten-inch one diagonally across his right side. Shortly after birth he had been operated on to remove a gastrointestinal block.

Wheaty puzzled me. From many long hours on guard duty with him, I knew his family background, but it didn't really fit his personality. He was born to a family on the skids in Norfolk, Virginia. The family had been well-off enough until his father lost a long-standing fight with the bottle. His mother was no help. The youngest of three children, Wheaty ran away from home when he was thirteen with a friend from a tenement down the street. They hitchhiked to Atlanta, where

Wheaty was arrested for stealing clothes in an Army and Navy store. He told the judge he was sixteen and received a suspended sentence. He went to Nashville, where he was busted for stealing candy, of all things. He lived on the road until he was fifteen and then, deciding he wanted a high-school diploma, returned home. For two years he went to school and worked nights and weekends at odd jobs. He had saved $250 and was thinking about going to college when the final blow came.

"It was Friday night and I had gotten paid. I was a curb hop at a drive-in. I went home to put my paycheck and tips in with my savings. I kept the money in a little box in my closet. I liked to count it. That night the box was missing. I tore the closet apart, and then I found my father passed out in the bathroom and my mother gone." Wheaty's words were bitter, but he had laughed at the end of each sentence, as if to show me that it didn't matter. "I knew what had happened. I found six bottles of whiskey, a new radio, and a pair of binoculars. Monday morning I joined the National Guard."

Wheaty got out after six months, returned to Norfolk, and, finding everything unchanged, enlisted in the regular Army. He drifted around the first two years and even was married for five months to a WAC. I've surmised that she left him. Wheaty's comments about women were usually limited to inanities like, "They're only good for one thing," and "Women are all dumb." But, in his own way, Wheaty persisted. He made it through OCS and into Special Forces.

If you've always wondered who wrote off for those "You can make big money by being a meatcutter" advertisements, wonder no more. People like Wheaty. He spent at least two nights a week at Bragg (and now here) poring over his books on the best way to slice a ham hock. Wheaty said he knew he would be booted out of the Army someday, and he wanted a good trade in reserve.

Wheaty gave the appearance of always trying to get away

33

with something or trying to put one over on you. Except that he really didn't try. And he didn't mind when you nailed him. I decided it was a wishy-washy front covering up a wishy-washy interior. The one thing Wheaty had going for him, if nothing else, was a high survival instinct.

A bobwhite whistled into my thoughts.

"Let's go," Wheaty said.

The night was incredibly quiet. In a few minutes we landed and hid the boats under brush. We were in Cambodia. The land looked the same, and, indeed, it was part of the same sprawling delta spewn forth over the centuries by the Mekong.

We walked slowly, with Top halting every so often for a compass reading. The sky began to lighten as a half-moon snuck up through the trees. After an hour and a half Top stopped.

"So far, so good," he whispered. "That stream we crossed must be the one about five hundred meters from Kompong Cheu. If our intelligence is right, the VC are as thick as mosquitoes on a fat man's ass. No smoking, no talking, no fires. Let's eat and get some sleep."

We divided guard duty and strung hammocks. I tied my poncho liner/hammock with quick-release ties to two small trees. My knapsack went underneath and my carbine was laid on top of it, within easy reach. Beside it, I laid my cartridge belt, which held four grenades, a forty-five pistol, five hundred rounds of thirty-caliber ammunition, a K-Bar double-edged knife, a collapsible canteen, my Special Forces survival kit and a first-aid package, now filled with a pack of Winstons and matches. It all weighed twenty pounds, but you could live for weeks in the jungle with it.

The next morning I woke at 0700 and looked out. Top sat cross-legged on the ground, eating from a C-ration can. The lieutenant was curled in his hammock, and the strikers were beginning to stir.

"*Chau*, Top."

34

"Good morning, *bac si*. Would you care for scrambled eggs and sausage or grits and country ham?" said Top. *Bac si*, by the way, is pronounced "boxy" and is Vietnamese for doctor. Everyone called me that.

I opened a can of cold stewed beef and potatoes. A number on the side read USAF-ComA44C59-201. I was convinced our C-rations were canned during World War II, at the latest. The bulk of our sixty- and eighty-one-millimeter mortar ammunition was dated 1942 to 1945. Surprisingly, only two had misfired, and in neither case had anyone been injured.

The lieutenant and the strikers were up in a few minutes, and, after they ate, we buried the cans and packed up. The day was already hot.

We moved slowly. We had yet to see a civilian or recent evidence of any. We were following an old trail through fairly dense jungle when the lead man stopped and pointed to two punji stakes in the path. Three inches of the sharp tips showed. From there on we picked our way carefully, walking in each other's tracks and watching for booby traps. The sun rose higher, and the constant tension and humidity soaked us with perspiration. My eyes stung from the sweat and salt.

Once we thought we heard voices to our left. We froze, but the noise drifted away. Punji stakes were everywhere, and I had seen four or five booby-trapped trees. The VC would sharpen a piece of bamboo to an ice-pick point and tie it to a tree, which would be bent backward and horizontally along a trail. If you touched the trip wire, two feet of bamboo moving at the speed of a bullet would be the last thing you saw. Crude but a hell of a lot cheaper than the thousand-dollar antipersonnel mines our Army favored.

We stopped for a quick lunch at 1300 hours, and I immediately started for the bushes.

"Where are you going?" asked Top.

"To take a crap. You want to give me a hand?"

"Cover it up."

35

I came back in a few minutes. They didn't get me that time. I had a recurring dream that the VC would capture me someday when I was defecating.

"Did everything come out all right?" asked Top.

"As well as can be expected," I said, opening a can of spaghetti and meat balls.

Top said, "That reminds me, did I ever tell you about Lieutenant Vaughn? He was XO on a training team, and he used to shit the biggest turds in the world. They were about the size and shape of beer cans. He had what they call, I think, a dysfunction of the colon. You'd go in the bathroom and you'd know if Vaughn had been in that day. There would be a giant turd floating around in the commode. They wouldn't flush down. You'd have to get a stick and break them up into pieces. I finally asked him about it one day, and he said he'd shit huge turds all his life. He admitted that they were so big that now and then one would rub against his prostate gland on the way out and he'd get a hard on and shoot off. I had always wondered why he seemed to smile a lot after taking a shit." Top laughed at the memory.

I finished a cold lunch, trying not to think about Lieutenant Vaughn and his giant turds.

At 1430 hours we hit the barbed wire. It was a single roll of concertina wire and was probably an outside perimeter. Top carried cutters and in five minutes we crawled through. We twisted the wire together so it would pass a fast inspection.

Two hundred yards further on, we smelled smoke and decided to get a little lower to mother earth. We sprawled on our bellies and saw the guard post before we had gone ten yards. It was a thatched hut, six feet off the ground. Two Viet Cong were lounging inside the doorway. Frenchy pointed to the left and there, through the leaves, we saw a guard, leaning against a banana tree. He was smoking a cigarette and drawing something in the dirt with a stick. Top motioned to our right, and we followed him on elbows and knees. A half-hour of slow worming, and we were 150 yards away and the first drops of rain were flicking the leaves.

Top whispered, "Warren, stay here with the strikers. The lieutenant and I are going in to see what we can see. The rain'll make good cover. It's—ah"—Top looked at his watch —"1530 now. If we're not back by 1830, head for the rendezvous point and wait. Keep your cock clean. Come on, sir."

Wheaty grinned nervously, and I thought, You might earn those medals yet, Lieutenant.

I gave the CIDG the plan and spread them twenty feet apart in a big circle. They didn't need to be told to keep under cover.

Frenchy and I leaned against a tree, facing the direction Top and Wheaty went.

"*Beaucoup* VC, huh?" asked Frenchy.

I nodded.

"Maybe many Japanese, too?"

"Maybe, Frenchy." Japanese, indeed.

Now and then Vietnamese voices would drift through the rain, but the tone was ordinary conversation. The raindrops were scaring the sensitive plants into folding their leaves. I wrapped my poncho closer and covered my carbine. God-damn, I thought, this is the highest cotton I've ever been in. But, hell, this is the stuff Special Forces is supposed to do. The whole theory of Special Forces had been to go in behind enemy lines for intelligence, sabotage, and guerrilla training. In the woods, not in a camp. I didn't understand why the regular Army insisted on fixed locations. Every time we built a camp, we gave up the countryside around it.

I felt a leech under my pants above my left boot. I squirted a few drops of K-4 mosquito repellent on the bloodsucker. He was two black, fat inches long. As soon as the liquid hit, he began wiggling, and a moment later he unfastened his teeth and dropped off. I raised my heel and squashed him.

The rain hurried to a downpour, and in spite of the poncho I was soaked to my skin. Top and Wheaty should be there by now or maybe on their way back. I had heard no shots.

My senses were acutely aware of every leaf, shadow, and noise, but inside I was somewhere else. My mind was singing "The Girl from Ipanema." The brain is jealously protective of itself. It was giving me a lovely memory, a warming thought about a girl, and, most of all, unspoken hope. Soft and tan and young and lovely . . . ah, it was going to be delicious to hold a real girl again. I was so horny that even the thought of talking to a female turned me on. The girl I had nearly married was Nina Buchanan, and she was in Bangkok, Thailand, with her father, a full colonel in the Army. We had started dating in our senior year at the University of North Carolina. Such a good-looking woman. Skin tones like honey. We had graduated and somehow, without really saying it, sensed that neither of us was ready for marriage. Her father was being transferred to Bangkok and she went along as a dependent. The thought of her wrapped around my mind like her legs around my waist.

A bobwhite called softly from nearby. I answered. Moments later Top and Wheaty crawled from under a betel nut vine. They looked as if they had been lying under a river for a month. Wheaty was grinning from ear to ear.

"How'd it go?" I asked.

"Jackpot," said Top.

"Any Japanese?" asked Frenchy.

"No, shithead, the Japs are busy making radios now," said Top. Frenchy smiled as if to say, I'll go along with your joke, because I know there are hundreds of Japanese in there.

"*Bac si*," said Wheaty, "I got this leech bite."

"So?" I asked.

"It's on my balls," he said, a flush creeping up his face.

Top said, "It fell off because it couldn't find anything big enough to get a hold of."

38

"I pulled it off an hour ago, but it's still bleeding," said Wheaty.

"It takes a long time to stop. Leeches have an anti-coagulant in their mouth that keeps the blood from clotting. Don't worry about it," I said.

"Let's haul ass," said Top.

It was nearly dark and the rain showed no sign of letting up. My elbows and knees were raw, and rarely used shoulder and back muscles gave me their opinion of all this. A half hour later we were back at the concertina wire. Since we were more confident about the location of the VC, we laid tree limbs over it and walked across. We moved due east, faster now. Once, in the dusk, I stepped on a punji stake, but the steel plate in my boot broke it. By 2230 we were a mile and a half from the VC camp and Top called a halt.

We strung hammocks in the pouring rain and gathered around for supper.

"Was it the 485th?" I asked.

"If it wasn't, it was close enough to count," said Top, chewing a mouthful of soggy ham. "We got to within a hundred yards of the main camp. They had an inner defense wire and a cleared area outside it. I think there were underground bunkers throughout the whole camp. I saw what looked like tunnel entrances under nearly every hooch. Two platoons of soldiers were attending a class of some kind. And get this—while we were watching they brought two elephants in, each one wearing a 105 recoilless on its back. Everyone was in khaki and wearing real boots. There were even women and kids. A minute's notice and it could pass for an ordinary village."

"Excuse me," said Wheaty in his officer's voice, "but you better look at my balls. They're still bleeding."

I was thinking about what a couple companies of VC could do to my young body, and then I was thinking it was odd the leech bite had not clotted yet.

"Drop your drawers, sir," I said.

"Whoopee, now we're going to see if officers have dicks after all," said Top.

The strikers were nudging each other and pointing.

Wheaty lowered his clothes, and I looked at his sac with a tiny flashlight, taped over except for a pinhole. The bite was at the very bottom and was bleeding rapidly. His undershorts were dripping blood.

"Maybe you can get a Purple Heart for wounds by a hostile leech," I said.

"You think so?" asked Wheaty in all seriousness.

"You know what standard medical treatment for this is? I'm supposed to put on a pressure bandage. But damned if I can figure how to get one tight enough when it's on your balls."

"Has he got a dick, Warren?" asked Top from within his poncho.

"Does it look like it's getting any less?" said Wheaty.

"You could always put a tourniquet on," said Top.

Suddenly I remembered from an obscure medical class that epinephrine, a drug normally used for heart failure, shock, or asthma, also had the property of acting as a vasoconstrictor when applied directly to blood vessels. I pulled out a vial, liberally doused a two-by-two, and pressed it against the bite.

"That feels better," said Wheaty.

Top piped up, "I knew it. Officers are queer."

I prepared another two-by-two, and while Wheaty held it, I taped the pad in place as best I could.

"I think that'll stop it," I said.

Wheaty suddenly realized that I had covered his balls with surgical tape. "How the hell am I supposed to get that tape off?" he asked.

I smiled.

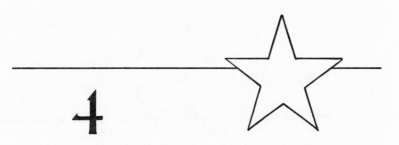

4

WE WERE up at dawn the next morning and after a quick breakfast headed northeast. Wheaty's leech bite had stopped bleeding during the night and he was already complaining about the tape.

At 1030 hours we reached the Chlong and estimated that we were one mile downriver from our SDC post. SDC meant Self-Defense Corps. The brainchild of some American in Saigon, SDC posts were small and manned by local men and their families. They were tucked around the border as listening posts. A nice theory, but their small size, inadequate defense systems, and lack of big guns made them essentially supply depots for the VC.

We paused on the bank while Wheaty radioed the post. They told us we were closer than we'd thought, apparently less than a click or so. Which also meant we were less than a click away from a Cambodian outpost. The two faced each other across the river, and by an unstated agreement neither had fired on the other. Yet. I had brought medical patrols to the post and seen Cambodians across the river. Once I had waved at a soldier eating lunch, and after a glance around he had waved back.

Our only problem now was crossing the river. Sampans in broad daylight were too risky. So we stripped to our skivvies, bundled our gear and clothes, except for the pants, into our ponchos, and tied the ponchos as airtight as possible. Then we knotted the bottoms of the pants legs, swooshed them through the air, and tied the waist with the belt. Presto! An inflated raft that would work for a short time.

Two of the strikers waded in first, a minute and ten yards apart. We knelt on the bank, wary of any sound. None came. The swift current carried the two several hundred feet downstream before they reached the other side.

The water was deep—I didn't touch anywhere—and warm. In a half hour we were all ashore and dressed. I lit my first cigarette in two days and felt like a teenager again—giddy-headed with the first puff.

"Put those cigarettes out! Hit the dirt!" shouted Top.

I was moving even as Top spoke. We all heard the motor at the same time. Whatever it was was big and close and moving toward us from behind a curve upriver. We slid back into the grass. Then it came into view. An ancient, dirty, and awesome patrol boat.

"That's the motherfucker," said Top hoarsely. "The one that pinned us down at Hiep Phung."

Although I hadn't been there, I remembered the battle from the bodies in my dispensary. Two stacks of three coffins each. Another twenty-one wounded. It had happened three months ago and the Army never really believed it. Hiep Phung was a hamlet on the Bassac north of our camp and literally on the border between Vietnam and Cambodia. The owner of the outdoor restaurant had a line down the middle of one table to mark the border. There had been no previous trouble. It started one morning when four men from D Company, camped outside Hiep Phung, entered town as usual to trade for food. Ten Viet Cong stepped out from behind a hut and began firing. Three strikers died instantly and the other was captured. Minutes later mortar shells started falling, and they fell . . . and they fell . . . all day long. It was three in the afternoon before Top, Hood, and Cranston, and C Company could get there. Two huts were still standing, and the VC had taken positions in the rubble.

The CIDG counterattacked. For a while it looked like we were going to take it back easily. Then a gunboat—this gunboat moving down the Chlong toward us now—appeared in the Bassac beside Hiep Phung. They swung a fifty-caliber anti-aircraft machine gun around and began sweeping Hiep Phung. Top called it "terrifying." "Those slugs ripped chunks the size of baseballs out of trees around us," he said.

That morning when we had received word of the attack at camp, we had radioed Can Tho where two South Vietnamese Navy gunboats were anchored. They got to Hiep Phung thirty minutes after the Cambodian gunboat had pinned our men down. Top said the Saigon fleet had approached to within a half mile when that fifty turned and loosed a few rounds over their decks. The pair spun around and had not been seen since. That night our men withdrew. In the course of the next week Choi and three hundred troops pushed the VC back into Cambodia. No one had seen the gunboat again. Until now.

In fact, no one but us and the VC believed the gunboat existed. Choi had reported the affair to the government. Saigon said that it wouldn't be best to antagonize such an old friend as Cambodia and that they doubted the gunboat was really there. Even our own officers in Can Tho would not okay our after-action report until they sent a first lieutenant out to "verify" our account. Top dragged the lad to Hiep Phung and braced him against a pine tree while he dug out a fifty-caliber slug. Reluctantly the officer admitted that someone had fired a fifty.

Now the gunboat moved heavily down the river. There was little chance they had seen us. I was glad I hadn't been with Top and Hood that day. You felt so helpless before such a monster of metal. The anti-aircraft gun, partially hidden under a tarpaulin, was mounted on the forward deck. I could see sixty-millimeter mortars mounted front and rear, and cases of ammunition with Chinese markings stacked around them. On deck a handful of khaki-clad North Vietnamese soldiers lounged.

"Good God Almighty," said Wheaty. "Did you see that?"

"Yeah, I've seen it before. From the fighting end," said Top.

The boat was still in view when the motor noise suddenly changed and the vessel turned sharply to the right. For a crazy moment I thought they had seen us and were coming back. It was four hundred yards downstream. There was a quick horn blast. Then an impossible thing happened—a curtain of jungle along the river started to move. Moments later there was a thirty-foot-wide opening into a man-made harbor. The brush was lashed to the sides of sampans, which were being paddled out of the way. The gunboat squeezed into the harbor, and the jungle closed back on itself. The river was empty once again.

"Japanese, huh?" asked Frenchy. "We blow up?"

"I don't know," said Top. "She must have come through special canals in Cambodia, or else the SDC post is blind."

I thought how close we must have come to that harbor when we were in Cambodia. Wheaty, showing surprising initiative, was on the radio giving the boat's position to the SDC post. In case something happened to us.

Top said, "What's the biggest mortar that post has?"

I said, "A sixty. They've got two. Range is a little more than fifteen hundred meters. They'd be shooting near maximum."

Top asked Wheaty, "Should we do it, sir? I owe 'em something." For Top to say "sir" was a rare concession to the lieutenant's rank, and it was clear that, in O'Hara's mind, we should.

"Hell, yes," said Wheaty. "Let's blow them out of the water."

Top already had the compass and map out. "Okay. Give them our position. Target azimuth is one hundred and eighty-six degrees. Range is fifteen hundred meters. Use HE." HE was high explosive. The rest of us spread out along the bank.

Top said, "They may try to run for it. Get your grenades ready. Lieutenant, tell them to fire three rounds when ready."

Wheaty called in the order.

A long minute passed. Jaws got tighter. Even the animals sensed something was afoot. We heard a whistle overhead and I knew it was too low. The first round hit a hundred yards downriver, near the opposite shore. The explosion was muffled and water sprayed into the air. Two more rounds bracketed that one.

Behind me, on the radio, Wheaty said, "Right thirty. Raise four hundred. Three rounds HE. Fire."

I fancied I heard shouts downriver, but it may have been my imagination. Suddenly the jungle where the vessel had gone in began moving.

Distant whistles passed above as the forth, fifth, and sixth rounds arched over and hit twenty-five yards from the harbor, but too far inland. Leaves and branches jumped into the air.

"Left fifty. Raise twenty-five. Three rounds HE. Fire."

Even as Wheaty spoke, the gunboat smashed through the brush before the sampans were out of the way. One boat flipped over and the man waved his arms like a dancing puppet until he disappeared under the gunboat. She was coming out fast and turning downstream.

"Goddamn, they're going to get away!" shouted Wheaty.

Then the first round in the new group hit, just behind a quartet of fifty-gallon drums on the stern. Mentally, I pushed the next round forward. It landed behind the rear mortar, blowing it, its mount and ammo cases high in the air. The big boat shuddered. The third round crashed somewhere amidships and the explosion was deadened. Then all hell broke loose as a secondary explosion went off. A man stumbled off the bow. More explosions rocked the boat. Wheaty gave an excited "Cease fire!" Flames were spreading too quickly over the boat—she must have been carrying gasoline or oil. Fire leaped into the water and covered the men trying to swim away. Their awful screams lasted only a moment in that heat.

"Sink, you mother! Sink!" Top shouted.

"Die Japanese!" screamed Frenchy. The other strikers had big grins and were slapping everyone on the back.

The stern lifted crookedly out of the water. She was breaking up. Ten minutes later there was only an oily mess burning in the water.

"Let's get out of here," said Top.

I glanced at my watch and was surprised to see it was only noon. We went cross-country until we met the Bassac and then headed south, walking on a skinny trail that became more and more familiar. The rains started at 1415 hours. We bundled up in our ponchos and kept going.

We were home in time for fried squash and onions, manioc, roast duck, and broiled glue.

After supper we (except for Wheaty who was showering and Top who was talking to Choi) were sitting around the table sipping coffee.

I asked Hood, "Do you think there'll be any repercussions from Cambodia?"

"I doubt it," he said. "They don't want it known the VC are using gunboats and hiding in Cambodia. I doubt we'll hear a word about it. Neither Cambodia nor Saigon will admit that Cambodia is a VC sanctuary, because it would strain both of their relations with Washington. In the world of politics the VC are only where it is expedient that they should be."

Santee said, "Say, Warren, you should've asked them if they'd let you ski down the Chlong."

46

Before I could think of a clever rejoinder, Hood said, "Which reminds me, did you know you were a saint now?"

"Well, I knew you guys liked me, but I never expected—"

"No, seriously. I dropped in to see the village chief in Nan Phuc yesterday and damned if he didn't have a picture of you on his altar. Incense, candles, flowers. The works."

"What?"

"It's true," added Cranston. "I saw one too. Nice frame and all. Really far out."

"Come off it. What are you all talking about? What kind of picture?"

Hood said, "You were waterskiing, naked except for your jockey shorts and a carbine over your shoulder. It must have been when you were coasting in for a stop. There was no rope and you have both arms outstretched. You can't see the skis. The chief said the villagers are calling you a '*than thanh*.' Which roughly means 'a saint.' '*Than thanh bac si dao bao*' or 'the saintly doctor who walks on water.' "

I think I was actually blushing. "That doesn't—" Then I knew. "Where'd they get those photographs? Who sold them the pictures?"

Santee found a hangnail that needed biting.

"Did you have anything to do with this?"

"Now, Warren—" Santee turned on a silky voice. "I didn't make any claims or anything. The villagers were thrilled the day you and Cranston went skiing. One of the strikers had a camera—an ancient old box camera—and took a picture. There's no harm in a few prints."

"How much?" I asked.

"Look, Phil, you can have one free. Heck—"

"Not for me, numbskull. How much are you charging the villagers?"

"Only a hundred P's. Framed and everything. That ain't bad. It's costing me eighty-eight P's for the print and the frame, so it's a fair price."

I had to laugh. The idea of me, a saint. In jockey shorts, no less.

While I was still chuckling, the door opened and Wheaty waved me outside.

"What's up, sir?"

"This damned tape you put on my balls is itching me to death. Don't you have something to take it off?"

The only thing that might help would be soaking in warm, soapy water and hydrogen peroxide. "You'll have to do it for an hour or so. Go back in the team house and I'll fix you up a bowl."

I warmed some water and sat Wheaty on one of his mail-order schoolbooks. He dropped his balls in the liquid.

Hood said, "You all missed hearing about the great tractor folly. A MAAG captain in Can Tho decided tractors worked so well in the United States that they had to work well here. So the Army spent thousands of dollars shipping a dozen Massey-Fergusons over. The brass held a big ceremony in Can Tho, inviting all the reporters and photographers down. The story goes the captain got on the tractor, drove it into a rice field, and promptly got stuck. They cranked up two more tractors to get that one unstuck and they all got mired in. Couldn't get any of them out. Even tried a deuce and a half. So somewhere near Can Tho there are three brand-new American tractors rusting and sinking into the ground." A deuce and a half was a two-and-a-half-ton truck, one of the biggest used by the Army in Vietnam.

"It makes you wonder what the Vietnamese must think of the Army," said Cranston.

"Hell, it makes me wonder what I think of the Army," said Santee.

Top came in from his debriefing with Major Choi and opened a beer. Spotting Wheaty's ball bath, he said, "Dear me, is the lieutenant washing hisself?" He turned to Hood. "Pick up anything while we were gone?"

48

"The only interesting tidbit is that the VC are closing the door in III Corps between Qui Nhon and Plei Khu. That's the same strategy Giap used against the French. He moved troops from Hue to Qui Nhon and turned inland. At the same time, two regiments snuck down the Ho Chi Minh trail to Plei Khu and turned left. The country was cut in half, and four months later Dien Bien Phu fell. They're going to try it again."

"Might as well," said Top. "It worked once, and I doubt that Westmoreland or any of these other jokers, except maybe Yarborough, can even spell guerrilla warfare."

General William Yarborough was the man who brought Special Forces to our finest hour. In the face of opposition from virtually every other general in the Army, Yarborough fought, finagled, and finally won the ear of President Kennedy and the money from Congress to build the type of fighting force he envisioned Special Forces should be—men who would be a fifth column, men who would recruit and train a guerrilla force in the back yard of the enemy. After Kennedy was assassinated, the Pentagon waited a decent interval and then shipped Yarborough off to Korea. Already our role was changing. Fixed camps. No patrols in Cambodia. TO&E's. Requisition forms.

Hood went on, "And I heard, again, the rumor that Westy's thinking about bringing in ground troops."

Top said, "That'd be one of the dumber moves. If we bring in American ground soldiers, the VC'll just go back in the jungle and wait twenty more years."

The big problem was that Westmoreland was not at all convinced guerrilla warfare tactics were any good. From everything I heard, he still thought in World War II terms, and that would be a tragic mistake. Our training consisted of Che Guevara, Mao Tse-tung, General Giap, and Ho Chi Minh, and our basic lesson had been "You cannot win a guerrilla war without the support of the people." We spoke

Vietnamese; we were familiar with the customs of the people, and we took great pains to treat them as our equals.

The only evidence I had seen that MAAG even knew civilians existed was the doling out of vitamin pills, a useless activity at best, and propaganda pamphlets to people who probably couldn't read. That sort of thing does more harm than good. People are given a pill or a shot, which they expect to do something good to them. So they take a pill and nothing happens. They still have a nagging backache or a dripping dick or a cough. And they naturally distrust MAAG or the government even more. They'll only remember the time they were given a pill that did nothing. Medically, it was even more dangerous: antibiotics, particularly the penicillins, must be given in large enough quantity and consistently over a period of time to prevent the germ from developing an immunity to the medicine.

I had no confidence in Westmoreland's idea that by bringing in ground troops he could engage the Viet Cong in major battles where our air power could wipe them out. The French deliberately stood at Dien Bien Phu to lure the Viet Minh into a set-piece battle where the superior French fire power would demolish them.

The door opened and Major Choi walked in. He wore severely tailored brown camouflaged fatigues—I couldn't remember having seen him in anything else—rubber sandals, and an ammo belt with a loaded forty-five on it. Choi was tall for a Vietnamese—about five feet nine. His smooth brown skin and coal-black hair belied his forty-two years. He was a handsome man, not so much in classic good looks, but in his friendly eyes, tiny smile wrinkles, and his open personality. He had the quiet but forceful manner of a good leader. One you trusted.

Top and Wheaty both stood up to offer him their chairs. We had dismissed such trivialities as saluting, except on formal occasions. Choi smiled and then noticed Wheaty's balls, sticking out of his pants. Soap suds dripped off the white tape.

"I hope I'm not interrupting anything," he said, staring at the lieutenant's privates.

Wheaty followed Choi's stare down and turned beet red. "I was, uh, just," Wheaty stuttered, stuffing his testicles inside his pants, ". . . soaking the tape. You see, I had this leech—" In his frantic movements Wheaty knocked over his chair, spilling the bowl and book onto the floor. The major picked them up and glanced at the book.

" 'How You Can Be a Successful Meat Cutter,' eh? Maybe you need to practice more," said Choi, handing the book back to Wheaty. "Please continue."

Top was in a spasm of coughing from trying not to laugh.

Choi addressed us all. "First, I want to congratulate Lieutenant Wheaty, Sergeant O'Hara, and Sergeant Warren for the brave and excellent work in sinking the VC gunboat. You acted wisely and well. That is one thing we won't have to worry about in the future. Second, I wanted to see Sergeant Santee a moment, if it is convenient."

Top said, "Go ahead, Santee. We were only shooting the shit. And, Lieutenant, wipe your pants off."

Forty-five minutes later Santee came back.

"What happened?" asked Top.

"Oh, a little problem. The police chief discovered the two women I have making VC flags. Except he didn't know they worked for me and arrested them, thinking they were VC. I got it straightened out. Choi went down with me. The police chief was disappointed because it was the first time he had ever arrested anyone. In fact, after I explained the flags, Choi wanted to go in as a partner. It would help the women, and us too, make a little extra money."

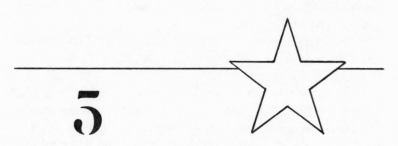

5

THREE DAYS later Choi asked us to become mercenaries for him.

During that time Wheaty and Choi had again attempted to radio to higher headquarters, but no luck. Our C-team refused to acknowledge us, and the Vietnamese Army said we had to go through our own channels. Wednesday evening after supper Top stood up and cleared his throat.

"It's been nearly a month since we were supposed to have been shipped back. Payday's coming and the water is still rising. Between us chickens, it don't look like anyone is hurrying to pick us up. Choi and I had a long talk this afternoon." Top coughed and scratched his ear.

"Choi has offered us a little deal to stay here and advise the Hoa Hao. Sort of consultants. He'll give us all a one-grade promotion, pay us the equivalent of what we were making, in dollars or piasters, and give us complete freedom of movement and training. We would report directly to him. Any time we can get out and want to go, we go. No questions asked.

Naturally, if the Army discovers its error, we are free to go. That, short and sweet, is his offer. Like I said before, whatever we do, we do together." Top sat down and laced his hands behind his head.

There was silence until Cranston said, "Far fucking out, man."

Suddenly we all had questions. Santee wanted to know if the salaries included jump pay. I asked what, specifically, we'd be doing. Wheaty wondered if our becoming soldiers in another army was legal. All of us except Hood. He had a faint smile and I knew he'd already decided.

"Knock it off," growled Top. "One at a time. I don't know about the regulations, Lieutenant. I figure no one has to know about this except Major Choi and us. A private agreement. It ain't our fault we're here. As for salaries, Santee, it'll be full salary, with jump pay. If in piasters, at whatever the going black-market rate is—right now a hundred eighty-five to the dollar. Now, Warren, our duties would remain basically the same—training cadre and soldiers. Choi did hint that we might take a few more exploratory patrols, like the one last week. Let's all think it over tonight. We'll decide tomorrow at lunch. There ain't much to add to what we talked about a couple weeks ago, except the water is higher and the VC still have the Bassac cut off."

After supper I sacked out because I had guard duty later. I dropped the mosquito net and tucked the bottoms under the mattress. So we were going to be on our own. Excitement and fear ran through me like a chill. It was close to the same feeling I'd had the day I volunteered for Special Forces. Two years ago. A lifetime. No one in my family had ever been in the Army, and I enlisted unassigned. I figured I'd start as a private, rise through the ranks as befitted my talents, and probably emerge a captain or major after three years. A harsh enlightenment, to say the least. Since I was unassigned, the Army tortured me through a battery of tests and in its infinite wisdom decided I should be a computer specialist. I could not believe it. The only course I had failed in my entire life was freshman mathematics. I was miserable.

It was in the last week of basic and in that frame of mind that I listened to a gnarled green-bereted sergeant hurry through a recruiting speech for Special Forces. He told of body-wrecking physical conditioning and mind-bending classroom work. He described eating snakes, blowing up bridges, crawling through the jungles to assassinate black-hearted Communists. All the things I dreamed about as a boy. Except I grew up and they said put away your childish things. I listened to him with growing excitement. Especially when he said that Special Forces took precedence over any previous assignment.

I argued with myself. Warren, you're a low-rent dip shit coward if you don't try it. All you have to do is go up and sign. But wait, what if I don't make it? Nobody'll know. You could flunk out of ten training schools and who would be the wiser? Are you going to spend three years programming computers? What did you do in the Army? I fearlessly and without regard for my own safety did, on the day of August 23, actually program four computers to give a variable cost analysis on the feasibility of using squeegee mop heads instead of cotton fiber mop heads. Three years of my life wasted. I watched the women come and go, talking of Michelangelo. Do I dare to eat a peach? Mr. Eliot, do I dare descend the stairs?

"Excuse me, Sergeant. Did you say that Special Forces took precedence over any assignment? I've been—"

"Put your John Henry right there, boy. It overrides any, I say, any assignment you have."

Two months of parachute school, three months of basic medical training, nine months of advanced medical training, three months of Special Forces dog lab training, three months of cross-training in light and heavy weapons, two months of language training, and three months of country training, and here I was.

I remembered the first time I saw Vietnam. We landed at night at Ton So Nhut airport in battle gear straight from Fort Bragg. An agency man met us, said as little as possible, and let us pick our personal weapons from a huge arms room. The next morning an Air America C-130 flew us to Can Tho. Half of me was scared because I was afraid the VC would shoot the plane down, but the other half was trying to memorize every detail. This is my country, I thought. Vietnam. My delta. God, the land was beautiful. A green checkerboard of rice fields and irrigation ditches. Rows of dark trees lined the canals. Flat for as far as I could see. Now and then we flew over a string of smoke from someone's breakfast fire.

And I had been falling more in love with the country and the people ever since.

A loud *thunk!* jarred me out of the sleep I was drifting into. Wheaty shouted happily, "I got one! I hit the little fucker!"

I stuck my head out of my door and nearly bumped into Wheaty, who was running down the hall carrying an arrow with a squirming rat impaled on the tip. Jesus Christ, the lieutenant has finally gone nuts. We did have a rat problem, especially now that the floods were driving the rats to higher ground. But an arrow?

"What happened, sir?" I asked, not sure that I wanted to know.

"I was lying there with my crossbow all loaded and waiting. Rats are always running around in the room at night, and I knew I'd get one sooner or later. Look at that, would you! I got me a goddamn rat!"

Santee was looking over the arrow. "Where did you get the crossbow?"

"A striker loaned it to me."

Top, who was on guard duty, had also come inside.

"Wheaty, you're going to shoot yourself in the ass or one of us with that thing. Sir, take the rat out of here."

Wheaty cackled to himself and walked out, waving the rat. I went back to bed, thinking I must be insane to stay with these madmen.

The next thing I knew, Top was shaking me. "Warren, 0200. Guard."

It was warm enough for the light cotton pajamas, so I slipped on rubber sandals, thinking with amusement that my taxes sent used Firestone tires to South Korea for a self-help AID program. The tires were cut into sandals, shipped to South Vietnam, and ended up on my feet.

I looked forward to guard with Hood. If I got him started on history, I would be in for several hours of pleasant earfuls. History was a hobby with him, and he had a good memory for facts.

Hood was thirty years old, stood six feet tall, and weighed 180 pounds. His blood pressure was a healthy 100/70. His blood type was O positive, the same as Wheaty's and mine. Heartbeat 60 times to the minute. There was no indication in his records why his face and neck were so scarred. But it had to be acne. There wasn't a place on his face or neck that wasn't pockmarked.

The last half inch of the formerly longest finger of his left hand was missing, sawed off accidentally when he was eighteen. Two years ago, on his first trip to Vietnam, he was hit in the left thigh by a dumdum round. A dumdum round is made by cutting a small X in the tip of a bullet. The bullet flattens and spreads out on impact. Dumdums were ruled illegal and inhumane by the Geneva Convention. The one that hit Hood shattered the femur, and doctors worked seven hours wiring the pieces together. Now, except for a slight favoring of that leg, you'd never know it. He also bore a long scar on his right knee from another accident with a saw when he was a teenager. He was allergic to primaquine phosphate, one of the primary prophylactic medicines for malaria. I substituted chloroquine easily enough.

Hood was the youngest of five children. He was born in Little Rock, Arkansas, and his mother died during his birth. I got the feeling from several comments that Hood's father never quite forgave him for causing, in his mind, his wife's death. Hood's father worked in a furniture factory, and after his wife died, the family barely survived. Hood graduated from high school with good grades and went to work in the same furniture factory. After a few years the management offered him a partial engineering scholarship to Arkansas State, but, Hood told me, he was scared of college and not confident he could make it. No one in his family had ever been to college. He was drafted a year later and had been in the Army since then, gravitating to Special Forces intelligence work six years ago. He was married to a home-town girl, who lived in Little Rock, but I knew little else about her, except that they had no children.

Top swore by Hood's intelligence network. Speaking both Vietnamese and French, Hood went straight to the hamlets for his contacts. None of this hiring a local Vietnamese who then in turn set up a spy net. Hood would sit for hours gnawing a rat bone and sipping rice wine with a villager for one piece of information. He respected the Vietnamese and they knew it. When we were switched over to the regular Army, our money for intelligence work was cut by 80 per cent. But that was only a temporary setback. He and Choi failed to report the next ten strikers who quit or retired or deserted (which was rare among the Hoa Hao), and used that money for intelligence work.

I poured a cup of coffee from the all-night pot Lon left on the stove and walked outside. Hood had moved the chairs against the shower so that one of us would face south and west and the other north and east.

" 'Lo, Hood. How is it tonight?"

"Peaceful. Very peaceful."

After a few minutes of silence Hood asked, "What do you think about Choi's offer?"

"I'll do whatever the team decides. Choi's a good man. I trust him and I wouldn't have any doubts about staying for a while."

Hood stood up. "I'll go make the round. If I'm not back in twenty minutes, run like hell." That was his standard joke. One of the few he told. We checked the guards on the wall every forty-five minutes or so, varying the time to set no pattern. Our camp was twice the size of a football field and literally built on a mud pile in the middle of a rice field. During the monsoons it was an island. The rest of the year a moat, thirty feet deep and thirty feet across, circled the camp and ran into the Bassac. Beyond the moat for two hundred feet in all directions was triple-decker concertina wire, decked with assorted booby traps and empty tin cans. The wall itself was a thicket of punji stakes and antipersonnel mines connected to the command bunker, under our fifty-caliber machine gun. The mines could be fired individually or as an entire wall at once. Also buried in the outer wall was our secret weapon: fifty-gallon drums filled with gasoline. They were rigged with C4 and, if exploded, would throw up a wall of fire around the camp. The idea for that came about by happenstance. Once during a supply drop by the Agency, a parachute on a gas drum failed to open and the drum buried itself five feet in the wall. While we were pondering how to get it out, Santee said, "Mine it." A machine-gun bunker guarded each corner, and two-man concrete bunkers ringed the inner wall. Around our team house were our own machine guns and mortar pits. The ammo dump also could be exploded from the command bunker or from the inside, if it came to that.

Hood padded up softly. "Only found one asleep. I snuck up behind him and put a knife to his throat and then woke him up. I don't think he'll fall asleep again."

"What do you think about Choi's offer?" I asked.

"It can't be much worse than this pile of shit we're in now. It isn't like it used to be. You've seen what's happening. We got an order a month ago telling us that standard Army uniforms would be worn at all times, complete with name tag, U.S. Army patch, and rank. Can you imagine going in the jungle with a white name tag? It makes a nice target."

"I never saw that order."

"O'Hara tore it up. And that isn't all. You know those SDC posts up next to the border with big arrows inside?"

The arrows were fifteen feet long and had empty cans nailed on top. If the post was hit and called in air support, the soldiers were to fill the cans with gasoline, light them and point the arrow in the direction of the attack, so the planes would know where to bomb.

Hood continued, "We got word just before the radio went out that American pilots had been ordered not to fly within five miles of the Cambodian border on the chance they might accidentally violate Cambodian airspace. We've got to tell those brave men out there that nobody is ever going to see their lighted arrows."

It was ironic that our Air Force was now bombing the hell out of North Vietnam and yet would not fly in support of our own camps. Only sketchy reports had come in about the bombing up north. Apparently it was in retaliation for some incident in the Tonkin Gulf more than a month ago. I could understand bombing an oil field or an air base, but Johnson was dropping tons of bombs on the jungle to knock out supplies and men coming south. That didn't make much sense to me. There was no way in hell a B-52 could stop thousands of men on foot and bicycle in jungle terrain unless, of course, they so devastated the jungle that there was nothing left. But that was a ridiculous possibility.

I thought about some other changes since the regular Army had taken over. Before that we had been controlled by the CIA, but we held occasional operations with MAAG. MAAG consisted of Army officers who theoretically lined up side by side with the South Vietnamese officers to lend them their experience.

Westmoreland had been given command of MAAG nine months ago, and he couldn't stand the idea that there were 5000 Special Forces men supervising 60,000 CIDG over whom he didn't have control. Three trips to Washington and six months later we were sold out. The highest bidder won, only the currency was political influence, not results.

In my own case the regular Army's stupidity was affecting some of my medical treatments. The previous medic left good records on the local villagers, particularly an elderly man named An Hoac Tien. Tien was a quiet, soft-spoken, shy man, who handled odd jobs around camp. He had advanced tuberculosis, endemic in the delta. We were trained to treat TB, provided no hospital was available and provided we could give the extended care needed. The CIA always gave us the proper drugs. The previous medic convinced Tien of the importance of taking his four pills every day, and he came promptly every two weeks to renew his supply. By the time I got here, his cough had decreased and he had gained thirteen pounds. We were making some progress.

Then Westy won his fight. MAAG answered my first requisition for medical supplies this way: "Isoniazid and aminosalicylic acid [two of the three necessary drugs to treat TB] are not on the list of approved drugs for use by Army medics in Vietnam."

I ranted and raved for days. Even Top got on the radio to the C-team, but it was all useless. I tried to buy the medicines on the black market in Chau An, but the only ones were French and were fifteen years old.

I had to tell Tien, "I'm sorry, we don't have your medicine any more." The corners of his mouth had twitched as if trying to form a polite smile, but then fell as he realized he had no hope left. He walked away slowly, looking at the ground. I go by and talk to Tien whenever I can and give him a little codeine for the cough. Yesterday his wife told me he coughed up some blood.

Hood interrupted my thoughts. "A hundred dollars says if an election were held today between Khanh and Ho Chi Minh, Uncle Ho would win hands down."

General Nguyen Khanh was the latest president, having been ousted once but reinstated with a little help from General Maxwell Taylor, and having survived two attempted coups, all since the beginning of September.

"Everything I've read indicates Ho is first a nationalist and second a Communist. More than anything else, I think he wants to get his country together again," I said.

"Sure. And he's playing China off against Russia to get guns and to keep from being forced into the arms of either one. Sometimes I think we should've made a deal with Ho to set up an independent Vietnam favorably disposed toward the U.S. A wedge between China and Russia. Then other times I'm not so sure. What about those hundred thousand Catholics who fled North Vietnam in 1954 and those hundred thousand more who didn't get out in time and are now six feet under somewhere?"

"If they could ever get together and let the people honestly vote, maybe that would settle it," I said, the eternal optimist speaking to the eternal pessimist.

"I'm not sure that most Vietnamese understand representative government. Their major concern is still survival. They don't understand highways, water-treatment plants, international relations, or other alleged signs of civilization," Hood said.

"Speaking of which, Lao, my nurse, thinks we have Viet Cong in America. Yesterday I told her I'd be getting out of the Army soon, and she didn't seem to understand. Finally she asked, 'You have no VC in America?' I explained that we didn't. She listened but I don't think she got it. She believes

61

VC are everywhere in the world and the rest of the world is like Vietnam."

"It's all she's ever seen," said Hood.

"She also thinks blacks have black blood. I tried to explain it, but she doesn't understand the idea of a germ, much less what blood and heredity are all about. She probably picked up the idea from Top," I added jokingly. Oddly, Hood didn't laugh.

Lao Thi Manh was my twenty-six-year-old nurse, having been trained by previous medics here. In spite of the above incident she was intelligent, funny, and, except for her eye, beautiful. She was born with a right eye that constantly pulled to the right and was always bloodshot. I had described it to our C-team doctor, and he thought two or three operations might help. She was afraid to see him. Otherwise she was lovely—flowing black hair and tawny, long legs. Lao had a crush on Cranston, and he seemed to be sweet on her, too. When she wasn't working in the dispensary, she hung around his radio room, giggling and carrying on. Maybe I was a little jealous.

As a nurse, she was good as long as she was supervised. She was conscientious and careful but had trouble with sterile techniques. Her parents were killed by the Viet Minh in 1953, and she had been raised by an elderly couple in Nan Phuc. Her only brother, four years older, was killed when Diem ambushed the Hoa Hao armies.

I made a tour of the wall. The air was warm and humid and blowing from the west.

"All quiet," I told Hood. "The striker you scared half to death told me three times how you held the knife up to his neck. Instead of being contrite, he's having a ball telling everyone about it."

A few minutes later the silence was stopped by loud boom-boom-booms from Nan Phuc. The mad drummer had started. Every morning, exactly at 0430 hours, he commenced to pound on a log. A slow, rhythmic beat that built to a peak, fell quickly, and began again. Each minute was punctuated by a loud metal bong. He stopped precisely at 0500. For the first few weeks here I had assumed the man was the local timekeeper or was performing some ancient Hoa Hao rite. I was finally told that he believed in an offshoot religious cult. A very small cult. He was the only member. His divine purpose was to make converts, and his method of persuasion was to pound on his hollow log every morning. Everyone in Nan Phuc hated the noise. The villagers had begged him to quit. Several men in the village were said to be plotting to steal his log and gong.

Not long after 0500, sunrise came swiftly across the Bassac. Lon was rattling dishes and guard duty was over.

After lunch Top called for a vote on Choi's offer. "Let's go around the table. If you have any doubts, speak up. This ain't a fucking PTA meeting."

Cranston, Santee, Hood, and I all said we would stay. Wheaty said, dropping his voice an octave, "I've thought long and hard about this. As near as I can tell it's against Army regulations to join a foreign army. But since we seem to be more or less trapped here and since Major Choi promised me captain, I guess we'll stay. But remember, when we go back, or if the Army finally finds us, we never worked for Choi."

"That's it, then," said Top. "You all have about as little sense as I hoped you'd have. I'll go give the main man the good news."

After Top left, we looked at each other with silly grins on our faces, much as if we'd all been thrown in jail for drunk and disorderly and we really didn't give a rat's ass.

That afternoon at 1600 hours we filed into Choi's briefing room, which was also his office and living room. He greeted us with smiles and nods as we sat down in small, straight-backed chairs.

"Sergeant O'Hara has told me about your decision and I welcome you to the Hoa Hao. I am sorry about your, ah, situation, but I am very pleased to have you with me now."

As he talked he absent-mindedly took his pig's teat from his pocket and worried it with his hand. It was the size of a half-dollar. The skin for a half inch around the nipple had been cut out. Nervous handling of it through the years had turned it soft, supple, and nearly black. Choi carried it as a good-luck charm from some untold episode long ago. It was grotesque.

He went on, "We have five companies of well-trained soldiers. We are doing a good job against the Communists. But I am troubled at reports of increasing activity across the border. We will take steps to verify these things. Again, let me congratulate Sergeants O'Hara and Warren and Lieutenant Wheaty for destroying the gunboat. That is a most significant victory. Yesterday I spoke on the radio with a Major Ban Hiao of the 485th VC regiment. I offered him a fight anywhere, any time with the Hoa Hao. He said he would fight in the Seven Mountains. I said we would fight on the Giap Phang." Giap Phang was a large plain four miles east of our camp.

"Excuse me, Major Choi," broke in Hood. "You mean you talked with a Viet Cong major on the radio?"

"Yes. You remember our SDC post at Ba Phuc lost a PRC-10 on a patrol several weeks ago? Hiao found the radio."

That didn't mean Hiao had been listening to all our communications for the last fourteen days. We used a half dozen different frequencies, changing them constantly. Choi continued, "Hiao sounded older and more bitter. You may not know this, but Hiao and I fought against the French together and then fought against Diem together. For a while. We were lieutenants then." Choi paused reflectively.

Then he said, "In two months we harvest the rice. Because the VC will try to capture the rice, I am trying to buy a large riverboat to carry it downriver. This will help my people very much, and it will help the many other Hoa Hao living in Cambodia near the border."

I remembered from my country training that the French had ruled both Cambodia and Cochin China, which was the South Vietnamese delta, as one state. Thus, there were still many families with relatives on both sides of the border, which had been defined arbitrarily in 1954. About 100,000 Vietnamese lived in eastern Cambodia and probably that many Cambodians in Vietnam.

"We want our Hoa Hao to get fair pay for their rice. With a boat and your help we may be able to safeguard the rice. My officers will give you whatever you need in the way of uniforms, medicine, weapons, and so forth. Are there any questions?"

I think the realization of what we had done was sinking in.

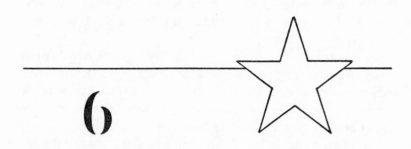

6

THE WATER, muddier than only two weeks before, sprayed from the boat as we motored upriver. Now and then a faint rainbow appeared in the droplets, and I wondered why rainbows were always curved, instead of straight or some other shape.

Today was exactly a month since we had been theoretically shipped back to Fort Bragg, and to celebrate the anniversary Cranston, four strikers, and I were taking a medical patrol to a village near C Company. Floodwaters were spreading over everything. A striker drove the boat from memory because it was impossible to see the main channel. Actually, "flood" is not quite the right word. The water moved slowly, and there was little danger of being swept away. It wasn't unusual to ride along a canal in Nan Phuc with ten feet of water under the boat and see children playing six feet away. The water would rise a few more feet and then stabilize for the next two months. It was eerie to know that we could turn the boat south and probably drive 250 miles straight into the China Sea. As far as a hundred miles inland at Can Tho, the paddies had a small tide.

Top had left two days ago, and the team house was strangely quiet. He was not only father confessor and comedian; he could sense problems between team members before they erupted and usually pierced the boil well ahead of time. Whatever a particular man reacted to, Top knew. With Cranston, it was a stern, fatherly talk; with Santee, an old-fashioned Army chewing out; with me, a little of both. Three days ago Choi's agents reported that American prisoners had been spotted in Cambodia, not far from the Mekong. Top was gone the next day in search of his former teammates. He and Wheaty got into a terrific shouting argument about whether or not he should go. It stopped when Top threatened to take Wheaty behind the team house and whip his ass. I think Top would have gone alone if Hood had not talked him into taking Frenchy. It was two years since the Viet Cong had overrun Hop Tac.

We reached C Company without trouble. C's headquarters were in an old and small pagoda just off the Bassac. It was a simple wooden building on stilts. One of Huynh Phu So's teachings was that money used to construct elaborate pagodas could better be used for other causes. Inside, paintings on the walls depicted the "Ten Good Things," similar to Christianity's Ten Commandments. A photograph, browned with age, of So sat on a wooden altar. Several brass Buddhas were perched on shelves. They bore the reversed swastika of the Dan Xa, the semi-secret political arm of the Hoa Hao.

The company commander detailed two medics to go with us, and we set off again. The village was two miles down the canal, and we were there in twenty minutes.

And for the next three hours there was bedlam. There was no such thing as standing in line—everyone wanted to watch. My patients were mostly mothers and babies, and a few old men. The young men were either strikers or Viet Cong. On my first patrols I'd been dismayed that everyone in a village appeared on sick call. Then I'd realized that at least half came to see the Americans and to view the show. Like a Baptist picnic.

Later I realized they were, in fact, probably all sick with something: leprosy, malaria, worms, cataracts, tuberculosis, skin rashes of all varieties, vitamin deficiencies. But it takes some education—even a smattering—for a person to know he has a disease and to transmit that fact to a doctor. So I got things like *bao lung* (backache). After questioning, I would discover the woman had paddled a sampan five miles to a rice paddy and worked there from dawn to dusk with two babies strapped on her back. But that I could handle, for a few hours at least. It was when I saw a baby nearly blind because of gonorrhea or an old man with leprosy that my heart broke.

A middle-aged, olive woman was pointing at a back tooth. *"Dao."*

"Dao, huh? *Neu lam?"* I followed the Vietnamese conversational gambit of repeating the last thing a person said and then going on.

"Neu lam. Dao neu lam," she said.

I looked inside her mouth. Because of the dark purple stain from betel nuts, it was hard to see anything. Betel nut chewing was practiced by nearly everyone. The nuts were mildly narcotic, similar to cigarettes, discouraged intestinal parasites, and caused some numbness in the mouth. In other words, good for what ailed you. I saw the problem. In her lower left rear molar was a hole, deep enough to have reached the pulp. She did not want it pulled. Hoa Hao women were proud of their teeth. I gently cleaned the tooth. I fashioned a cotton filling with zinc oxide and clove oil and tapped it in. The filling might hold for two weeks.

I recalled the first tooth I pulled. The father of one of our strikers appeared at sick call one day and asked me to pull a tooth. No ifs and buts. I looked and agreed. I concealed my nervousness and copped a peek at my medical notes. After the Novocain I began to work the tooth loose. I was terribly afraid of hurting him, so I proceeded slowly. Then I positioned the extractor on the tooth and cautiously rotated the tooth. I stopped once to wipe the perspiration from my face. Finally the old man could stand it no longer. He clamped his hands around mine. My first thought was that the pain was too much. Then he tightened his hold, jerked hard, and pulled the tooth himself. He spit out a mouthful of blood and smiled. After thanking him, I asked him to spit in the bucket, not on my floor.

The next woman said something that I didn't understand. The second time around, I realized she was addressing me as "the doctor who walks saintlike on the water." I denied it, but she only giggled. She complained of being weak and tired. She had no other symptoms, so I gave her fourteen vitamin pills and explained how to take them. I would be back in two weeks. Maybe, I told myself, she'll take them correctly. She knew they were vitamins but was obviously disappointed.

One legacy of the French was that drugs, including vitamins, should be given via injections. Unfortunately, the American Army used injections as little as possible, to avoid hepatitis and the problem of sterilization. After realizing this, I tried to get drugs in injection form. Not on the TO&E, MAAG said. Compounding the problem was that a variation of Chinese acupuncture, a holdover from the thousand years that China ruled Vietnam, was still practiced. Every village had its "Chinese doctor," who rubbed, scraped, punctured, and otherwise expelled bad spirits. My strikers came to me only after their "Chinese doctor" failed. But I had seen too many illnesses cured by a foot-long brass needle to be skeptical any more.

At last my footlocker was empty. Forty-five minutes later we were on the Bassac and the rain was pouring down. After a month and a half of rain, it had become part of life. You even looked forward to it.

Cranston faced me on the front seat. Charcoal-black hair and horn-rimmed glasses dressed a round face. Small eyes, small nose, ordinary mouth. In civilian clothes he could have been an insurance salesman or, at best, an assistant professor of theology. Until he opened his mouth.

"Far fucking out, man."

"What's that, Lance?"

He pointed. Going by was one of the larger sampans, home for an entire family. They were the emerging rural middle class: traders, travelers on the river, and dealers in pans, pots, cloth, and a little opium. The towns had their own middle class, and it was frighteningly like ours: hustlers, Honda salesmen, and whores. On this thirty-foot sampan a young woman hunkered in the rain, fanning a fire in a stone enclosure. The boat had a bamboo deckhouse with cut-out openings for windows. Fishing lines raced down the sides. One kid, pot-bellied, naked, and smiling, was peeing over the side. Two others were scrambling around the deck. All were being watched by their father, who pushed a giant tiller back and forth for propulsion.

"Man, that's what's happening. Going down the river, a few fishing lines out for supper. That's the life," said Cranston.

"Except for getting held up by the VC and shot at by Americans and ambushed by the Cambodians and questioned by the CIDG."

"Yeah. That's a hassle, all right," he said softly.

Cranston was weird, maybe even crazy. He was twenty-three and grew up in Brooklyn. The son of a dock worker, he had learned the fine art of street fighting as easily and normally as I, an only child, had learned to entertain myself. He had two older sisters, both of whom were married. Cranston was also brilliant. He entered the University of Maryland on a scholarship and attended off and on for four years. He never completed the necessary courses. Only ones like Italian, Russian, math, and psychology. Lance said that when he liked a course, he did well, usually an A. When he didn't, he dropped it. For six months he lived in one of the first communes in New Mexico. But it wasn't for him, and he was drafted while trying to win a surfing contest at Malibu Beach. Outwardly slow and offbeat, Lance was a miracle man with the radio and had graduated from Special Forces training with honors. He was one of those people who, when they decide to do something, do it incredibly well.

At five feet ten, he was deep-chested and broad, carrying his 185 pounds easily. He wore glasses for nearsightedness and slight astigmatism. Both appendix and tonsils had been removed. His blood pressure was 110/80, and his heartbeat was a steady 65. His only scar was on his left forearm, fading evidence of a teen-age fight. As a child he had had bad teeth—every tooth but four had fillings. He was allergic to poison ivy, but I had yet to see any in Vietnam.

"Lance, you got a thing going with Lao?" I asked, out of curiosity and perverseness.

"We kinda dig each other. She's one fine chick. She doesn't play the role all the time. Just sort of relaxed and calm. Nice body, too."

"What about when we leave?"

"That's something else now. My discharge is in a month. I've been thinking about getting out over here."

"Are you seriously thinking about staying on?" I asked.

"I don't know. I might try for a job with AID. If they bring in ground troops, though, it could get real bad. I'm not going to hurt Lao. We're only playing around with each other," he said. Then he added quietly, "I think."

As we turned the last bend in the river, we saw a huge wooden boat tied up to the main pier at Nan Phuc. We docked beside her, and I estimated she was a good fifty feet long. She had nice lines; a low hull swept up to a fifteen-foot bowsprit. Then I recognized it: a sloop-rigged skipjack. The skipjack was used during the nineteenth century, mainly by Chesapeake Bay oystermen. A two-foot wood railing encircled the twelve-foot-wide deck. It was at least fifty years old, but looked like it had been well cared for. Major Choi, followed by the village elders, climbed out of the aft cabin. Speaking through a grin, Choi invited us on board.

"I think this is our rice-carrying ship," he said.

"Where did you find it?" asked Cranston.

"A merchant in Saigon bought it from a retired American Naval officer who sailed it to Hong Kong many years ago. The rice merchant is going to import air conditioners."

She needed painting, and as we toured the boat I noticed water in the hold. Some replanking would be necessary. Four and a half feet of cargo space ran the length of the ship beneath the deck.

Choi was so proud of the boat that he had the strikers raise and lower the mains'l three times before we left.

Cranston and I motored around to the dock. With water so high, we could bring the boat through the moat that ran around the camp and dock beside the catfish latrine. The latrine embodied a fine symbiotic relationship. We shit through chairs with no seats in them. The fish ate the shit and we ate the fish. A baited line, dropped through a chair, would snag a fish within a minute.

After supper I held sick call for B Company, now in camp for its week off. The fourth man in had what looked suspiciously like an arrow wound. It was the third such wound in the past two weeks.

"How did you do this?"

"With a stick."

"What kind of stick?"

"A stick with a pointed end."

"Were you shooting a crossbow?" I asked, feeling like the straight man in a comedy team.

72

"Ah, no, no." Several strikers were giggling and poking each other.

I grabbed B Company's medic, who was helping me, and asked him what happened.

"He and a friend were shooting arrows at rats, but his friend hit him instead of the rat. Everyone is now shooting at rats like *Thieu Uy* Wheaty." *Thieu Uy,* pronounced "teewee," was Vietnamese for second lieutenant.

My God, I thought. Crazy Wheaty has started a fad now. We were getting more casualties from CIDG shooting each other with crossbows than from the VC.

The next few days passed quietly as we waited for some word from Top. The VC probed two SDC posts, wounding two soldiers and a woman. A hamlet south of us was entered by a VC psychological warfare team, who talked for several hours with the people. Choi was putting machine guns on the sailboat and Santee was hunting armor plating for the sides. The village chief's son, the police captain, beat Cranston in a game of pool. I talked with "Teewee" Wheaty (we, too, called him "Teewee") about the rat situation. I think he was secretly thrilled that somebody was emulating him.

Friday night, October 21, I was helping Hood with the Viet Cong propaganda when I found out he thought he was black. Over the past few weeks we had received more than the usual amount of propaganda leaflets. Most of it had been captured by strikers, but we were getting a goodly amount turned over to us from villagers. Hood kept a running tally of the dominant VC themes and the target groups so he could dream up counterthemes. Most of the propaganda was mimeographed on cheap manilla paper that turned brown in a few days.

"Listen to this one," I said, reading from a "Liberation News Letter":

> "Dear Friends, the more deaths the American Imperialists and their servants sustain, the deeper their dissen-

> sion becomes. *Coup d'états* and counter *coup d'états* were
> staged continuously by their generals in order to dispute
> power and positions. Two *coup d'états* within two days!
> This caused bloodshed among the soldiers themselves.
> Deceived by the Americans and their savage servants
> whom they hate for having forced them into a war against
> their own compatriots, hundred of soldiers have dropped
> their weapons on the battlefields when clashing with the
> Front's troops, thousands and thousands of soldiers have
> deserted with their weapons after firing in the head of the
> Americans and their leaders. The Hoa Hao Buddhist
> youths will not let speculators sell their blood to the
> American advisers and make them traitors of their
> country.

"Themes?" I asked.

"Several. Mark it number two, 'You are on the wrong side.
You are a dupe of the U.S.–Saigon clique, which is not worth
fighting for, certainly not worth dying for,' and number four,
'Desert. Everyone is doing it.' "

"Target?"

"The soldier and the young person."

"Here's a funny one," I said. " 'Down with McNamara's
Pacification Program!' How many Vietnamese farmers do you
reckon know who McNamara is?"

"Probably about as many as know who the new prime
minister is. Here's one for you: 'The U.S.–Saigon clique has a
long record of mistreating members of religious sects,' which is
true, 'You are being denied freedom to religion,' which is true,
and 'The U.S.–Saigon clique is using the religious sects for its
own political purposes,' which is mostly true. It's hard to argue
against those things."

Not all of the propaganda was pleasant. A consistent theme
was that Americans raped women and ate babies. The first

time I heard that, I laughed. But then I overheard Hoa Hao talking about the Vietnamese mountain people and how they drank blood and killed children. The Hoa Hao could conceive of such a possibility.

Later we were talking about staying in Vietnam, when Hood said, "In the first place, it's only temporary. And secondly, I don't figure we're really deserting the Army. They deserted us along the way. Even so, the Army ain't so bad. I've been in eight years. Made first sergeant two years ago." He paused a moment, as if deciding something, and then went on. "Then, too, it's more pleasant over here. You know how discrimination is such a problem in the States."

Hood almost slipped that by me. I glanced at him as I tried to figure out what he meant. He tanned easily and his hair was curly, but he certainly wasn't black or Mexican or anything noticeable. I knew he was married. Maybe his wife was black.

I phrased my words carefully. "I don't quite follow you. About that discrimination."

"Look, Phil, you've been to college and you're from the South. You know how they treat blacks down there. Even in the Army."

"Ahh. Yes. I think I see what you mean. But, uh, Hood, you, uh, is your wife . . . ?"

"Oh, no. I married white."

I looked at him again. Jesus, the man's putting me on.

"You mean you think you're black?" I asked, trying to put enough sarcasm in my voice so he'd pick it up and tell me it was all a joke.

Hood stared at me, his eyes dark and distant. "I may not look it, but I am." Not only was he serious; he rarely joked, and never the sort of jokes that involved deceiving someone else.

I didn't know what to say. The man was as white as I was. I tried to shift Hood over into that whole framework of a black, tried to fit him into some category, but he didn't match up anywhere. Even if he was, I couldn't say, "Hell, that's too bad. I'm very sorry to hear it."

I changed the subject.

Top returned on Sunday. He'd been gone a full week. As soon as we saw his face, we knew he'd found nothing. He said they had followed rumors thirty miles into the country. A few farmers reported they had seen American prisoners, but none matched the descriptions of Top's old team members, even after subtracting thirty or forty pounds a man. They had one close call when they accidentally walked into a small VC camp. Before they could backpedal, a guard asked for a password. Top, standing in shadows behind Frenchy, carefully raised his rifle. Frenchy immediately cursed the man for making noise and then asked him for a light. The guard was so flustered he gave Frenchy a match and sat down. Top and Frenchy strolled out.

Top uncovered one interesting piece of intelligence: those recoilless rifles we had seen at the 485th headquarters were stolen from a Special Forces camp fifty miles north of us. Top knew the first sergeant there and had advised him not to get recoilless rifles. As soon as the VC heard about them, Top had said, they would take them. Which is what happened. Top said the Cong attacked the camp, opposite the end where the new rifles were. While the defense was busy at that end, a VC suicide squad with two elephants crept in, loaded the rifles on the elephants, and crept out. Now those rifles were pointed down our throats less than five miles away.

That night, after supper, I got Top aside.

"Do you know that Hood thinks he's black?" I asked.

Top gave me a quizzical look. "Did he say that?"

"Yes."

"He usually don't talk about it."

"You mean he is?" I had a feeling that the whole team was mad.

"No, he ain't no more a nigger than I am. He's said something like that to me a couple times."

I wasn't getting the right answer. "Why the hell does he think he's black?"

Top gazed out across the camp. "I don't really know. One thing was that his birth certificate has a C in the place where it asks for race. His old man had put C for Caucasian. But down in Arkansas most whites put in W for white and niggers either put N for nigger or C for colored. And when Hood, who was a teenager at the time, asked his old man about it, he said it meant colored. He was probably joking. Then, too, in school, the kids teased him about having dark skin and curly hair. No mother, either. But I think what really convinced him was when somebody once told him that if your—what do you call these things? Half-moons?—in your fingernails were dark, you were part nigger. And his are dark. But he ain't no nigger. I've told him all that stuff is a bunch of bull. He's just got a thick head."

If I'd been Cranston, I would've said, "Far fucking out."

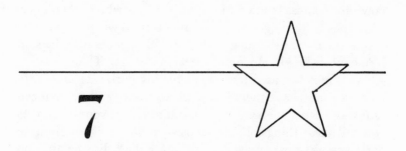

7

THREE DAYS later I killed my first man. It started Wednesday morning when I was preparing my surgical kits. In the absence of an autoclave, I had to make do. I scrubbed my instruments, washed them with Phisohex, sorted them into special packs, and pressure-cooked them for several hours.

Teewee Wheaty opened the door. "*Bac si,* you want to capture some VC?"

"Oh, hell, yes," I said without enthusiasm. Reports came in weekly that VC were at such and such a location. Mostly they fled before we arrived, or the rumors were just that.

Also going were Top, Major Choi, and a platoon of strikers. Wheaty explained that a defector had surrendered late last night and claimed three companions were in caves along the Bassac—about the same location where Cranston and I had gone skiing.

We crossed the Bassac in sampans and walked to within a hundred yards of a small bamboo thicket on the eastern bank. Nobody was taking it seriously. One striker was climbing a grapefruit tree, and two others were arguing about the source of rain. At least this might be good training. We lined the troops up in a semblance of order, while Choi walked into the field between us and the thicket.

Cupping his hands around his mouth, he shouted in Vietnamese, "This is the commander of the Hoa Hao army at Nan Phuc. We have you surrounded. We invite you to surrender now or else you will die. We will not shoot if you come out now."

There was no answer. Choi is a brave man and a good leader, but this is ridiculous, I thought. There are no VC in there. Choi walked back and spoke with the defector. The man pointed to the southern end of the thicket. Choi called us over.

"He said VC are in tunnels. They will not come out. We will fire for a few minutes and use rifle grenades."

During the next ten minutes thousands of bullets, each moving at three thousand miles per hour, and a dozen rifle grenades ripped the trees and bushes to pieces. Twigs, leaves, and bark clouded the air. The noise was terrific.

"Cease fire," Choi shouted. He stood and repeated his surrender offer.

Suddenly a half dozen words in Vietnamese were flung out from the trees.

"What did they say?" I asked a striker.

"He said, 'Come in and get us.' "

My first thought was about a bad John Wayne movie, then I realized there really were VC in there. I fell to the ground. A buzz ran through the strikers. Assholes were audibly tightened. This was no longer a training exercise. Why hadn't they shot? They could've killed half of us.

Top, lying with a squad thirty feet away, shouted, "Warren, let's move in. We'll go first. Cover us and go ahead on my signal." I signaled okay.

Rifle shots cracked, and Top and his men zigzagged fifty

feet before falling down. Top waved at me, and his men opened up. We leapfrogged Top's squad and ran to within seventy-five feet of the trees. I still had heard no return fire. But if I were a VC, I wouldn't be poking my head out either. We jumped squads again.

We were only a few feet from the trees and shooting like death was going out of style. My eight men flanked the lower end of the thicket, around to the Bassac. I shouted, "Stop firing!" but gave up after the third time. The shooting would die down and then some idiot would start and everyone would chime in. Even if the VC were shooting, you wouldn't be able to hear it. We could not see into the thicket. Vines and underbrush merged into a solid green wall.

Suddenly a striker jumped up, tore a grenade off his belt, jerked the pin and threw it. It slammed into a tree, bounced off, and, as I watched in horror, rolled to a stop fifteen feet in front of me.

Jesus Christ! The pin had been pulled two or three seconds. Not enough time to get there. Goddamn! I threw my arms around my head and shoved my teeth into the mud. The grenade exploded with a shrieking noise, and the air above snapped like sticks as the shrapnel smashed through it. I looked around. Nobody seemed hurt. A minor miracle.

"Stop throwing those goddamned grenades," I shouted. Everyone started shooting. I think they thought the VC had thrown the grenade. Down the line, Frenchy screamed, "Death to the Japanese!"

Sweat poured off me. It was hot and I had to piss. Top was arguing with two strikers. A moment later he crawled over to me. "Those yellow bastards won't go in," he spat out disgustedly.

I didn't say anything. I wasn't sure I wanted to find out if I was the hero type.

"Have you heard any return fire?"

"No. They're in a cave."

Wheaty and Choi ran up and slid into the dirt beside us. Wheaty wouldn't miss a chance at a medal, especially since no one was shooting at us yet.

"What's up?" said Wheaty, grinning like a possum.

"Major," said Top, "can't you get these men to stop shooting for a while?"

"It keeps the VC from shooting back," said Choi with unassailable logic. But he did order the men to fire in short bursts and less often. The din quieted to occasional chaos.

"I tell you what," said Top. "Warren, you, me, and Wheaty and a couple strikers will slip over the bank and go in from the river side." It was the best idea anyone had. It was the only idea anyone had.

Top grabbed three strikers and we crawled over the bank, dropping six feet down to the river. The water was about a foot deep. Somehow I found myself in front. I had started sliding along, hugging the bank, when another burst of fire from our own men blasted a shower of dirt on our heads.

"Lieutenant," Top said, "go back and get those bastards to stop shooting while we're down here."

A few feet farther on, Top stopped us. "We should be about even with the tunnels now."

"Okay," I said. Everything suddenly fell into place. Now I was calm. Every page of my combat training was spread out like an open book. I smiled at myself, as I knew that I wasn't afraid, or perhaps I was crazy. I turned to the closest striker. "Go up the bank and see if you see any caves."

Our own men had stopped shooting. I saw Wheaty coming back down the bank. He stumbled and fell headfirst into the river. Good Lord, I thought, a leader of men.

The striker scrambled up the bank. As he stepped forward, his eyes widened. He started to speak but instead opened fire at a point that must have been about eight feet inside the thicket. The barrel of his gun started to rise. He held the trigger down instead of firing short bursts. He stepped backward and the gun kept rising. He was now firing at the sky. Suddenly, throwing his arms up, he toppled off the bank into the river. For a second I thought he'd been hit, then I realized, no, the dumb fool let the gun kick him into the river.

Top shouted, "Warren, throw a grenade up there."

Which was fine with me. The striker had seen something. I untaped a grenade from my belt—taped to prevent a limb or vine from tearing it loose—pulled the pin, and crawled up the bank. I stuck my head over, wishing I had a steel pot, and saw a small, cleared area about ten feet straight ahead. That must be the place. Perhaps the striker had seen something move. I released the safety handle, counted three seconds, and lobbed the grenade forward. I ducked and it exploded almost instantly.

"One more," shouted Top.

I looked into the clearing. A three-foot circle of woven bamboo lay against a bush. The first grenade had blown off the top of a tunnel, but obviously had exploded above ground. I pulled the pin and crawled to within a few feet of the hole, fully expecting a bullet in my face at any moment. I let the handle fly off. The *ping* was quickly loud in the silence. I ticked off three seconds, rolled it in the hole, and scrambled as I'd never scrambled before. I leaped over the bank, and as my feet cleared, the grenade exploded. Unfortunately, the striker who had fallen into the river was directly under me, and I crashed headfirst into him. His eyes were wide with terror. No doubt he thought I was a flying Viet Cong. We untangled ourselves. Top was shaking his head in disgust. I turned around and found myself staring into a large hole in the bank. The grenade had blown out an air hole. Or a shooting hole. For what seemed like minutes, I stared down the hole before I realized that if a live VC was in there I was a dead man. I twisted sideways and fell against the bank.

"The grenade," I shouted to Top, "blew out this lookout hole here."

"Put another down to be safe," said Top.

As I started to move, I heard a faint noise. It sounded like somebody inside the cave moaning. It came again, fainter. A man, a living man, was wounded in there. Maybe dying. Top was giving orders to a striker to drop another grenade.

"Wait," I said. "I think I heard someone in there." I switched to Vietnamese. "Go up and ask them to surrender. Tell them we won't shoot if they come out. *Biet?*"

"Biet," the striker said.

He crawled up and made the offer. There was no answer. My mind raced. If they're wounded badly, they may not be able to answer. Should I, or this striker, go in and try to bring them out? What if it's a trick, a ruse to get someone to the entrance and then take as many of us as they can before we kill them? What if that second grenade didn't go all the way in, or what if there are other underground rooms and they're hiding farther back? What if they're lying there, bleeding, torn with shrapnel, trying to surrender?

I heard no more noise. Maybe it wasn't a man. Maybe they were talking. Maybe the noise had been just earth falling down inside. Maybe I imagined it all. It was going to be us or them.

"Drop the grenade," I said.

The striker pulled the pin, threw it down the hole, and flipped over the bank. The explosion was deeply muted.

"There can't be nobody alive in there now," said Top. "Let's go over."

We climbed up and I covered the striker while he approached the cave. He began shooting into it five feet away, going through an entire clip before reaching it. He reloaded and crawled inside.

"Dead VC!" he shouted happily. "Bring a light."

I gave him my Zippo. He said, "Two dead VC. And guns!"

I looked into the hole. Something round and wet lay there. I stared at it. A shirt? Some food? Then I knew. It was a man's leg, torn off at the hip. I was staring at the shattered bone and nerves and blood vessels. The pants leg was still on. My stomach turned over and I had a moment of dizziness. Then something hardened. Something that said, he would've killed you, given the chance. And anyway, he's dead now. He doesn't feel anything any more. Just a piece of meat, like a butchered cow.

That was what part of my mind was saying. The other part was remembering that the first thing I had ever killed was a dog when I was nine. We lived in the country, and one afternoon a dog, which may have been rabid or sick, showed up in our back yard. A rib-thin, brown, long-eared mutt, barely able to keep its balance. My mother said, "Get your father's rifle and shoot him. He may be mad." There was froth on his mouth, but he only stood there weaving back and forth, looking at me. My mother told me to shoot him. I had to. I was the man of the house because my father was away. "Shoot him in the head. It's quicker," she said. I could barely see him through the tears as I pulled the trigger. He screamed only once and collapsed in a pile of brown. Something lost forever. Can never be brought back. Every man ultimately standing alone.

I realized the striker was handing me stuff: rifles, pamphlets, a Hoa Hao bible, a picture of a man, another rifle, a small brass cooking pot, more propaganda leaflets.

I dropped inside the cave. It was small. That first grenade had probably wounded them. The cave was eight feet long, three feet wide, and tall enough to crawl around in. A shelf, which was cut into one wall, held a candle and a tiny brass Buddha. Blood was everywhere. I made myself look at the bodies. The man whose leg had been blown off was not a man. Just a boy. Fourteen or fifteen years old. A teenager. I couldn't see the face of the other one. Only torn clothing stuffed with torn flesh. I climbed out weakly, shutting doors in my mind.

Top stared at me with a crooked smile on his face. He

wanted to see how I was taking it. I, too, wondered how I was taking it.

"Two dead VC. Three rifles and a couple hundred rounds of ammo. One of them couldn't have been more than fifteen," I said.

Someone shouted and I swung around, bringing my rifle up. Ten feet away, beneath a papaya tree, the earth was moving. A piece moved back and two empty hands appeared. A striker pointed madly as if we had no eyes. A man climbed out and as he stood, the striker opened fire on him. I jumped forward and slammed the gun to one side. Luckily, the striker was so excited he forgot to aim and only shot the bark off the tree.

The Viet Cong, with tears streaming down his face, talked so fast I couldn't understand him. He probably thought we were going to shoot him on the spot. Top told him to relax and calm down. He was an old man, maybe forty-five or fifty years old. He wore a homemade patch over one eye and wrinkles around the other. We tied his hands behind him. From his cave we retrieved two rifles, ammunition, and more pamphlets.

We left the two dead VC in their cave. Several CIDG were detailed to remain and fill their grave with dirt.

We searched the thicket but found no more caves. Finally I stopped to piss. The human body is amazing. One can be suffering a swollen bladder, a migraine headache, or the agonizing torture of psoriasis, but let bullets start flying and it's all forgotten.

On the boat ride back, I thought that if we had had gas or water we could've flushed the men out without killing them. And the Army knew that a favorite VC tactic was the use of caves. Why hadn't something been developed? For lack of a tear-gas canister, two men were dead.

Or was it the lack of the right decision? I couldn't get over how young the boy had been. When I was his age I was sneaking a drag off someone's cigarette at the Community

Center in Hickory, North Carolina. Did he know what he was fighting for? A kid, wearing thin cotton pajamas, carrying a gun and living in a hole in the ground. How did he eat? We found a handful of rice, wrapped neatly in a red handkerchief and tied with a vine. And the man we captured was an old man, with one eye. He should be playing with his grandchildren. What the hell kind of soldier was that? Dead now, two of them. And they were fighting to get a piece of their land back. But they would've shot me. Maybe they were even the ones who shot at Cranston and me that day on the river. And they would've shot other Hoa Hao. Yes, they were Hoa Hao, too. Choi knew their families. The old man had lived up the river until a year ago. Several strikers said they knew the boy. He had been a quiet one.

I pulled out of my pocket the Hoa Hao bible that he had been carrying. It was printed on old, ratty-looking rice paper. The printing was even crooked. A red stain edged the pages. Blood from a man who'd been alive two hours ago.

Something lost forever.

"Hey, *bac si*, we kill VC today!" a striker shouted exuberantly.

I grinned, but my mouth was stiff and dry.

Later that day B Company and the team gathered on the western wall of the camp to watch their company commander test-fire a mortar from a sampan. We were drinking Ba Muoi Bas and not talking about this morning's action.

"Hey, Hogjaw," asked Top, "how's your VC flag factory coming?"

"You laugh. We've got six ladies working in the old schoolhouse. We can turn out close to a dozen flags a day. Got regular tea breaks and two hours off for pok time," Santee said.

"Who buys them all?" I asked.

"Most go south, eventually to Can Tho and probably to

Saigon, but we got a new contract for some that are likely going across the border," Santee said.

Top took the bait. "What do you mean, across the border?"

Santee said, "You know money don't have no color. All I know is a man contracted for two dozen flags a week, and we send them up the Bassac and they're transferred to another sampan near Beo Con. He specified the flags not be all fucked up. We have a special squad to shoot holes in them, tear them and rub them in mud—those flags go downriver as genuine VC souvenirs. The ones upriver are clean, folded, and pressed. Before you say anything, we made over a hundred and fifty dollars U.S. profit last week."

"It's blood money, if you ask me," said Top.

"Look," I said, "they're ready." Three sampans were being paddled around the end of the camp outside the barbed wire. Only the top two strands showed above the water. B's commander was convinced that if he could mount sixty-millimeter mortars in sampans, they would be a great mobile fire force. We argued that a mortar would be too unstable and that a sampan couldn't carry the weight. Also, it probably wouldn't be terribly accurate. But he wanted to try.

The sun rested low on the horizon as the sampans drifted across the yellow water. I could easily imagine boats such as these on a rice field here two thousand years ago. Somewhere off to my right a small bell was ringing on a water buffalo's neck. Funny that such a big animal as the water buffalo could make no noise except a weak grunt. Only a cold dullness in my stomach reminded me of this morning.

One sampan pulled a few yards away from the others, and in it Captain Dan, the commander, knelt while two soldiers held the base plate. They would fire a flare round toward Cambodia.

Dan dropped a round down the tube. I heard the muffled *dwump!*, and immediately a geyser of water blew up through the middle of the boat. I thought the round had exploded in the tube, then I realized what had happened and burst out laughing. The mortar blew itself right through the paper-thin bottom of the sampan. Dan fell out of the boat and was shouting and floundering around in the water. The two strikers were still sitting there looking dazedly at their empty hands while the boat sank under them. By now we were all cracking up. Cranston fell on the ground, screaming. Even Major Choi was hiding a chuckle behind his hand. High in the west a white star exploded above the sun.

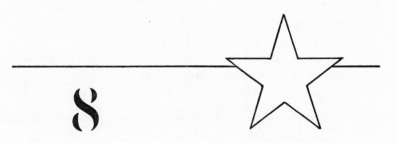

8

TOP LISTENED stoically to my fretting for five minutes before finally answering, "Look at it this way, Warren, either we'll get our asses in a bodacious sling or"—he paused—"we won't."

Ah. A leap into lucidity. He was absolutely right. It was, after all, that simple. Either there were VC on the riverbanks ahead or there weren't. And it really didn't matter because we would find out, one way or the other.

It was a little after 0900 hours and we were sailing past the island Tan Dao on the way to Chau An. Thanksgiving had been two days ago, and the mercury still passed 90 degrees daily. There were only two seasons in the delta—rainy and dry. And it was still raining.

This was my first trip on *Granny's Ghost*, our nickname for the skipjack, and it was fast turning into a love affair. If not classically beautiful, *Granny* was, like Eleanor Roosevelt, memorable. She had been replanked, tarred, sanded, and painted bright orange and purple. She also flew the maroon

Hoa Hao flag. Maroon was considered not to be a separate color but a combination of all colors, signifying the idea of all people, regardless of race, living together in harmony.

With centerboard down, *Granny* needed five feet of water. Up, she could glide across a paddy. The four hundred square feet of mains'l stretched from a fifty-foot mast to a thirty-foot boom. She was old, cumbersome, and cranky, but, under sail, she could sneak up on a tiger. Which was why we dubbed her *Granny's Ghost.* Her real name was *Hoa Hao Lua Viec Lam Tua*, the Hoa Hao Rice and Trading Boat.

When the wind was down, two Peugeot engines drove twin screws that prodded *Granny* up to ten knots.

Choi had rebuilt the aft cabin into a small apartment for himself: carpets, beer cooler, transistor radio, bed, brass Buddhas, a picture of Huynh Phu So, and two green-and-white webbed, folding lawn chairs. On a recent trip to Chau An, Choi had discovered lawn chairs for the first time and convinced himself they were the epitome of Western civilization. I suppose they were.

Mounted on the cabins were thirty-caliber Brownings. *Granny* also boasted two sixty-millimeter mortars, ten feet apart on each side of the mast. These mortars wouldn't blast themselves through the bottom of the boat. One of Santee's nefarious flag smugglers had traded six cases of "genuine" VC souvenirs to a MAAG adviser in Can Tho for enough one-inch armor plating to give the skipjack protection from small arms fire.

Choi had removed a ton of encrusted oyster-dredging equipment that once filled the hold. We had also hauled off hundreds of rocks hidden in dark corners of the hold. Cranston told us that boat crews often snuck rocks aboard boats which they believed did not carry enough ballast.

Granny was profitably plying the waters between Chau An and the border. In Chau An, Choi would pick up pots, pans, root beer, medicine, radios, brassieres, hardware, and some canned foods. He would add vegetables and fruits grown in Nan Phuc. All of which was sold at a slight markup to the outlying villages and hamlets. Soon *Granny* would be bringing back the rice harvest.

So popular were brassieres that Santee and Choi switched half of their fifteen-woman production line from making VC flags to making brassieres. Santee had scrounged up eight Stone Age treadle-type Singer sewing machines, and the women loved them. I, for one, was sad at the appearance of the bras under the tight-fitting blouses Hoa Hao women wore. The bras were considered a luxury, a sign of wealth and sophistication.

Santee and Choi named their Viet Cong flag- and brassiere-making enterprise Hoa Hao Unlimited Ltd. and set up shop in half of the old school building. At night the women used the sewing machines to make clothes for themselves. Hoa Hao Unlimited Ltd. was also producing a dozen fake AK-47s a week. The pseudo-Russian rifles were perfect except that the barrels were a shade too large for thirty-caliber ammunition. If the VC got them, they would be quite useless. Like the flags, the rifles followed a circuitous route south, passing through many hands before reaching Americans or Australians or Koreans. I asked Hood why we didn't make real guns, and he said the Hoa Hao had mountains of hidden guns and ammunition left over from the Japanese, French, Americans, and Viet Minh. Enough to keep the Hoa Hao going for a long, long time.

The people of Nan Phuc were taking great pride in the small factory. Not only was it becoming a social must to wear a bra made by Hoa Hao Unlimited Ltd., we had many more requests for jobs than were available. For the first time people were earning a living without the harsh labor that made men and women bent and wrinkled at thirty.

During the past month Teewee and Major Choi had attempted again to reach headquarters about our situation, but no luck. Superficially, the team attitude was that any day the Army would discover our abandonment. But I think that inwardly we were accepting that we might be here until the water went down.

As for myself, I enjoyed the adventure. Never had I even considered an Army career, although I was fascinated with being a medic. The thought of medical school someday had crossed my mind, but in the meantime I was able to help here. Choi made it easier. He was obtaining my medical supplies on the black market, and I had ordered the correct medicine for tuberculosis. It was going to be nip and tuck at saving Tien's life. His TB had been untreated for five months.

Of all of us, Cranston was the most content and several times said he might stay. It was common knowledge that he and Lao were sleeping together. She was radiant and Cranston was doing foolish things like writing poetry and giving her flowers.

Top, a lifer, was not as content as Cranston and I, but his attitudes were changing. One night on guard duty he talked about the Army. "I'm not sure I understand the Army any more. Westmoreland wouldn't recognize a guerrilla war if it bit him on the thigh. And this candy-ass crap back in the States. They spend more money on demonstrations for politicians than on salaries for us. And these court suits over hitting recruits. 'Be nice to my son, or I'll call up Senator Pissant and tell him you said a naughty word.' "

I said, "Shit, Top, you can't go around whomping on recruits."

"You don't really hurt them," he said. "Sometimes it's the only way to get the point across. I don't know. Maybe it's changing and I'm not. Out here it ain't so bad, not taking orders from Saigon. You know," Top grinned suddenly, "I was thinking about the red tape and huge command staff we got. I figure the Saigon desk jockeys might work their balls off, churning out great ideas, passing the shit back and forth for years, and never realize the entire country had been lost to the VC long ago and Saigon had just been ignored." We both laughed at the image. Top concluded, "And there's always the chance I might run across my old team members."

That was the real reason Top didn't mind staying on.

Santee, on the other hand, loved every minute of our new life. He was getting richer and crazier. "Phil, where am I going to find a deal like this stateside?" he said one day with his feet propped up beside Choi's new abacus. "Me and the major have a little factory going. I guess you could call me an executive vice-president." He threw his head back and laughed. "Shit! I reckon. Can you see me an executive vice-president?

"But then," he added, "have you noticed how quickly I've picked up Vietnamese?"

"No, I haven't," I said.

"It's because many Southerners in the United States have Oriental blood in them. Yessir," he said with a conspiratorial gleam in his eyes. Something told me I should leave.

"Did you read," he said, "where they've found more evidence that North America was once connected to Asia by a land bridge? It stands to reason that thousands of years ago the Chinese came over, turned into what we call Indians, who then interbred with the first Southerners." He kept a beady eye fixed on me. I kept a beady eye fixed on his boots, while arranging what I hoped was a thoughtful, pondering look on my face.

He went on, talking more to himself than to me. "Yes, it all fits in. Southerners have a more relaxed, calm way of life. Close to the soil. A lot of our eyes—look at mine—have a decided slant to them." I looked at Santee's eyes. They were as round as mine.

"We also talk differently, and we know how to work the land. Did you know rice was one of the biggest crops in the South, before tobacco?"

I shook my head. Maybe they all get crazy after a few years in the Army.

"Some say we're inscrutable," he added.

For the life of me, I couldn't figure out how to tell Santee he was black as midnight. I nodded dumbly, thinking that if the truth were known, I did have an aunt from South Carolina, with beautiful skinny eyes and yellow-brown skin.

"I feel a kinship here," Santee said, looking out the window. "This land stirs deep, nearly lost racial memories of a time and a country before this life."

He turned to me. "Yes, Phil, there is no doubt about it. These"—he threw his arms out—"are my people. Our people."

Santee and Hood were both crazy. Hood, who thought he was black, was really white. Santee, who was really black, thought he was Oriental.

And our only officer, Wheaty, wanted to be a meatcutter. Since his "promotion," Wheaty had been adjusting with mixed feelings, I thought. He'd never understood the Army anyway, and Lord knows the Army never understood him. Wheaty liked the structured life of the Army. He was the only one who wore his rank insignia, even sewing captain's bars on his T-shirts. That made no difference, much to his chagrin. We called him Wheaty, and the strikers called him Teewee, because Cranston told the soldiers Teewee was a funny word in English. All of which reinforced Wheaty's suspicion that while he deserved to be a captain of men, there was an elusive quality of leadership that was not his to have. So he continued to toil diligently on his meat-cutting course, pessimistically waiting for the day the world discovered his true worthlessness.

We now had a mail-delivery system of sorts. *Granny's Ghost* carried letters to the Cambodian border. There they were hauled by sampan to Takeo, toted by sicylo to Phnom Penh, and then to the States. We told our families our tours had been extended. Hood and O'Hara were the only ones with real families anyway—Hood's wife lived with her parents in Little Rock, and Top's children were kept by his sister-in-law.

Thus, Wheaty had taken his first test and, much to his astonishment, received an A in Part I of basic meat cutting. You would've thought it was a Rhodes Scholarship. Since then he had pestered Lon to death in the kitchen, slicing up what little meat we had. On meatless days Wheaty attacked the fruits and vegetables. For Thanksgiving our plates were filled with delicately carved pickles and tomatoes that resembled Swiss cheese. Once he fashioned part of a bread loaf into pork chops. Top took one look at his serving and threw the plate at Wheaty.

I admired the shore sliding by and felt the breeze taking the sweat away. *Granny* was beautiful. Maybe I should be a sailor. Top went to chat with Hood, who was sitting on the forward cabin roof.

Hood. Now there was an odd one. He was as unchanging as ever, quiet, collected, and somehow always exuding a faint air of pessimism. He seemed least affected by our situation. A competent man with no ambition except to continue being competent. Not a bad way to have worked things out for yourself.

I was going to buy myself something in Chau An. I had a need, a gut desire, to buy something expensive and something I didn't need. I had a little more than ten thousand piasters (about sixty dollars) on me. Two weeks ago, our second month as mercenaries had ended and Choi had paid us in piasters at 185 to the dollar. When we left Vietnam, the Army would cash our piasters in at the official rate of 65 to the dollar. If you think five or six hundred dollars in dollars is a handful, you should see that much in piasters. The largest commonly circulated Vietnamese bill was a thousand-piaster note, about six dollars. We took pillow cases to collect our pay.

But quick-thinking Santee and Choi were ready last payday. "Fortunately for you, I have the solution to all your problems," said J. P. Morgan, disguised as a black Oriental Santee. He was sitting at Choi's bamboo desk, behind several ledger books and a metal box. "Where are you going to keep your money, plus get a fifteen or twenty per cent return?"

Top asked, "What the fuck are you talking about, shithead?"

"Sergeant O'Hara, fellow team members, as you know, Major Choi and I have a modest business operation called Hoa Hao Unlimited Ltd. But like all young companies, we need additional capital. One of the most common methods of raising money is the selling of common stock. Now there are several types of common stock—"

"Come on, Hogjaw, get to the point. For a nigger, you sure are longwinded," said Top.

"Ain't it true, though," said Santee, grinning. Hood wasn't smiling.

"As I was saying, we are offering you nonvoting class-A common at a thousand piasters a share. This is what you might call our initial offering. Here's how it works." Santee leaned forward. "You buy as much stock as you want at a thousand P's a share. We will invest your money in sewing machines, looms, lathes, vegetable sorters, boats—anything that will help Hoa Hao Unlimited Ltd. make money for you."

Across the room Major Choi was hunched over a desk, looking like he was busy trying to look busy while listening to every word.

"Far fucking out," said Cranston.

"I don't understand how we get our money back," said Teewee.

Santee said, "In a couple weeks we will go to the company commanders, the troops, the townspeople, with this same offer. We are going to sell only a maximum of eighty thousand shares of class A. As Hoa Hao Unlimited Ltd. becomes more and more prosperous, we will divide the profits up into dividends. Secondly, once Hoa Hao Unlimited Ltd. really starts moving, there will be more demand for its stock, and that will make the price go up. Your thousand-piaster stock may be worth two thousand piasters in six months. A hundred per cent return."

"That sounds like a big gamble to me," said Wheaty.

"It sounds like a bunch of horseshit to me," said Top.

"I tell you what I'll do," said Santee, catching the eye of Choi, who gave a scant nod. "I am so confident that I guarantee to buy back, at any time, your stock for one thousand piasters. And after two months I'll buy it back for twelve hundred P's. What we are trying to do, simply, is to raise enough capital to buy bigger and better equipment."

"Hogjaw, where the fuck did you learn so much about business?" asked Top wearily.

"Sergeant O'Hara, I ain't been in the Army all my life. Me and a friend once had a real-estate operation in Georgia," said Santee.

"For niggers?" asked Top skeptically.

"There's a few niggers that manage to tuck some money away."

"What ever happened to your company?" I asked.

Santee picked up a ledger. "We ran into a little problem with the SEC. That's the"—he looked around—"zoning people in Georgia. Now, tell me how many shares you want."

So here we were on *Granny's Ghost*, carrying capitalism to the Hoa Hao. As for the war, we were getting more of that: Lots of sniping, probings, propaganda, and movement in Cambodia. A minor village official from Se Toi had been kidnaped two weeks ago. We had heard nothing about the missing village chief from Tan Dao. We assumed he was dead. We learned the 485th believed our camp was defended by a thousand well-armed men. That was good news. On one hand. On the other was that if the VC ever attacked, they would come prepared for two battalions, instead of 150 men, and probably obliterate our camp.

Well, as Top would say, either they would attack . . . or
. . . they wouldn't.

We turned the last bend in the Bassac, and Chau An lay
dead ahead. We relaxed. Frenchy, who was sailing the
skipjack today—Choi was working on a method for the
company to make lawn chairs—took twenty minutes maneu-
vering through heavy traffic before docking. At least seventy-
five sampans of all sizes and smells were anchored in the bay.

Chau An was a small town of about three thousand people,
lying in the shadows of the Seven Mountains, fifteen miles
southwestward. I had been here several times before and liked
the town. It had no tinsel and no ragtag ugliness. There were
no GIs here.

We strolled down the dirt street beside the river, passing a
dozen food venders. Odors of fish, people, incense, urine, and
open fire were heavy in the air. One lady offered homemade
popsicles wrapped in banana leaves. The ice cream tasted like
slightly rotten fruit, but it was only two piasters. Next to her a
woman sold hot soups and rice. She had prepared the food at
home or, more likely, on her sampan. The food was arranged
in metal bowls, stacked eight high, and carried on each end of
a long pole balanced across her shoulders. She now hunkered
placidly in the shade, fanning herself with a palm frond. I
waved a hello. She grinned and covered her mouth with her
hand. A giggle leaked out.

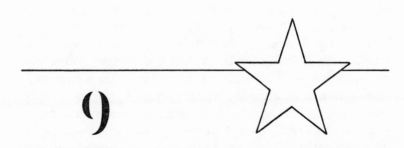

DOWNTOWN WE split up. We would meet at 1600 hours at Bien's Bar, the only bar in Chau An. Top was off to find liquor, cigarettes, and food items. Hood and I were looking for razor blades, toothpaste, soap, and a meat cleaver for Wheaty. The strikers would be buying supplies for their comrades.

Americans were still a rarity, and the crowds threw oblique glances as we threaded our way to *Tuy Hoc Tiem*, Tuy's Drugstore. Tuy's was dark and cramped but stocked everything from Indian incense to American prophylactics. We found Gillette razor blades, Colgate toothpaste, and Ivory soap. On a back shelf I spied jars of Tiger Balm, a dark red salve made of herbs. Its sharp odor was a mixture of fresh mint, camphor, lime, and red pepper. The strikers rubbed it on their upper lip and around their nostrils. They said Tiger Balm repelled evil spirits and bad winds that might fly in through your nose. I tried it and found it pleasantly refreshing. I came to use it as much as the strikers, either from unadmitted superstition or because it smelled so good. I bought four jars.

Next we drifted into the central marketplace, an open-air market much like a county fair. People shopped shoulder-to-shoulder, shouting out gossip and arguing over prices. On my first shopping trip I had been embarrassed at the thought of suggesting to someone that his merchandise was not worth the price on it. But after learning the routine, I appreciated and enjoyed the finesse and style of good bartering.

Hood went on when I paused before an assortment of oil lanterns. I picked up a small, delicate one. The ribbed glass base was the size of an ink bottle. But what caught my eye was the reflector: shiny aluminum with fluted edges and rays leading to a rice-harvesting scene in the center. This is really fine, I thought. I'll read by it at night after the generators are switched off. Sturdy, honest artisans working into the night to shape the metal. . . . Then I turned the reflector around and read, "Sunkist Lemon Juice, Coral Gables, Fla." I had to have it now. Local artisans, my ass.

A few yards farther on, I stopped before a religious trinkets store. On sale were Hoa Hao bibles, statues of Buddha, candles, religious calendars, incense—much like a religious store back in North Carolina. The proprietor, a middle-aged, monkey-faced man, padded up and bid me a good day.

"Toi chi co thay, cam on ong," I said. Meaning, "I'm only looking."

He wandered off, but moments later I caught him staring at me—an impolite social act in Vietnam. Maybe I had ice cream on my face. I had started to leave when he rushed up and said, "Excuse me, but would you mind removing your hat for a moment?"

I pulled my beret off and inspected it for traces of bird shit or some other oddity. Most likely he suspected I was bald (people always know) and wanted to see my naked pate. Bald Vietnamese men were rare.

"Choi oi!" he exclaimed. *"Choi oi"* is a favorite Vietnamese expression of joy, loosely meaning, "Oh, my God!" *"Than thanh bac si dao bao!"* He all but jumped up and down. Asking me to wait a moment, he ran into another room. The translation of what he said—the doctor who walks on water—hit me at the same time I recognized a picture of myself, propped up on a shelf. Jockey shorts and water skis. Oh, no. A legend in my own time. The man, his wife, and two teen-age girls came running out.

Bowing low, he nervously held out an unframed picture of myself and asked me to sign it. I hesitated because I couldn't quite believe it. His wife whispered to him. He shook his head, and I sensed he felt he had offended me.

I smiled and said I would be glad to. He gave me a pencil. "What is your name?" I asked.

"Minh Thi Cao," he said.

I wrote in Vietnamese, "To my good friend, Minh Thi Cao. Good luck, long life, and health. *Than thanh bac si dao bao.*"

He took it back gingerly and when he read his own name, let out another *"Choi oi!"* He showed the picture to his family, bowed to me, and thanked me all the way out the door.

Thirty minutes later I found Hood at the far end of the market. It was nearly 1400 hours and we decided to seek a brew in the shade. We had taken no more than twenty steps when Hood stopped and, looking straight ahead, said, "Stay here and watch out." I saw only a crowded street.

I unfastened the holster flap on my pistol. We had left our rifles on *Granny*, because Chau An had had little trouble with VC. Hood walked over to a small boy, perhaps nine or ten years old, standing near a clothing store. He wore short pants and a ragged T-shirt. The boy had one hand in his pocket. Hood hunkered and began talking. The boy put his other hand in his mouth. After a moment the boy withdrew the hand from his pocket, and I froze. He clutched a grenade. He held it out. Hood, moving quickly but carefully, took the

101

grenade with both hands. Several Vietnamese passed, but if they noticed, they chose not to stop. Hood talked to the boy a moment more and then scooted him off with a slap on the fanny.

Hood walked back, sweat pouring down his face. When I saw the grenade closer, a chill ran through me. The pin had been pulled, and only the pressure on the handle from Hood's fingers—and before that the boy's fingers—kept it from exploding.

"Jesus, Hood, how did you see that?"

"I happened to glance at him at the right time. He was putting the grenade in his pocket because his hand was tired of holding the lever down. He said that an hour ago a man gave it to him and paid him twenty-five piasters to throw it at the first American he saw. The kid wasn't really sure what he was holding. The man had pulled the pin and told him to keep the lever down until he threw it. Goddamned VC. They could've killed that boy and a half dozen other innocent people. The boy was scared to death. He knew something was wrong," said Hood, his eyes darker than ever.

We fashioned a pin from wire and tied the handle down with string as an added precaution. The grenade was a standard U.S. Army M-3 grenade.

I tucked my holster flap behind my pistol so it could be drawn in a hurry. Fat chance a pistol had against a grenade, though.

More watchful now, we walked to an outdoor restaurant at the end of the street. The café overlooked the river, and we sat under a cloth umbrella at a table. The humidity was wilting me. We ordered Ba Muoi Bas with ice. Because of the lack of refrigeration, restaurants kept their beer only lukewarm. Like the Vietnamese, we drank our beer on the rocks. Long fingers of sweat tickled my sides. I briefly considered stripping and leaping into the Bassac.

A half hour later a MAAG captain strolled around the corner, spotted us, and with a great-to-see-fellow-Americans-in-this-Godforsaken-country grin, headed our way.

I hadn't known there were any MAAG personnel in Chau An, and Hood's raised eyebrows told me he hadn't either. Looking back, I realize it's curious I didn't consider the possibility that this might be a way out for us.

Hood muttered, "Don't say anything about the camp."

"Good afternoon—may I join you?" the captain asked.

Hood motioned to a chair. The captain was blond, slightly taller than I, and still wore his baby fat, although he looked in his late twenties. I inspected his insignia. Not only does insignia give you an immediate pigeonhole of an Army man; it tells you how much money he makes, what he has done and where, and what ambitions he has. It's superficial but handy. His name was Clow. He'd probably been in the Army about four years, no less than three. Could be a lifer. He wore no Ranger or Airborne tabs, so he wasn't terribly ambitious. An officer with an eye to the future would definitely have been through those schools. His base pay was $415 a month, plus cost of living, plus separation, if married, plus foreign-duty pay, plus clothing, plus quarters allowance, plus hostile-fire pay. His total salary was about $700.

Hood and I had the advantage: our camouflaged uniforms bore no markings.

"Where are you men from?"

Hood motioned upriver. "North." The captain glanced at me. I sipped my beer.

"What about your uniforms? I'm not familiar with them," he said, frost forming on his words.

Hood hesitated a moment, looked around, and said in a low voice, "Actually, Captain, we're doing some special work for the Agency. You understand if we can't say more."

Clow sat up, his eyes widening. "You mean the CIA?"

Hood said nothing.

"Oh, sure, sure. I understand." Clow looked at us again, reappraising his impressions.

He said, "Say, you probably heard there were Viet Cong near Nan Phuc impersonating a Special Forces team that used to be there."

Hood said, "Yes. That's one of the things we're checking into."

"Boy, it must be exciting working with the Agency. Better than being cooped up in backwater junctions like Can Tho. These gooks are so fucking lazy. As bad as niggers. Even the whores are lazy. You're lucky, you probably don't have to work with many."

Hood was getting a case of tight jaws. The tops of his ears were turning bright red. "As a matter of fact, Captain, we have worked with these people"—he emphasized "people"—"and found them not particularly better but certainly no worse than the average U.S. Army recruit."

It sailed over the captain's head. "You're lucky out there in the boonies. The slopes in town are something else."

Where was the boy with the grenade when we needed him? I asked, "What are you doing here?"

"I came up the Bassac with a South Vietnamese gunboat to bust through the VC blockade. We made it, but it took three hours of air strikes. I'm not looking forward to going back. They sank two government boats last week. For all practical purposes, the river is still closed. The VC are raising hell all over the delta now. The only operation the South Vietnamese have been able to put together was one in the Seven Mountains a couple of weeks back. Did you hear about it?"

"Can't say we have," said Hood.

I knew Hood's agents had reported the operation three days before it began.

"We ran a sweeping operation across Monkey's Head, the largest of the mountains. We heard the VC had a training

104

camp up there. We sent four companies of Arvin [Army, Republic of Vietnam] up the mountain and dropped a company of Arvin paratroopers on top. It was early morning, and I was in the second element. I came over a little rise, and there—I swear this is true—were naked men shooting at us. I couldn't believe what I saw. Not thirty feet from me there was a bare-assed Cong running like hell. Somebody figured out the VC had stripped so they could shoot anything wearing clothes. So our major ordered us to strip down. You never saw such a thing. It was mass confusion. A couple hundred men tearing their clothes off and trying not to get shot at the same time."

In spite of ourselves Hood and I were laughing.

"How many VC did you get?" Hood asked.

"We found thirty-six bodies and twenty weapons. Didn't find anything else except a bunch of tunnels."

That wasn't surprising. The Seven Mountains, which rose suddenly out of the delta, were not mountains by American standards; perhaps hills, for they topped only 900 feet. Their north face fell to within a half mile of the Cambodian border. We suspected there was a fix in between the Special Forces camp on the far side of the mountains and the Viet Cong. That camp rarely held operations in the mountains and had not been hit with anything bigger than occasional sniper fire. Yet it was common knowledge the Seven Mountains was a major supply and staging location for the VC.

Clow was babbling on about the lack of decent women in Vietnam, and my dislike for him was coming to a boil.

While I was thinking of a way to leave gracefully or even not so gracefully, a Chau An district soldier wearing first lieutenant's bars walked up, carrying a bundle of cloth. After today's grenade incident my hand slid to the butt of my pistol. He saluted briskly and said, "Excuse me, sirs. We have operation recently and captured several Viet Cong flags. Perhaps you would like to purchase as, ah, souvenirs?"

He unfolded several flags. They were torn, dirty, and had bullet holes in them.

"Nice stitching," Hood said pointedly.

There was no doubt about it. Second-generation flags from the Singer sewing machines of Hoa Hao Unlimited Ltd. A faint smile toyed with Hood's mouth.

He said, "This looks like a good buy, Captain."

Clow said to the lieutenant, "We don't want any today."

The officer thanked us and left.

Clow smirked. "I didn't want to say anything to him, but last week I bought fifteen VC flags. Province had captured some and a soldier sold me fifteen for only fifty dollars. Not a bad deal at all. They all looked just like those."

He smiled.

We smiled.

I computed that he had paid more than three dollars apiece for flags that cost us thirty cents to make.

When Clow ordered another beer, I said to Hood, "We better be getting back."

Hood flashed me a thankful look. "See you around, Captain." We started to leave.

Clow said, "Good luck with the Agency, and remember if you can get 'em by the balls, their hearts and minds will follow."

Hood broke stride, and his ears went scarlet. But the moment passed. Hood said to me, "Stupid son of a bitch."

Afternoon storm clouds crowded the sky as we hurried to the bar to meet Top. The first drops were falling when we stepped into Bien's, a dimly lit bar so small that six pizza-size tables filled it.

"Come in, shitheads," shouted the only person in the world who would shout that at us in a bar.

Top was sprawled out at a table, one arm around a bar girl and a happy grin on his face. We were the only patrons.

Hood sent the girl away and gave Top a verbatim account of our conversation with the captain.

"So we didn't say anything about who we were or where we were from. He's probably still here in town—" Hood left the sentence open.

Top thought a moment and said, "We got men back at camp, and I doubt we could convince the yellow-bellied Saigon fleet to go to Nan Phuc. Anyway, he sounds like one of those wonder boys that won't do anything unless he goes back and checks the story. And that would be a dead end for us. Fuck him." Top ordered a round of beer. "Tell me again about the naked VC."

We did and it got funnier the more we drank. Top motioned for the girl to come back. She was attractive with her long black hair done up in a nest on her head. She walked over, exaggerating her walk. Smooth, pouting lips.

Top said, "Hello, honey, how's your hammer-holder hanging?" He broke up at his own wit. The girl creased her brow, shrugged, and said, "Okay, I guess."

For the next hour we drank more beer and ate bowls of pretzels, while the rain pounded down outside. Another girl, who, judging from her yawns and puffy eyes, had just awakened, came on duty and joined us. This was the first time since Saigon four months ago that I was allowing myself to get drunk. And the more I talked to these brown-skinned women, the hornier I got. Both wore cheap dresses that fell to their knees but had slits up the side, suggesting delights I could scarcely, but did, imagine. The skin of Vietnamese women made your mouth water: smooth, soft, and a natural golden.

But Top's coarseness and the memory of Clow's stupidity pressed in. My body ached for a girl, but damned if I was going to be another big, hairy GI looking for a quick lay. I told myself that these girls were merely working at their profession. No dice. I told myself I was different from Clow and Top. But the girls wouldn't know that. And maybe I wasn't. Gradually I became aware that neither Top nor Hood, both as drunk as myself, was going with the girls. Hood mumbled sadly that no self-respecting whore would fuck a black man. Top said he wasn't in the mood. Finally, it dawned on me that both men were hiding behind their own excuses. The girls sensed it and they began to relax and even ordered real beers for themselves instead of the tea they had been drinking. They, too, realized that Top's loudness and heavy-handed passes were attempts to impress Hood and me, or himself, rather than them.

Much later Hood asked them, "Do you know a Captain Clow from Can Tho? He probably comes to Chau An now and then."

The girls glanced at each other. "A friend?" asked one.

"Not at all," answered Hood.

Both girls giggled, and one said, "He's no good at fucking. One, two, three, boom! He's done!" She laughed, clapping her hands together.

Finally, reluctantly, we paid and ran sloppily through the rain to the skipjack. It was 1615 hours. We waited another forty-five minutes for the last of the strikers to find their way back, and we weren't the only ones less than sober.

10

GRANNY was gliding by a place where the bank disappeared under the swollen Bassac, and as far as I could see to the west the flooded rice fields seemed on fire. The sun was eerily large and red and only inches above the horizon. A light breeze played across the water, sending sparks of sunlight dancing for miles. It was achingly beautiful. Peaceful. Primitive. Like pictures I had seen of the Orient as a child. The sun's bottom rim tipped the horizon, and a river of orange-red ran from me to the sun.

Most of the strikers were sleeping off the beer. One had strung a hammock between a jib stay and a mains'l stay. Sound asleep, he swayed from the deck out across the water and back. The only noises were the muffled Peugeot engines, three strikers quietly playing cards in Choi's apartment, and the soft splashing of water beneath *Granny*.

"That's ah rat purty pitcher, ain't it?" said Top in a hillbilly accent. He had walked up behind me.

"Yep, it are indeed," I said, without enthusiasm for the

109

accent. My mind was out there in the rice paddies, thinking old Chinese thoughts and being wise.

Top leaned against the railing. He was silent for a long time. Finally he said, "Makes you wonder."

"What?"

"Who made it all. These rice fields, the land, the sun."

"Why, Top, I didn't know you were a churchgoer," I said, knowing he wasn't.

"I don't have much use for churches. As to the rest of it, I don't know. I got into a church once, believe it or not. I was going with a preacher's daughter—that's some of the best you'll ever get—up in Nashville. She talked me into attending services one Sunday. I sat there listening to all this crap. Mind, I was still about half hit from the night before. It was during the silent prayer that I looked around and saw all the people that I had been with on Saturday, drinking and fucking. So I said, right out loud, 'There ain't nothing in here but a bunch of fucking hypocrites.' The preacher asked me to leave the church then and there. I did, but I waited outside until after the service and then offered to shoot dice with him for the collection plate. He nearly slugged me, right there on the church steps. I thought that was the funniest thing."

"What ever happened to the daughter?"

"She wanted to get married. I wouldn't have any of that."

In the distance the silhouette of a man and his water buffalo moved across a paddy.

Top said, "These people are a lot like those back in Alabama. Mostly uneducated, simple farmers trying to get by. Shit, I know what they're thinking. They're thinking, What if the water rises too high? What if a typhoon ruins this year's crops? What if there's more locusts than usual and they eat up the crops?"

Top lit a cigarette. He blew the smoke out in a long stream. "And when they go to bed and pray to Buddha or whoever, they don't ask for guidance on deciding between a Communist

110

or a democratic government or any of that. They ask him to help them through the monsoons and to make their rice grow strong and tall. Except for being yellow and having slanted eyes, they could be Alabama tobacco farmers."

Santee's Oriental theory of Southerners flitted through my mind.

Top said, "Hell, that's half the problem back in the South. The do-gooders should've started integration up North. The whites in the South are just as ignorant as the niggers. What did they expect but trouble?"

Top's words reminded me of once when I went home from college and found out that my father wasn't as dumb as I'd thought a few years earlier. I was surprised and saddened. He had deep, serious reasons for his attitudes, but they weren't mutable. I knew that he, like Top, understood much more than his words implied, and I also knew that he, like Top, wasn't going to change.

Top started to say something, but the popping of distant gunfire interrupted. It sounded like several rifles and came from the direction of Chau An. The shooting stopped after a dozen shots. We listened for a few minutes but heard nothing more.

"I'll bet somebody got drunk and decided to shoot up the town," said Top. "Did I ever tell you about the time we almost took tanks into Phoenix City, Alabama?"

"No."

"Goddamn, but that was fun." Top laughed at the memory. "It was back when I was with The Baby Rapers. Phoenix City was a rotten, crooked town. It was a Saturday night and we were downtown drinking. Somebody—I don't remember who —got in a fight and this mean-ass cop split his skull open with a billy club. Laid him out cold. We carried him back to Benning, and we were just drunk enough that we decided to get our tanks and go back. We got the ammunition and the gas and fired up five Shermans. We planned to drive them to the middle of town and level everything in sight. We got all the way to the main gate and there, standing on the hood of his jeep, was our battalion commander, Colonel Nadan. All by himself, with a forty-five in his hand. He said he'd shoot the first man that moved a tank. Then he said if a cop in Phoenix City ever beat up a member of the 185th again, he personally would drive the first tank into town. We turned them around. Word must have gotten to the cops, because we never had any more trouble."

A few moments later Top asked, "Did you hear about the Marines? The skinny has it that Johnson has sent in two regiments from Lejeune to build a base at Cam Ran Bay. It hasn't been announced officially yet."

That ruffled the hairs on my neck. Things must be getting pretty bad if the Marines were landing.

Top went on, "Those jarheads are going to get their asses kicked back in the ocean. The average Hoa Hao kid of eight knows more about guerrilla warfare."

Only a fading orange edge of the sun remained above the distant water. An awful sadness and longing came over me. I had a premonition that something terrible was going to happen to this beautiful land of mine.

Neither of us said anything for a few minutes. The sun disappeared, leaving pale yellow light bouncing off the underside of the clouds. It would be completely dark soon; night came fast in this flat country.

"Those strikers have the right idea," said Top, coughing. He went forward to the jib, spread a place in the canvas, and lay down.

A short time later Hood came up from Choi's apartment. Since leaving Chau An, he had been gathering intelligence from the strikers, fitting all the rumors and gossip together. He walked over. Maybe he could shake this melancholy from me.

"Finding out much?" I asked.

"A little here and there. There may be more MAAG

advisers coming to Can Tho and probably some regular Army troops for defense. Also, I heard the KKK were seen in this area last month. They usually don't stray this far north."

"Who?" It was the first I had heard of the KKK.

"You don't know about the KKK?"

"No. At least not the ones here in Vietnam."

Hood said, "KKK means Khmer Kampuchea Krom, which roughly translates to Free Cambodians for Cambodia. They're a group of three to four thousand armed Cambodians living in the South Vietnamese delta, who are fighting to return part of the delta to Cambodia."

"What?" I said. That didn't make any sense.

"All of the delta of South Vietnam was once part of Cambodia. Saigon itself was Cambodian until late in the seventeenth century, and the area below Saigon wasn't brought under Vietnamese control until the eighteenth century. The KKK want Vietnam to return to Cambodia the eight provinces around and including this one. And it gets even more complicated. The KKK are old guard, peasant soldiers and pro-Sihanouk, who probably slips them money and guns now and then. Thus, the KKK see their duty as opposing the Khmer Serei, who are fighting for the overthrow of Sihanouk."

At the puzzled expression on my face, Hood went on, "The Khmer Serei are also a group of a couple thousand armed men that roam back and forth between the delta and Cambodia. They started in 1935 as a secret society to free Cambodia from the French. The man who started it was Son Ngo Thanh, who was chief librarian at the Phnom Penh library at the time. During World War Two the French cracked down on them and Thanh fled to Japan. The society died down until the early 1950s when Cambodia was given its independence and Sihanouk, who had been a puppet king for the French, established a dictatorship. The old revolutionaries got together and dusted off the Khmer Serei to fight, once

113

again, for independence. This time from Sihanouk. It's rumored that Thanh is living in the delta now and directs the Khmer Serei from here."

"How do you know all that?" I asked.

"I read a lot and I went through the Army's Asian intelligence school at Carlisle, Pennsylvania. I really enjoy history. Someday I'd like to be a high-school teacher." He laughed self-consciously. "I'm getting a little old, though, to go to college."

I said, "So we have the KKK raising hell around the delta and fighting the Khmer Serei and fighting the South Vietnamese government as well?"

"Right. The KKK get a lot of weapons from raiding government camps or VC camps. They're anti-Communist, too, because they want to free the delta from everybody, including the Viet Cong. Every now and then we get a report of a fire fight out in the boondocks somewhere. And there are no government or CIDG forces involved. It must be either the KKK and the Cong or maybe the KKK and the Khmer Serei or a run-in with the border bandits."

What madness. I had nearly forgotten that there were also several well-armed bandit gangs who weren't interested in any government—just stealing, fighting, and smuggling opium.

"Strange country, isn't it?" said Hood, echoing my own thoughts. "Here we are with Colgate toothpaste, the latest razor blades, and out there is a world living a hundred years ago. Except for the guns."

"What's the story on opium, anyway?" I asked. Although I'd heard many stories of opium smuggling and even had smoked it twice in Saigon, I had yet to see any poppy fields or processed opium in the villages.

Hood said, "Probably one-fourth of all the river traffic on the Mekong is bringing opium out of the Cambodian highlands on its way to Saigon and then to the West. More used to come down the Bassac, but Choi's stopped a lot of that. Gold and opium are the two most stable currencies in this part of the world."

I had noticed that Vietnamese hoarded gold, usually as jewelry, the way Westerners had savings accounts and stock. It made good sense. In the eight months we'd been here, the black-market rate on piasters had gone from 110 per dollar to 185.

"Except for the opium dens in Saigon, probably very little stays in this country. The Chinese control most of the exporting."

"Who grows it?"

"Primarily the Meo tribes that live in Northern Laos and I Corps and in southern North Vietnam. The Tho and Yao also grow a lot. The French, in an effort to make these colonies profitable, encouraged the growing of opium. I wouldn't be surprised to see some high-ranking officials in all three countries involved in it. Nasty business."

I agreed. Opium was a narcotic made from the dried sap of the poppy and medically useful for controlling diarrhea and pain. Ah, but the mythology: an evil, mind-bending drug inhabiting dark alleyways, strange dens, and obscure paragraphs in novels my parents kept on the top shelf. In spite of the dangers, I rationalized to myself one night four months ago in Saigon, I would probably never have another chance to smoke it. So, after five scotch-and-waters, I asked three taxi drivers before the fourth one said, "Sure. I know where. Hop in."

He drove me deep into Cholon, the old Chinese city in Saigon, at last stopping in front of a house, indistinguishable from the other shacks. He knocked on a door that trembled with every rap. An elderly Chinese man, wearing a shirt that buttoned to the neck, baggy pants, and slippers, answered and talked with the taxi driver in Chinese. The driver told me to go in.

The Chinese introduced himself as Tan and led me into a

candle-lit bedroom. He spoke little Vietnamese, but with sign language we arranged the prices. The opium was two hundred piasters a pipe, a little over one dollar, and fifteen hundred piasters for a girl if I stayed overnight.

I asked how many pipes I should smoke. Tan grinned sillily, shrugged, and said, "Maybe five, maybe three."

He was a bit high himself. From under a bed he brought out a brass box. While Tan prepared the pipe, a woman and another elderly man came in. She was his wife, and the man was a relative. They chatted in Chinese, and I followed their example and sat cross-legged on the floor.

With great care Tan heated several pinches of brown powder in a tablespoon until it melted into a red-black liquid. After it cooled, he rolled it into a small ball, the size of a pencil eraser. Then he placed it in the tiny bowl of an ornately carved ivory pipe and lit it. As soon as it was going, he handed the pipe to me. He motioned for me to breathe deeply. I did and passed the pipe to his wife. It tasted bittersweet, like a stale, strong cigarette with sugar in it. We finished that pipe and started another. The woman left and brought back beers.

Although nothing swept over me, as such, I began to feel friendly and warm. I wanted to talk to these people, tell them how I understood the war, get them to know me, and at the same time I really didn't need to speak. Because, somehow, they already knew these things. We had two more pipes. Now and then someone would say a few words and we all nodded. Even though I spoke no Chinese, the sounds were good and noble. Occasionally I said something incisive and intelligent like, "Boy it sure is nice in here." And everyone smiled and nodded. The other man climbed onto a small bed, his eyes closed and a faint smile on his lips. But the earth was still stable, so I asked Tan to make me three more pipes, which I smoked by myself. I began to get slightly dizzy and my body felt delightful. The idea of a woman intrigued me, and I told Tan I would like to spend the night with a woman. It wasn't that I had a sudden raging sex desire, but that I wanted to lie down and it would be nice to have a soft, warm woman beside me. Tan showed me to another bedroom. It wasn't a real bedroom. A curtain had turned a large hallway into a small hallway and a smaller bedroom. I stretched out on the bed.

Every muscle floated gently in the air. I was completely relaxed. I moved my leg. There was no weight, no effort. The curtain parted, and a lovely face smiled at me and a slender arm held out a Ba Muoi Ba.

"*Choi oi! Thuoc huoc*, huh?" she teased.

"Come in. I'm Phil Warren."

"Toi Luan." Instead of getting in, Luan led me to a shower. The smarter prostitutes always bathed their clients to cut down the chances of disease. I immediately noticed her perfectly proportioned body as we stepped into the small shower, a worn curtain around a drain in the floor. What breasts! Most of the Vietnamese and Chinese women I had seen had small breasts. But this girl, Lord! Two mouth-watering globes that pointed straight out and rubbed against me every time one of us turned. Her skin was a little whiter than most Chinese and her cheekbones not so high. She was probably Eurasian. Her eyes were set far apart but still delightfully canted. A small waist and boyish hips led to long, muscular legs. By the time we rinsed off, I had an erection.

We raced to the bed. I turned on my side and stroked her satin skin. My eyes explored those lovely breasts lying inches away. I moved my hand up and drew S's around the hardening nipples. Time moved ever so slowly. I loved it. I leaned over and placed my mouth around the dark brown circle, running my tongue back and forth across the nipple. My right hand slid down her waist to her thigh and to the soft flesh inside. She moaned and caressed the back of my neck. I could have fondled her body for days. We went slow because for me it was more than the idea of ejaculation; it was the sheer sensuousness of flesh. I slid my hand back up the inside

117

of her leg and across her nearly hairless pussy. I paused to touch her outer lips and then moved to the other thigh. Her legs opened. She pulled my head to hers and, opening her mouth, kissed me long and deep. With one hand, she reached over and felt my penis, moving around and under to play with my balls. Time crept along. It seemed we made love for hours. Finally we were ready and I rolled over on top. She slipped down in the bed, raising her legs high in a V. She took my penis and rubbed it up and down her wet vagina. Then, moaning, she pushed her hips forward, driving me deep. Back and forth, in and out, slowly at first, then faster. And once in a while, circular, because it felt so good. Suddenly she uttered a deep guttural cry. Her fingernails bit into my back. We were one person, sharing the same thing: uncluttered, uncomplicated, pure sex. And loving it. Moments later we lay side by side, breathing heavily.

She fell asleep almost immediately, her head on my shoulder. I lay awake and felt my body from the inside out.

The next thing I knew I was waking up with the sickening knowledge that you have five seconds before you throw up. I ran for the bathroom and vomited into the toilet, painfully and long. Toward the end a wet washcloth was pressed against my forehead. I leaned against naked thighs.

"Too much opium, Phil," Luan said. "It often happens the first time."

I looked at my watch. It was 0500 hours. "I'd better go," I said, embarrassed.

After a shower I dressed and left. No sad words, no unmeant platitudes. Honest smiles that said no more than, "Last night was good."

I smoked opium once again, on another trip to Saigon. Same place. Same girl. But this time I had only a few drinks and took only four pipes. Except for the vomiting, it was a repeat of the first evening.

That was the last time I smoked opium. I had no craving or

desire to try it again. Although the physical effects were euphoric, I was too proud of my own independence to enjoy the dizziness, confusion, and dreamlike quality of it. I was glad I did it. Twice.

Ahead of us the island of Tan Dao appeared as a black hulk in mid-river. It was 2030 hours and a few lights were flickering on the bank as we approached Nan Phuc.

It was good to be home.

11

"ALL RIGHT," I said. "Let's try this. *Bao nao?*"

"*Bao nao?* What means *bao nao?*"

"*Bao nu-h?*"

"Can I see that?" said Luc. He squinted at my notes. "You are trying to say, 'What time is it?' "

"Yes."

"Here they say, '*may gio.*' '*May ya.*' Remember the '*gio*' has a *huyen* over it, so the sound is low and falling."

"*May ya?*" I said, repeating it twice.

It was after chow the next evening, and Luc, one of our three interpreters, and I were sitting on the sandbags, practicing each other's language. Our interpreters remained here even though we had been shipped back to the States, because the Vietnamese government paid and placed the interpreters. Like bureaucracies everywhere that spend someone else's money, the South Vietnamese government would rather continue three men on full salary than see that money disappear from Uncle's outstretched pocketbook come next year's budget.

Luc was twenty-four and a lean five feet seven. Under a high forehead was a long, thin face with a large mouth, traces of northern Chinese blood. His father had been an administrative officer under the French. Because of that, Luc told me, his family had enough money to put him through high school, but not enough to buy him out of the army. The going rate was five hundred dollars, U.S. His high-school degree, called a baccalauréat, meant that he should have been one of the elite. For in a country of fourteen million, only one and a half million children even started school and less than thirty thousand finished high school last year, 1963, according to my country training. In peacetime Luc would have been a successful professional man.

I had picked up Vietnamese from scratch. When A-376 began training for Vietnam, the Army decreed that eleven team members would be taught Vietnamese and one would learn French. You guessed it. I learned such conversational French as *"Où sont les mitrailleuses? La grenade est sur la table. Où sont les communistes?"* Then our half team was assigned to Nan Phuc, where few people spoke French at all and those few would not admit it. Fortunately, I was quick with languages and learned Vietnamese easily in spite of its tonality. Like Chinese, Vietnamese word meanings depend on the inflection of the speaker.

Our lesson was interrupted by two strikers. One was Phu, C Company's chief medic. The other was a gunner named Soc. Phu said Soc's back hurt fiercely and was giving him much pain because today's high winds blew out of the south. What he really meant was that the evil winds had blown in through Soc's nose and lodged in his back.

I questioned Soc. Finally he remembered lifting five cases of mortar ammunition yesterday. Ammo cases weighed seventy-five pounds. He didn't see the connection. We walked to the dispensary, and I gave him two sodium salicylate tablets, a muscle relaxer and painkiller. I told him to stay overnight in one of my four sick-bay cots because I doubted he would rest in the barracks. Phu wanted to stay with him.

I walked back to Luc.

"Say, *bac si,* where did you learn to say *'bao nao'* for 'what time is it?' " he asked.

"Top brought me a Vietnamese dictionary from Danang when he went back in October. Here." I handed it to him.

Luc opened it. *"Thinh Zuat Ban,* huh?" he muttered. "That's what I thought, *bac si,*" he said, grinning. "You've been learning Communist."

"What?"

He pointed to the author's name. "Thinh teaches at the University of Saigon. But he taught in Hanoi until he escaped a few years ago. And here, it was published in Hanoi in 1958. You've been learning North Vietnamese dialect."

That explained a few things. Since getting the dictionary, I'd memorized a half dozen words a day and tried to use them. With a notable lack of success. Sometimes I would finally be understood, only to have the person tell me the right way to say it was something else. These people must think I'm crazy. First I speak French and then when I learn some Vietnamese it's North Vietnamese.

"Did everyone know I was speaking North Vietnamese?"

"Oh, no. There are many dialects in Vietnam. They think it's just another dialect from somewhere."

Luc seemed in a garrulous mood, so I asked, "How did you get to be an interpreter?"

Luc said, "I was drafted after I finished high school. I . . . did not want to be a soldier. I don't like fighting, so I asked the Army not to draft me. I wanted to try for a scholarship to the university, but the Army said no. I had to choose between being a monk or a soldier. In our country that's all the choice

122

a man has, unless his parents are wealthy. So I asked to be an interpreter, because then maybe I won't get sent out to fight. I took English in high school and the Army sent me to six months of English school in Hue."

"And you were sent here to a Special Forces camp beside Cambodia. You've been in more fire fights than I have."

"I know," he said, laughing. "Very dangerous. But at least this is better than with regular Army troops. They live very bad."

"How long are you in for?"

"For a long time," he said. He rubbed a long fingernail across the sandbag. "Until the war is over."

"Maybe someday it'll be over and you can go back to school," I said, dumbly and angrily. Luc was smart. Such a waste of brains and talent. Thirty-seven U.S. dollars a month. For the duration.

Suddenly there was a commotion at the main gate. In the twilight we could make out a group of strikers surrounding somebody. I saw a bushy-headed white man and a red-headed girl with their hands tied behind them. Major Choi, Top, and the rest of the team were gathering around. As Luc and I came up, I caught the tail end of the man's sentence.

". . . surrounded us. Believe me, we're not dangerous. Boy, am I glad to see Westerners," he said. They were Americans. The man looked in his late twenties, was more than six feet tall, and wore long, curly blond hair that stood electrically a good five inches in all directions. A long Roman nose ended in a magnificent handlebar mustache which, combined with deep wrinkles at the corners of his eyes, gave his face the appearance of rugged openness. The girl was tall and rather heavy—no, she wasn't. I was so used to the petiteness of Vietnamese women that she seemed big to me. She was five feet six or so and had titian hair that hung carelessly past her shoulders. A pretty face made attractive by dark eyes and a wide mouth. She wore a man's patched shirt outside jeans and, except for two large, unencumbered tits, I couldn't tell much about her figure. Her breasts were the type that pointed off to the left and right and clearly were full and weighty. With her arms tied behind her, her breasts stood out and quivered whenever she moved. I've always thought a better measurement of a woman's breasts would be by the pound rather than by the inch. Many girls with large backs and small breasts end up with numbers that sound great. But what about something like, "four pounds each-24-37"? A much fairer comparison.

Their arms were untied and the two were led to Choi's office. As we moved forward, Top growled, "Just me and the major are talking to these folks. The rest of you stop drooling and go about your business."

Back in the team room, we discussed various theories of who the couple might be. The strikers said they had been captured without a fight near Phu Duc on the border. They'd been unarmed and carrying only rucksacks.

While I was pondering if the agony of another Ba Muoi Ba beer was worth it, Hood reminded me about his wart. It grew on the knuckle of his trigger finger, and he was constantly bruising or cutting it. I was dropping silver nitrate on it each night in the hope that would burn it off. It seemed to be working.

While in the dispensary, I remembered Soc's back and glanced in the sick bay. He lay face down on a cot while Phu was straddling him and scraping his back with a piece of broken glass. He wasn't cutting the skin, but he was raising patches of ugly red welts. The ancient art of Chinese medicine.

"Wait, Phu," I said in Vietnamese. "Let's try this instead." I handed him a bottle of methyl salicylate. "It's very good medicine for sore backs. It makes the evil spirits go out. Use this and wait a little while. If that doesn't help, use your Chinese medicine."

Phu nodded.

I went into the front room. Hood asked who was sick.

124

"One of the strikers has a sore back, and Phu was laying some Chinese torture on him. It wasn't three days ago that I gave a class, and Phu was in it, on how to treat pulled muscles."

I finished with Hood's finger and decided to have a last look at Soc. There sat Phu, on Soc's back as before, vigorously rubbing the bottle of methyl salicylate up and down Soc's back. The bottle, mind you, turned sideways. Phu looked up and smiled proudly. I had explained everything, except to say that the medicine was in the bottle; it wasn't the bottle itself. One had to start so far back.

Phu got a quick lesson in opening the bottle, pouring methyl salicylate on cotton, and rubbing that on Soc's back. Phu, at thirty, was older than most of the strikers and was my best medic, by far. But it was hard for me to remember that to him the idea of rubbing a glass bottle on a man's back made as much sense as rubbing a colorless liquid on it.

It was nearly dark now. A faint gray-yellow ribbon hemmed up the western sky. I was halfway to the team house before I saw the American couple sitting on sandbags, talking to Cranston. I wished I had my beret on to hide my baldness. First impressions and all that.

"Good evening," I said. "They've decided you aren't clever Oriental agents?"

"Yeah," said the man. "What a scene. We don't even look Vietnamese." He shook his head in amazement. I was trying to check out the lady's tits before the light failed completely.

"I'm Phil Warren," I said, sticking out my hand.

"Oh, excuse me," said Cranston. "This is Hamilton Dupree, known as the Aristocrat, and Jasmine Banks. Phil Warren."

"The Artistocrat, huh?" I said. "Why are you called that?"

"I guess it's 'cause I admire the true aristocrats of the—say, where are you from?"

"A little town called Hickory in North Carolina. You probably never heard of it."

"Like fish. Are you familiar with Baton, outside of Lenoir?" he asked.

"You're kidding. I'll be goddamned." Baton was fourteen miles up the Catawba River from my home. We shook hands again, with much arm slapping and laughing.

"Wait," I said. "Let me give you a test. What's a raddy aral?"

"Raddy aral?" said Hamilton, frowning. "I got it. A radio aerial. Whoeehotdamn. Here's one for you. If we's at home, working in one of the mills, what would we have for a midmorning snack, or maybe even for breakfast?"

I came up with, "A Nehi Grape with salted peanuts in it."

"That's good, but not what I was thinking. How about a big orange—"

"—a Moonpie and a Goody Powder. Goddamn, yes!" Hamilton and I were laughing and grinning and feeling all warm and friendly. Cranston and Jasmine looked at each other as if to say, "It must be some sort of mystical rite." It was.

"Anyway," I said, "how come you're the Aristocrat?"

"Like I was saying, I'm rather fond of the gentle, slower way of life. The old Southern plantation aristocrat, without the slaves. There are so few men of quality, of true aristocraticness left in the world," said Hamilton. "And also, did you ever hear of the Dupree Textile Mills?"

The name rang a distant bell.

"My grandfather, Martin Dupree, founded the Dupree Mills during Reconstruction. He made a lot of money until the Depression. Then the family lost everything but the house and some land. As a matter of fact, I was working third shift at a dollar eighty an hour in the mill last spring before I left. It was a strange feeling, working in a mill founded by your grandfather and now owned by the bank. The men there, of course, found out who I was and gave me a lot of ribbing. That's where I really picked up the name Aristocrat."

"Say," broke in Jasmine, "I hate to interrupt Old Home Week, but where do I find the crapper around here?"

Cranston said, "Over there, through that gate, around the . . . ah, look, we better go with you. It's dark and you'll never find it."

"What are you all doing here?" I asked as we started.

"We're hitching across the East on our way back to America. If we can get to Saigon, we want to catch a boat or plane to Australia to see the down under and out back. I was sent to France on a Lions Club scholarship."

"What?" Cranston and I said simultaneously.

"Yes. I was in France this summer speaking to French Lions clubs about today's young people and stuff like that. I met Jasmine in Cannes."

Cranston unhooked the barbed-wire gate beside the moat. "Watch out along here," he said, shining a flashlight on the water a couple feet away. We walked carefully along a narrow mud path between the wire and the overflowing canal.

"Far out," said Jasmine.

"Yeah, it is kind of far out. Get it? Far outside?" said Cranston.

Jasmine and Cranston laughed. They were both strange.

"What were you doing in Cannes?" I asked Jasmine, offering her my hand for balance, but hoping she would give me a tit.

"Bumming around. I was a waitress when I met Ham. Back in the States I was working on a doctorate in political science. But I got up-tight with everything and decided to split. Where the hell is this shit house anyway?"

The lady minced no words. But it wasn't affected. From her it was a simple question.

"There," said Cranston, flashing the light ahead. At the same moment the light went on, a giant turd, reminiscent of what Lieutenant Vaughn's must have been like, fell into the water. A great splashing arose as the catfish fought for it.

"Good grief, what's going on?" asked Jasmine.

Cranston explained the inner workings of a catfish latrine. Through the one open door I recognized a radio man named Chien, who was fishing through a seatless lawn chair. Seeing us, he pulled up a string of four nice cats. The strikers—there were a half dozen or more behind us—chatted with Chien about his fish.

"What are all these people doing here?" asked the Aristocrat.

"They're curious about Jasmine and you. I don't think they've seen a Western woman before. Certainly not one with such good-sized . . . uh, ah, I mean, such a well-developed one," I finished lamely. Get a hold of yourself, Phil.

The other door opened and a striker came out, buttoning his pants. He and Chien walked over the boards to us.

"Okay," said Cranston, shining the light over the planks. "Go ahead."

"This is ridiculous," said Jasmine. "I'm supposed to walk on those boards out to a lawn chair with no seat in it with those . . . those fish down there and all of you standing here?"

"Now, now, Jas," soothed Hamilton. "I'm going with you. The door'll be closed."

"By the way," I said, "wipe off the seat. The Vietnamese squat on the seat instead of sitting in it. There may be dirt on top." Like all Orientals, except the Chinese, the Vietnamese rarely used chairs.

Hamilton led the way across.

"Also," called Cranston, "there's usually an old *Newsweek* in there. Rip off a couple of pages."

The strikers tittered. Several carried flashlights, and beams lit up the latrine and the water below.

We didn't say much. There's little one can say while waiting for two strangers to shit. I tried to imagine what a Viet Cong would think if he was hidden out there watching.

Suddenly a great cheer went up from the strikers as two

dainty turds tumbled from Jasmine's side. The water boiled and the soldiers shouted, *"Choi oi!"* and other Vietnamese hurrahs.

A faint female voice said, "Jesus fucking Christ!"

I said, "Okay, knock it off. And turn those lights off. A girl's got a right to her privacy."

The lights blinked out. That was even worse. There was only darkness and dead silence, broken by an occasional *plop!* which brought hearty shouts each time.

A few minutes later they finished.

"That's the first time I've ever been cheered for taking a shit," said Jasmine.

We walked back into camp, followed by even more strikers, who were discussing the quality and quantity of American shit.

"I don't understand why they follow us," she said.

I said, "They don't have anything else to do. We're funny-looking in their eyes. Big, hairy, coarse people with long noses and sickly-looking skin. I tell you what, come with me."

I led them into my dispensary, locked the door, took them through the supply room and out the back door. We climbed the ladder to the water tower. Forty feet up was the three-thousand-gallon rubber water tank, circled by a small wooden platform. We sat down, hung our feet over the edge, and leaned against the tank.

"How did you all happen to come through here?" asked Cranston.

"We were in Bangkok and heard about those fabulous ruins in Cambodia. Since we wanted to come this way anyway, we took off. Have you ever seen Angkor Wat? Gigantic old temples and buildings falling apart in the middle of the jungle. It was the site of a Cambodian civilization hundreds of years ago, and then, for some unknown reason, everyone left. There are dozens of old stone structures scattered through the trees for miles. We caught a boat from Angkor Wat to Phnom

Penh. Not much there, so we decided to take the Mekong to Saigon. A fisherman said he'd give us a ride to the border for three dollars. We hopped in and two days later he dropped us off up there." He waved northward. "We started walking, and an hour later your men captured us."

"You came down the Bassac River. It splits off the Mekong some five miles south of Phnom Penh," I said.

Cranston said, "You're lucky you didn't run into VC."

"That's what Major Choi kept telling us. He asked a lot of questions about the VC, but we didn't see anyone except fishermen. Which reminds me of something. Let me see that flashlight a second."

Cranston handed him the light. He shone it in my face. I raised my hand in reflex.

"Sorry," said the Aristocrat. "This may sound crazy, but I think I saw a picture of you in that fishing boat that we rode down in. There was a picture of a man in jockey shorts who was waterskiing. Isn't that the damnedest thing? It was framed and sitting on a shelf with candles and joss sticks around it. There must be a religious person who looks like you."

Cranston, damn his eyes, started laughing. "Oh, wow, yes. That's great. Let me tell you the whole story. One Sunday afternoon me and Phil didn't have anything to do—"

Rather than hear it for the fiftieth time, I snuck down to the team house and got us all Ba Muoi Bas. When I got back, Cranston was saying, "Dope? Sure. I'm growing some down by a cemetery outside Nan Phuc. Not great booje, but good booje."

Jasmine said, "Really weird, isn't it? Here we are halfway around the world and we meet a guy who's from Hickory and the other guy's growing marijuana."

The Aristocrat said, "Would you all like to share a little joint?"

Cranston, who didn't have guard tonight, said, "Sure."

"None for me, thanks," I said. "Guard duty." That was

130

partially true. I did have guard, but more than that, I didn't really enjoy grass that much. I had smoked some back in Hickory, but, like opium, the stuff put too much cotton candy on reality for me.

The Aristocrat said as he rolled a joint, "Cranston, you are about to have some of the world's greatest grass. Home-grown in Baton, North Carolina. Called by those who have smoked it aristograss. It's change-of-life dope. I started four years ago, and this past summer I put in about two acres."

"Do you use any fertilizer?" asked Cranston.

"I planted in an old cornfield and put the seedlings about three feet apart in hills, like watermelons. It's best to start them indoors and then transplant when they're about five inches tall. Put a little phosphate and nitrogen in the ground in the early spring and a little more about midsummer. When your plants are a couple feet tall, pinch off the top leaves. The plant will bunch out at the bottom with more branches instead of growing tall and skinny."

Like two farmers sitting around talking about the tobacco crop.

Cranston said, "You say you had some growing this past summer. Who was looking after it?"

The Aristocrat lit the joint, took a deep breath, and handed it to Cranston. "My mother."

"Your mother?" I said. "Your mother was taking care of your marijuana?"

"She makes tea from it every afternoon. She's sixty now and we've been real close, especially after Dad died ten years ago. She lives alone in the old homestead. It's one of those three-story Southern-style, neo-Wallace mansions, except it's pretty run-down now. She lives in five rooms on the first floor. A couple of years ago I decided to give her a little grass. She's liberal and a spunky old gal. One afternoon we lit up on the veranda and she loved it. We sat up the entire night. She told me marvelous stories about my father and what they did when

131

they were young. She doesn't like to smoke grass—it makes her cough—so she figured out how to make tea. Every afternoon about five o'clock she goes in and brews a pot. She sits there on our falling-down porch and sips marijuana tea till dark. Smiling and rocking and looking at the sunset. Now and then one of her lady friends—they're all about sixty or seventy—will drop in and they'll sit there and drink tea and laugh for hours. She never tells them what's in the tea. I don't think that's bad."

"Real nice," said Cranston.

Jasmine said, "What's with that black sergeant, Santee? He tried to sell us stock in something called ha ha."

I laughed. "Hoa Hao Unlimited Ltd. That's a little company we started to make clothes and flags and stuff like that."

"Like a textile mill?" Hamilton asked with interest.

"Yes, but we only have eight sewing machines."

"Can I look at your setup tomorrow? I know a little about sewing. Maybe give you some advice."

Hamilton passed the aristograss and leaned back. "This sure is a beautiful area. That was a pretty little village we came through. Primitive and clean and happy."

"I know," said Cranston. "I've been giving some serious thought to staying on here after . . . the Army. Man, I don't want to go back to all that garbage in the States. People breaking windows, riots in the streets, strikes, shootings on campus, television, cars, dirty air. What a hassle."

In a way Cranston was right. Even though we were getting shot at here, we knew who the enemy was. Maybe not specifically, but generally. When the VC weren't around, life was very pleasant.

He continued. "Maybe I'm copping out. But I've been going through a lot of changes. There's a bunch of stuff in the world I realized I'm never going to figure out. But there's some I can. When I'm out there working with my hands in a rice field, I feel like I'm getting it all together. If I plant a rice seedling right, it'll grow straight and tall and true. It's part of me. Something I did. Something I did right. Does that make any sense?"

"I can dig it, man," said the Aristocrat.

"Beautiful," said Jasmine.

Hamilton said, "For me, I think life is absurd, but you can't just stop there. You have to decide what is best for you to do and go on and do it. Everything is still absurd, even more so, but you're doing something, even through the irony and heartbreak."

On that note, I decided we needed more beer. I ran into Top in the team room and told him we were getting drunk on top of the water tower. He said if Jasmine started giving it away, to holler. I said I would, afterwards.

I got back in time to hear Cranston mumble, "This sure is some dynamite shit."

"Yes," said the Aristocrat. "Let me tell you about the time—"

And for the next three hours it was like being at home, sitting on our cars at the Snack Bar, telling lies and drinking. Cranston told us about when he accidentally smoked rabbit tobacco and got high as hell, because he thought it was grass. Jasmine told us about the time her dog pissed on her boyfriend's new transistor radio. And the Aristocrat broke us up with a story about the time he rode a huge Harley-Davidson motorcycle through the halls of Baton High School, nearly running down the principal and two teachers. And I told about the time I passed out in a parking space in San Antonio, Texas, but remembered to put my dime in the meter. The cop who arrested me had no sense of humor.

That kind of evening.

12

UNTIL A week ago the road from our camp to Nan Phuc was dry. But the floodwaters breached that at last, and today we waded across. The water was only a couple feet deep, but our newcomers stepped warily, since for as far as they could see, both left and right, there was water.

"How did you all sleep?" I asked. We had given them cots in the dispensary.

"Fine, we were tired," said the Aristocrat. "Except for one strange thing. About four in the morning I woke up and I swear I heard someone singing. It was a man's voice, singing in Vietnamese. Maybe I dreamed it all."

"No," I laughed. "That was one of our guards. They sometimes sing at night to stay awake. At first we tried to stop it, but then they fell asleep, so we ignore it as best we can."

We walked through the back door of Hoa Hao Unlimited Ltd. School, taught by a woman who had finished elementary school, was being held in a room on our left. Two families lived in another room on the right. The factory occupied the rest of the building, which consisted of one large room the size of a basketball court and two small rooms at the far end.

Santee, wearing the traditional white shirt and black pants of the Vietnamese businessman, trotted over.

"Welcome to Hoa Hao Unlimited Ltd.," he said, holding out both arms expansively. "You are Hamilton Dupree and this simply gorgeous woman is Jasmine Banks." He all but kissed her hand.

"The pleasure is all ours, sah," said Hamilton, returning the partial bow in fine aristocratic fashion.

Straight down the middle of the room were our foot-powered Singers. On the right four women sat at tables, measuring and cutting cloth. Along the other wall women were putting the finishing stitches in brassieres and Viet Cong flags. A dozen crumb crunchers scurried around the floor.

"Today is bra day," said Santee, whose eyes were tracking the rise and fall of Jasmine's breasts. "We make bras Monday through Wednesday and flags on Thursday and Friday, although we may switch to a four-day bra week soon. They're becoming our best seller."

He walked to the first sewing machine. "She's making a size twenty-four A. That's our smallest size. Our women here are somewhat smaller than in America. The next woman is working on a twenty-six and so on up to a thirty-six C, our largest."

He turned. "Over there we cut the pattern. They're attaching a little number to each piece, indicating its size."

"Where do you get your material?" asked Hamilton, picking up a handful.

"That's a problem. We buy it when and where we can find it. Right now our man in Tan Chau gets it from Japan through an AID program. However, his shipments are irregular and the quality is never consistent."

We stepped over children to the other side. "Here they check the stitching, sew the straps on, and sew our tag in. Our trademark is 'Granny's Ghost.' "

I explained about *Granny*.

The Aristocrat examined the bra. "What do you think of these, Jas?" Hamilton asked.

She held the bra at arm's length. The women stopped working and giggled behind their hands. The size of Jasmine's breasts would disquiet most women—Asian or American. She wore only a T-shirt.

"Hell, Ham, I haven't bought a bra in years. Let me see now." She inspected it carefully and held it close.

Oh, Heavenly Father, I prayed, let her try it on. Right here and now.

My Heavenly Father wasn't listening.

She said, "Why not put a bow between the cups? You know it might look cute and a little fancier. I'll show you." Rummaging through the scrap-cloth pile, she found an orange ribbon. She tied a tiny bow and pinned it between the cups. The other women nodded approvingly.

"Great," said Santee. "That's just the right touch. Fantastic." A happy Santee was a getting-richer Santee. "We've also been thinking about expanding into other lines. Maybe blouses."

Gunshots suddenly broke out behind the building. Hamilton and Jasmine dove to the floor and started burrowing under a pile of brassieres. I myself was reaching for my pistol before I realized what the shooting was.

Santee shouted, "It's okay," but another burst drowned out his words. All we saw were two pairs of feet disappearing under A cups. The gunfire stopped as abruptly as it had begun.

"It's all right now," I said, tugging on a foot. "That was us shooting. Come out."

Jasmine and Hamilton emerged, pale and shaken.

136

"We were shooting holes in our flags," said Santee, seizing the opportunity to help Jasmine brush her fanny off.

"Why?" she asked.

"We make the standard platoon-size flags as well as the larger company and battalion size. Half are sold or traded to GIs as souvenirs. So we shoot holes in them, mess them up, so they look authentic."

"What about the rest?" asked Hamilton.

Santee lowered his voice. "We sell them to the VC. Maybe the women know, but it's not something we talk about openly. We make more money selling them as souvenirs than as actual flags. The VC are real tight with their money. If it weren't for the fact that their flags have to be brought down from North Vietnam, they wouldn't buy any from us."

The Aristocrat looked at me and back at Santee. "Isn't that odd? You making flags for the enemy?"

"It's not as if we were making bullets," said Santee. "After all, a flag is just a piece of pretty cloth."

"A piece of pretty cloth," repeated Jasmine.

Hamilton said, "I've got a couple ideas. Instead of each woman sewing a bra from beginning to end, have each one sew a particular part of the bra and pass it along. You'd get economy of effort, because each woman has only one job, which she can do faster and more efficiently."

"Hmmm," said Santee. "I believe it would work."

"Secondly, your cutting area is over there. When a woman wants more material, she has to get up, walk over there, find it, and walk back. Move those tables close behind the sewing machines. Then run a ramp from the table to the left side of the sewing machine. Put sides on it so the material doesn't fall on the floor. As the cloth is cut, the woman slides it across the table and down the ramp. It would be in arm's reach of the person sewing."

"Another good idea," said Santee. "Thank you again. Where are you from?"

"Baton, North Carolina. About fifteen miles from where Warren was raised."

"Your family born and raised in the South?"

"Yes," said the Aristocrat.

"Don't you feel a special kinship for all our people here?" Santee asked.

"You mean because they're working in a textile mill?"

"No. No. Because they're Oriental."

Hamilton looked at me. I scratched my ear.

Santee went on. "Doesn't all this—the smells, the sounds, the weather, the rice, the eyes—especially the eyes—stir a lost chord in your soul? A distant memory from centuries past?"

"I'm not sure. There is something stirring in my mind."

"Let it out, let it free. The Southern-Oriental mystique. We Southerners are mighty lucky," said Santee, looking from Hamilton to Jasmine. "We instinctively understand the yin and the yang. The uncanny canniness of the East. Yes, I love it here. Love it." He paused. "Enough of this. Come, let me show you the back rooms."

Jasmine and Hamilton exchanged glances.

At the far end we entered the room on the right. Four strikers were sanding stocks, cutting barrels on a metal lathe, and assembling metal parts.

"In here we're making AK-47s. They're very popular with the MAAG officers. Naturally, we beat them up a bit, nick the stocks and so forth."

We crossed the hall. Santee said, "Here's a new project. Major Choi wants to make lawn chairs. We can get the plastic webbing easily enough, but the aluminum framing is more difficult. We're trying to find a substitute material for the frame."

"What's your pay scale?" asked Hamilton.

"We pay a hundred and ten piasters a day. That's more than a corporal in the Army makes, but it's not so far out of line that it disrupts the local economy. At the end of the first year we plan to divide up the profits among the employees."

Santee looked down the length of the big room. "Also we let the women come in after hours and use the machines. We sell them material at cost. It's a rare night when every machine isn't working. Some of our women have turned out beautiful designs. There are a couple blouse patterns we're thinking about using."

"What were all these people doing before your factory started?" asked Jasmine.

"You probably noticed the women are in their forties and fifties, which is old in Vietnam. They're too old to work in the fields, but instead of sitting at home all day watching the children, they work here. The kids run loose in a sort of group kindergarten. These women are making money and are feeling useful again. They're happy. The families are happy. And you saw the kids."

We said our good-byes.

Jasmine waited till we were out of earshot to ask, "What's the story on that guy? I can dig the idea of the factory and everybody making money, but what's this about 'us Orientals' and 'my people'?"

"Santee thinks he's Oriental," I said.

"Oriental?" asked Hamilton.

"Something to do with the Chinese migrating to Georgia thousands of years ago and turning into Cherokees and marrying Southerners."

"But he's black," said Jasmine.

"Yes, but he thinks he's Oriental."

"Strange," she said.

I almost said, "If you think he's weird, let me tell you about Hood."

An hour later Hamilton and Jasmine left Nan Phuc. They were shooting pool with Cranston in the police captain's living room when they found out a fisherman was going to Chau An today.

Later Cranston excitedly told me that Hamilton had given him a dozen carefully selected aristograss seeds.

We never saw or heard of them again. Now and then I find myself wondering if Hamilton Dupree is still out there somewhere, dropping off seeds around the world. The Johnny Appleseed of a new generation. Compliments of the Baton Lions Club.

After sick call that afternoon (Soc said the wind had departed from his back shortly before noon) I went into the team room for a beer. Top lounged at the table with one in his hand, and Teewee and Lon were hollering at each other in the kitchen.

"Hello, baldy, how's your hammer hanging?" greeted Top.

"Hanging high after that sweet round eye," I said.

"She could lay a lip lock on my dick any time she wanted to," said Top.

"Do you think they'll make it to Can Tho?" I asked.

"If they were lucky enough to get from Phnom Penh to here, they might luck up enough to get to Can Tho. Except for a few AID officials, who were probably Agency men, the VC haven't fucked with U.S. civilians. Yet."

"Lon, goddamnit, look at this picture," said Wheaty. "You're supposed to cut the leg from the back forward, coming in and under the joint."

Lon unraveled a string of Chinese words.

Top said, "I'd like to give that woman one big wide-on."

"A what?"

"A wide-on. Come on, college boy, haven't you ever heard of a wide-on?"

"I can't say that I have," I said.

"Men get hard-ons, right?"

"Yes."

"So women got to get something. I figure it must be a wide-on."

"A wide-on. I like that," I laughed. The image it brought to mind was deliciously sexy.

Teewee shouted from the kitchen, "That's why enlisted men are enlisted men. You always got your mind in the gutter."

Top said, "Speaking of meat, how's your meat cutting coming?"

"Okay, except there's not enough around here to practice on. This is the first pig we've had in over a month."

Overhead the afternoon rain turned our tin roof into a drum. "I can't see why cows—cows like we have, Jerseys, Guernseys, and Angus—wouldn't live over here. God knows they need milk and meat," Top said.

I pointed at the roof.

"True, but the highest stage of the flood only lasts about a month and a half or two. There are a few high places left. They could be fed by hand for a while, which means hay. It might work. I've ordered some hybrids from Sears Roebuck— tomatoes, okra, beans, peas, and corn. I thought I'd make a test garden downtown to see if we can get better crops."

"Good idea, Top," I said. O'Hara had surprised me again.

Hood, wearing a creased forehead and olive-drab boxer shorts, walked through the team door, saying, "The shit has hit the fan. Remember the other night on the way back from Chau An we heard gunfire? From what Choi can piece together, some Hoa Hao soldiers from Vinh Gia and some South Vietnamese Navy types got in a fracas, and the next morning the Hoa Hao sank one of the Navy junks."

Moans ran around the table. I couldn't believe we'd sunk part of our own Navy. Vinh Gia was a small Hoa Hao outpost a few miles below Chau An. It was not part of our area, but it was Hoa Hao.

Hood went on. "Apparently, there was a fight downtown over a girl after we left—"

"What did I tell you?" Top asked me.

"—and it turned into a shootout. One Hoa Hao soldier was killed. During the night the Hoa Hao went back to their post, got a mortar and two machine guns, and the next morning ambushed the junks as they went by. One junk was sunk, two South Vietnamese sailors killed and a half dozen wounded. There's a big stink with the province chief threatening to send in GVN troops and take over the area. Choi's been on the radio with the other Hoa Hao generals for an hour."

"Goddamn," said Top. "That's all we need. Our own men ambushing the South Vietnamese Navy."

"Was Clow hurt?" I asked hopefully.

"Apparently not."

Funny that they made it through the Viet Cong blockade only to be ambushed by their own people. Of course, the Viet Cong were their own people, too.

Hood said, "Something even stranger. Choi got a radio message from GVN to look out for a team of Viet Cong, disguised as an American Special Forces team, operating in this area."

"That's us," said Wheaty.

"Of course that's us," said Top.

I said, "How could they think that the Viet Cong could disguise themselves to look like Americans?"

"They could hire men who look like Santee," said Top.

"He's black," I said.

"But he thinks he's Oriental."

"You're as crazy as he is," I said.

From the kitchen Teewee asked, "Speaking of Choi, how long has he been a major?"

"About six years," said Hood. "But you know he can't go any higher than major, don't you?"

"No, why?"

"The government of Vietnam forbids any Hoa Hao from holding a rank higher than major in the Army. Afraid they'll get too much power, I guess."

That must be terribly frustrating to Choi, I thought. Not only did Diem destroy three of the four Hoa Hao armies in 1957 (after promising amnesty), he moved thousands of Catholic refugees from North Vietnam into the provinces around the Hoa Hao to contain them. A Catholic himself, Diem also must have admired John Foster Dulles's foreign policy.

And Diem's attempts at containment were about as successful as Dulles's. Instead of stopping the spread of the Hoa Hao religion, his methods only reinforced the Hoa Hao political and social cohesiveness. The Hoa Hao became more independent, more secretive, and more hostile to the South Vietnamese government. They had demonstrated time and time again, with words and guns, that all they wanted was to be left alone.

Hood said, "Speaking of the illustrious government, I heard there was another coup that failed two days ago."

Since Diem had been killed, there had been several successful coups and several failures. An unknown civilian named Tran Van Huong was president at the moment.

Hood said, "The II Corps commander and the head of the Navy, an admiral named Dong Tinh Tri, tried to kick Huong out but couldn't find him. It seems Huong heard about the coup, borrowed a Piper Cub from you-can-guess-who, and flew around over the city, protected by Sabre jets, until it was all over. They couldn't find anything to overthrow."

"Goddamn, I don't know who's crazier, us or them," said Top disgustedly.

Heated rivalry had existed between the corps commanders, especially since Diem's murder. Vietnam was divided into four corps, each headed by a general. The generals took their duties quite seriously. So seriously that each kept more than half of his men nearby and ready to move on Saigon at all times, either to join in a coup or to fight against one. Needless to say, this cut down on the war effort.

"Did I ever tell you all about my steaks and defense budgets theory?" I asked.

Nobody answered.

I said, "First you take all the defense budgets of all the nations in the world. That would be two hundred billion dollars a year. You divide that by the three billion people in the world and you get two hundred and sixty-five dollars a year for an average family of four people. With that you could buy every family on earth, once a week, every week, say on Saturday night, a complete steak dinner with baked potatoes, tossed salad, champagne, and a cigar. Since you're buying three billion of everything, you'd get a good price. Everybody would be so happy that there wouldn't be any more wars."

Top said, "You thought this up all by yourself?"

"Yep."

"Thank goodness. I was afraid someone else had a hand in it. Is that what they teach in college these days?"

Wheaty came in, holding up something made out of meat. It was long and pink and carved out of a pig's back leg.

"A possum," said Hood.

"An apple pie," I said.

"A pig's back leg," said Top.

"Look." Wheaty held it sideways. "A duck. See, this is the wing and this is . . ."

Top got up and opened another beer.

13

SMALL WAVES lapped against *Granny's Ghost* as I walked up the gangplank. Without rain, the afternoon seemed all wrong. Today, Christmas Eve, was the first day in months that dark clouds weren't banked across the sky, and even the air felt drier and cooler. A week ago the villagers, relying on instinct and subtle changes in the weather, had said the water would rise no more. It had not.

A dozen strikers covered *Granny* like bees, hammering, nailing, cutting, and sanding. Choi was raising the deck three feet between the fore and aft cabins so customers could stroll through the cargo area, inspecting the merchandise firsthand. A floating Macy's. Shelves and display counters, to be lit by lanterns, were being built in the hold. I could almost see the signs, "Special! Today only! Tran Van Huong's birthday sale—20 per cent off!"

"Chao, bac si," said Frenchy, walking toward me. He hooked an ancient, double-headed French hammer with an elaborately carved handle into his belt.

"Merry Christmas, Frenchy. I'm looking for Cranston. Is he here?"

"*Non, mon bac si.* He is in rice fields." He pointed to the west.

I should have known. Cranston had been in the paddies more and more, helping with the rice harvesting. It was not an entirely altruistic endeavor. He worked with Lao's foster parents in their field. The romance was blossoming into a full-grown love affair. Hand-holding and night walks along the Bassac. A couple of weeks ago I'd entered my dispensary early one morning and heard those unmistakable sounds coming from the tiny attic. A blushing Cranston had glared over a rafter and told me to stop laughing.

Glancing around *Granny*, I spied Nguyen Van Linh at the far end of the boat, pulling nails out of a board. A Company had captured Linh three weeks ago near the border. Six VC were ambushed. Five died. Linh had dropped his gun and surrendered. Choi and Hood had interrogated him for three days and were convinced he was sincere in saying he had been on the brink of defecting. He was kept under guard for two weeks and now worked as an honor prisoner.

Linh was small, a little more than five feet tall. He wore his hair long—it touched his ears—and styled it in late rag mop. Only eighteen years old, he had been shy, and it wasn't until after three or four conversations with me that he began to relax. He was intelligent with a quick sense of humor. I think his difficulty in making friends was due to more than the fact that he had been a VC; it was because he had one brown eye and one blue eye. Half the strikers contended he had the evil eye, and the other half said it was good luck but that he was still possessed. I found it discomforting, since I could never decide which eye to look at.

I walked to the stern.

"*Chao,* Linh, how goes it?"

"Fine, *bac si.* How are you?" Linh spoke good English, having taken it at the high school in Can Tho, where he was raised. He laid his tools down and lit a Nguoi Can Dam, a foul Cambodian cigarette that smelled and tasted of ground-up cigar butts.

We chatted about the weather. The rains may have stopped. Yes, they were very heavy this year. Soon the river will begin to fall. The rice harvest begins.

I was curious about Linh's family and asked what his father did in Can Tho.

"He is a weatherman with the province airport. At least, the last I heard. I suppose he still is. He was old-fashioned and conservative. That was probably one reason I joined the Viet Cong. He didn't like my music. He didn't want me smoking. He didn't like politics. Stubborn as an old female water buffalo."

I smiled, remembering my same thoughts when I was a teenager.

"I'd like to see him again," said Linh, flipping his cigarette into the river.

"What changed your mind?" Maybe it would be easier if I looked at the blue eye.

"About him?" said Linh.

"About everything."

"A lot of things, I guess." Linh switched to Vietnamese. "The realities of war. Endless training and lectures took the fun out of it real quick. Things like taking orders from someone dumber than you are. Training for suicide attacks. At first I was thrilled and excited to be part of the revolution. I was trained as an anti-aircraft gunner. Did you know that?"

"No." I tried looking at a spot between his eyes.

"I spent five months on a mountaintop shooting into a valley at a chalk outline of a B-52. We couldn't afford real planes, so we shot at drawings on the ground. Learning how far to lead the planes. Except we were so short of ammunition I only fired twenty rounds during the training. The rest of the time I aimed. As it turned out, it didn't matter. I was assigned as a rifleman to a company coming south. I complained, but I was told I'd go where I was told and do what I was told. It's hard to keep an ideal in mind when you're tired and hungry, being fucked over and getting bombed day and night."

"Our planes?"

"Every day on the way south. There are tunnels along the trails, and except for a few shrapnel wounds, no one was hurt. But I became very nervous. The bombs fell all the time."

Linh turned to face the muddy Bassac. "Sometimes the planes hit villages near us. I saw a boy, about my age, with half a face. Napalm had burned his face down to the bone. He was eating through half a mouth, breaking the food into little pieces and stuffing them into a black hole. I don't understand how he lived. In another village bombs hit a schoolhouse and we buried six children that afternoon. It was awful. Somewhere along the way I lost my taste for war. A lot of our men were different. It made them hate Americans even more. I still hate the planes. But we had teams of terrorists working in the south, doing the same thing with grenades and bombs."

I remembered the nine-year-old boy in Chau An who was paid fifteen cents to throw a live grenade at the first American he saw.

Linh said, "Maybe not on as big a scale, but the same thing. It started not to make much sense. After a while you wonder if it's worth it. And you wonder why the men who disagree aren't out here fighting."

Linh turned around and changed the subject. "Have you ever been to Chicago?"

"Once, when I was twelve. I don't remember much about it. Why?" Maybe if I just looked at his nose . . .

"I have a brother who lives in Chicago."

"What? You're kidding." His nose won't do. He'll think there's something wrong with his nose.

"He's lived there for four years. He went to the U.S.A. for

148

the government of South Vietnam to learn how to set up a police force. He had been a policeman in Saigon. But he didn't come back when the time came. He goes to the university and used to send me records when I was in high school. I remember one good album he sent. It was the Beach Boys?"

"Hell, yes," I said. "The Beach Boys are great. Remember 'Little Deuce Coupe?' 'Gonna shut 'em down . . .' " We laughed and sang several lines together.

We chatted a few minutes more and I left, after inviting him over to listen to the Supremes on Cranston's portable record player. Cranston had only three albums; two by the Supremes and one by Jonathan Winters.

I found Cranston clearing out an irrigation ditch near the Tran Tri canal. I told him we were having a special Christmas Eve supper tonight and Top wanted the whole team together, and also that one radio wasn't working and would he check on it. He said he'd be along.

On the way back I passed the fast-growing factory of Hoa Hao Unlimited Ltd. Since Thanksgiving Santee had added four more sewing machines, a line of blouses and pants, and crossbows. The crossbows were a recent brainstorm, conceived after Wheaty killed his second rat with one. They might sell even better than the AK-47s. Unlike the guns, the crossbows didn't have to be smuggled into the States. The bows could be manufactured easily and sold at a good profit.

The profits from Hoa Hao Unlimited Ltd. had already built two houses for the families who had lived in the back room at the factory. Their old room became a second classroom.

Santee and Choi were also selling eighty thousand shares of common stock, class B, voting, for 100 piasters each. Since the company had sold us our original shares at 1000 P's apiece, we were given new certificates with ten-for-one convertibility into class B. I think that's the way it went. Like the rest of the

149

team, I was putting most of my salary into the company. I now owned sixty shares, and it was exciting to watch my investment.

Santee had also succeeded in getting us involved in the business. Teewee was handling bookkeeping. Hood was channeling part of his vast intelligence network into industrial spying—to find out the techniques, wage scales, and prices that other textile companies used. That shouldn't be too hard. There were only three other textile factories in South Vietnam. As a medic, stockholder, and director (yes, we were all directors), I held sick call once a week for the employees. Another fringe benefit.

Counting the men on *Granny*, there were thirty-five strikers working for the company now.

Which was one reason we had just hired a hundred Chinese mercenaries called Nungs. Another reason was, as Choi said, "Why risk good Hoa Hao men?" The profits from the company could cover their salaries. The third reason was that VC were getting bolder. Sniping and small patrol action had increased in the month since Thanksgiving. Two outposts were probed, a recon patrol near Giap Phung was ambushed (two wounded), and three teenagers from Se Toi were kidnaped. On my medical patrols I could sense an undercurrent of tension and fear, particularly in the villages around the border.

VC activity had also increased throughout the country, especially after 25,000 U.S. ground troops had arrived a few weeks back. GIs were operational in II Corps, trying to stop the Cong from cutting the country in half. According to the grapevine, our men were literally and figuratively following in the footsteps of the French. Huge, sweeping operations on the slopes of the Chaîne Annamitique. Civilians were forcibly moved to "relocation hamlets," and anything left would be shot or burned. I'd heard the term "free-fire zone" for the first time two weeks ago. It left a bad taste in my mouth.

Although Major Choi had been the first to mention mercenaries, I suspected the seed had been planted by Top or Hood, who had worked with the Chinese before.

The Nungs were recruited from Phouc Long in the mountains of III Corps. They had signed a six-month contract with us, insisting that that was standard procedure.

Three days ago they had marched into camp. They had slipped from the mountains down through the Cambodian jungles to the border. We escorted them the rest of the way. Their weapons wrote a story of Indochina: two Red Chinese mortars, a half dozen French submachine guns, a couple Russian PP-41s, and a large assortment of American carbines, Browning Automatic Rifles (BARs), and Garands. The Nungs' self-confidence was tangible. I had yet to see a Nung carry his gun at anything but the ready. Most were middle-aged, in their thirties and forties. A few looked over fifty. Their clothes were as varied as their guns: black pajamas, camouflaged fatigues, and olive-drab uniforms. These men were generally heavier, slightly taller, and older than our strikers.

Hood had briefed us on the Nungs: "They're about the best fighters in Indochina. The name is a tribal one that refers to the Chinese who were once natives of the Yunnan Province in Southern China. Part are remnants of the old Kuomintang, the Nationalist Chinese, 93rd Division, which was driven out of China by the Communists in 1949. They refused to be repatriated to Formosa. Most of the 93rd is now in Northern Laos and controls opium there. The rest moved south out of China when the Communists took over. Part of them moved south again into South Vietnam when the country was split in half. Fighting is a family tradition, passed from father to son. They've worked for the French, the CIA, MAAG, and Special Forces. Because of their family ties and the fact that few speak Vietnamese, the Nungs are close-knit and clannish. Not necessarily unfriendly, but cautious and reserved. And they're damn cool fighters."

151

When the Nungs arrived, we put together a training schedule. I was teaching advanced first aid. Their ten medics had had no formal training, but experience had been a good teacher. To be sure, acupuncture was their favorite procedure, but when that didn't work—it usually did work for most minor ailments—they turned to Western medicines with no hesitation.

The Nungs had brought a new excitement into camp. Or perhaps just to us. The routine of CIDG training, combined with our isolation from the Army, had become depressing. Cranston was involved with Lao and Santee with the company. But it was clear we had been drifting apart. We had heard nothing from MAAG about our situation.

It was only 1730 hours and the sun was already sinking fast beyond the flooded fields. Winter was here, which meant that on a cold night the temperature might fall to 50 degrees.

The odor of freshly baked bread and a mood of recent asperity hung in the air when I stepped into the team room. The bread and the reason for the asperity were both on the table. Since morning Lon had been cooking a pig for Christmas. But the thing sitting between heaping bowls of USOM mashed potatoes and local string beans resembled what might be left after a moose was run over by six tanks. Two of the pig's feet had been stitched to its sides. The other feet were missing and seams crisscrossed the body, forcing it into what looked like a deformed turkey.

Top, pulling out a chair, said, "Lon, what the hell is that?"

"You ask Teewee," Lon said, slamming a bowl of fresh pineapple on the table.

Wheaty said, "Come on, Lon. You're not still mad?"

Lon spit out a mouthful of Chinese.

The rest of the team gathered around the table.

"Wheaty, what is this?" asked Top.

"What better way to celebrate Christmas than with a turkey?"

"That's a turkey?" asked Hood.

"That's a pig," shouted Lon.

"That's the worst-looking turkey or pig I've ever seen," said Santee, trying to tear a leg off.

"Wait," said Wheaty. "I'll have to cut the stitches for you. You guys don't appreciate art."

"Wheaty," asked Top, "have you ever thought about being a plumber?"

"I don't know anything about plumbing," said Wheaty.

"That's all right, because you don't know anything about art either." Top laughed, punching Santee in the ribs.

When Top recovered, he said, "Lieutenant, do—"

"Captain," corrected Wheaty.

"You're still a lieutenant in Uncle Sam's Army. Shithead. Do you know that meat cutting don't mean you're supposed to carve meat like it was a fucking piece of sculpture?"

"Pass the wine, Hogjaw," Cranston said. From somewhere Lon had dug up a bottle of Vietnamese red wine. A little sharp, but still wine.

"Anyway," Wheaty went on, "I'm through with meat cutting. I've graduated and have a diploma. But I've been thinking that when you get right down to it meat cutting is kind of low-class. The money isn't bad, according to the school, but it isn't something I'd want to do the rest of my life."

"I don't see how you'd make much money at it," said Top.

"So I've sent off for a private-investigator course," said Wheaty, grinning and looking around the table.

"Oh, my God," groaned Santee.

"Far fucking out," said Cranston.

"It just came to me one day. This sounds silly, maybe, but I was reading one of those men's magazines"—Teewee chuckled hesitantly—"and I saw an advertisement with a picture of a man introducing himself to a really sharp-looking woman. He was holding out an ID card. Under the picture it said, 'You,

153

too, can be a private investigator!' My Army training would come in handy. I know you don't meet beautiful women every day, but it might happen once in a while."

Santee changed the subject. "How's your garden coming, Top?"

"Pretty good, considering. Can't beat those Sears Roebuck hybrids. The only thing we need is fertilizer. The floods leach the minerals out every year. I've been trying to convince the farmers to save their shit and use it. But they believe it's dirty and unclean."

"To say nothing of parasites, diarrhea, and a half dozen other diseases," I said.

"I got the goddamn garden going, and in a month or so you'll have the finest mess of collards and black-eyes you've ever ate. Hey, Lon, you know how to cook collards?"

"Corrards?" said Lon. "No, but I fix special rice pudding for Christmas," he said, setting bowls beside our plates.

The only thing special I could find was that it was burned a little more than usual.

"By the way," said Top, "the latest MAAG directive came down today through Vietnamese channels: 'Because of the nature of this conflict, captured Viet Cong will not be referred to as prisoners of war. The term "captured enemy" will henceforth be used in all oral and written communications. Particularly in the presence of members of the press.' "

"Captured enemy? Crock of shit," snorted Hood. "But that reminds me, our 'captured enemy,' Linh, said the reason his team was on a patrol the day they were ambushed was that their headquarters had intercepted a Vietnamese radio report that said there were Viet Cong disguised as Americans in this area. Linh said his company commander figured the disguised VC must be a secret intelligence team from North Vietnam. Linh's patrol was trying to link up with them."

"Damn. They're as crazy as MAAG," said Top.

Santee, who was hiding his rice pudding under a pig/turkey

bone, asked, "Anybody got any ideas on how to make a lightweight frame for lawn chairs? Bamboo splits when we put screws in it."

"Hell, Hogjaw, the company ought to be rich enough to buy an aluminum rolling machine," said Top.

"An aluminum rolling machine?"

"It could make frames for you. When I was sixteen, I worked in a rolling plant. But I was only kidding. Those things cost ten or fifteen thousand dollars."

"Well, now," Santee said smugly, "today Choi and I did a little addition, and so far we've raised about eighteen thousand dollars from the stock offering. We've sold nearly thirty-two thousand shares. Tell me more about these rolling machines."

"Back home the company made aluminum clothesline poles. The aluminum came in eight-by-ten-foot sheets. I laid the sheet under the stamper, kicked a pedal, and the pattern was cut out. The machine then rolled and bradded it together. The great thing is it can handle dozens of different templates. You could make poles, shelves, boxes, practically anything."

"Pass the wine," I said.

Maybe if I had enough to drink I could forget that I was stranded in the middle of Southeastern Asia with six madmen, one of whom was talking about importing heavy machinery to make lawn chairs and another was selling common stock to rice farmers. Not to mention our officer, who spent half a day cutting a pig apart and sewing it back together so it would look like a fucking turkey.

14

AT 1615 hours the next day the call came from Bac Lam, our SDC post on the Chlong River nine miles southwest: "Platoon of Viet Cong attacking. Send help." The message ended and Cranston could not raise the post again. He radioed B Company, seven miles upriver, and then told Choi.

Twenty minutes later a platoon of Nungs, twenty strikers, Choi, Teewee, Hood, Top, and I were aboard *Granny*.

Bac Lam was the southernmost post in our area. It sat on the edge of a large swamp forest, four hundred yards from Cambodia. The land was poor and the area was thinly populated. Bac Lam was manned by twenty men and their families. "Manned" is not really the word; perhaps "lived in." Primarily a lookout position, its defense was a couple strands of barbed wire and two concrete bunkers. The post had received only sniper fire before.

We sailed from Nan Phuc through the Tran Van Tri canal, mains'l and jib up to capture the light breeze and both Peugeot engines under full throttle.

Everyone was getting right with their own god. The chief

Nung medicine man, a humorless middle-aged man named Chung, lit a bundle of red joss sticks tied to the barrel of his BAR. The strikers rubbed Tiger Balm under their noses and pinched their chests to exorcise any last-minute devils. I had called on my own gods and brought my emergency medical footlocker, permanently packed for fire fights such as this.

We swung left into the Tri-Chlong canal which angled southwest to the Chlong. The eastern sky was darkening. It would be a bad time for an ambush. Any time the VC hit something, the relief force had to be aware that it might be a trap. Since this was *Granny*'s first foray into combat, we would have some element of surprise. Plus, she was armor-plated.

Top was leaning against the forward cabin. "What do you think we'll find?" I asked.

"I figure it's a probe to see what kind of guts the SDC have or to see what reaction force we can put together or the VC wanted some weapons. Or all three."

Unspoken was the fear that this could be the big one. Whenever the VC decided to come across for real, it would start with something small, like this, to draw away part of the camp's defenses.

I smeared Tiger Balm under my nose.

"You going native, too?" asked Top.

"It keeps evil spirits away," I kidded Top. "Try some?"

"Shit. You a medic and a white man, too."

We didn't hear the gunfire until we entered the Chlong. It sounded like rifles. That was good. And if the fire fight was still going on, there weren't a whole hell of a lot of VC. Top ordered everyone flat on the deck, because of our nearness to Cambodia. The border ran north and south only a few hundred yards west of the river, but for all practical purposes the river was the border. No one lived in the thin strip of land to our right.

We were within two miles of Bac Lam, and there was no sign of B Company's sampans. We were probably ahead of them. The closer we got, the less gunfire we heard. Only occasional rounds now.

A half mile from the post Choi dropped the sails for more maneuverability and visibility. The sun had set and the shoreline was fading into grays and blacks. There was no shooting now.

One of Bac Lam's corner bunkers appeared, dark against the deep purple sky. The rest of the post was hidden among the pine, mango, and palm trees. Choi cut the engines to a crawl and we drifted closer. Still no light or noise. In Choi's cabin Wheaty was trying to raise the post on the radio. There was no answer. Clicks underscored the tension as men released their safeties. Choi reversed the props to maintain our position.

I lay on the port side, my gun propped in one of the V's Santee had cut every two feet along the armor plating. Forty-five yards away loomed Bac Lam. I could think of only one thing: Either the VC were inside watching us . . . or . . . they weren't. Minutes passed.

Then it happened. One moment there was silence, and the next, bullets screamed around us, ricocheting off the armor, karumping into the mast, and whap-whapping overhead.

Jesus Christ, I thought, curling against the plating. We got us a live one now. The first barrage caught us unaware. Only a half dozen scattered shots were returned. Through the noise, I picked out twenty-five or thirty guns. No heavy weapons.

"Merry goddamn Christmas!" Top shouted.

As the first volley slackened, strikers began poking their guns into firing positions. The Nungs were getting themselves organized and firing back. Fire from the VC became sporadic.

There was a shout behind me, and I turned to see Teewee disappearing headfirst down an open hatch. Hood crawled to the opening.

"Is he hit?" I shouted.

"No. He tripped and fell in," said Hood, giving Wheaty a hand.

158

"What's the matter, Lieutenant? Trying to get away from them bees?" asked Top.

Somewhere up front a voice shouted, "Die Japanese!"

Through my firing hole I picked out a muzzle blast a few feet from the corner bunker. I steadied my carbine and fired a short burst. Tracers told me I was high. I dropped my barrel an inch and fired again. Even as I watched the red streaks race to the target, a bullet slammed into the armor not two inches away, showering me with tiny bits of metal. The bullet whined into the water.

Behind, Choi was hollering at the machine-gun crews to get the thirties going. The Nungs, like the pros they were, fired either single shots or in bursts of three or four.

I had just emptied the rest of my clip when I heard a striker shouting in pain, *"Bac si! Bac si!"*

I grabbed my shoulder bag and crawled back to the voice. The wounded man lay next to the railing. He was Vinh Lan Nha, an eighteen-year-old rifleman from Tan Dao. I had treated his six-year-old sister for worms the week before. Nha was pale and holding his left arm. Blood soaked his shirt sleeve and ran between his fingers.

"Dau, bac si. Dau. Neu—" His words were lost as the machine gun behind us began firing. We both winced at the wall of bullets two feet over our heads.

It might not be too bad, I thought. He'd lost maybe half a pint of blood. I cut the sleeve off and sponged up the blood. The entry hole was two inches forward of his elbow. A clean hole, no bigger around than a pencil, with blood steadily oozing out. I saw no exit hole, and before I could explore further, Nha moaned loudly. He was white. Most likely going into psychological shock, for he hadn't bled that much.

"It doesn't look bad, Nha. You're going to be okay." Right now he had about three pints of blood collected in his stomach from fear. I laid him flat and pushed an ammo box under his feet to pour blood back to his brain.

Out of a corner of my consciousness I realized our firing had nearly stopped.

I cleaned Nha's upper arm and there I found the exit hole. It was the size of a quarter and had ragged edges. Blood ran out in a smooth stream, but I detected no arterial pumping. That was an odd place for the exit. I tied pressure bandages over both wounds.

"It looks okay, Nha. Not serious." I quickly examined him for other wounds. Once in Special Forces medical school I learned that lesson the hard way. On a simulated casualty test my victim had a sucking chest wound, which I promptly patched up. I stood by proudly, while my instructor marked an F on my card. He asked the victim to turn over. In his back was a knife.

"Your patient died, medic, while you stood here and assumed he had only one injury," the captain said.

Nha had no other wounds. A shape materialized out of the dark, and Major Choi picked up Nha's hand. "How is he, *bac si?*"

I told him.

Choi looked at Nha. "Vinh Lan Nha, you will be healthy again soon. Do not worry. I will tell your father and your mother that you have been brave."

Nha smiled. Better medicine than mine.

"Stay here, Nha," I said. "We'll be going back soon. You'll be all right, and if you need anything, call me."

Looking around, I gathered that the fight was over. The strikers and Nungs were chattering like chickens, and some were standing up. I told one of A Company's medics to stay with Nha and to get him to drink as much water as possible.

I found Choi hunkered with Top and Teewee. Choi was saying, "I think they have gone now. We scared them off."

Top said, "I saw some men jumping off the back wall."

Teewee interrupted, "Here comes B Company."

Silhouettes of several dozen sampans on the water moved

toward us. Someone was softly calling, "Nan Phuc? Camp Nan Phuc? Major Choi?"

Choi answered, "Yes, Minh. Be quiet. Get up here."

We helped fat Captain Minh aboard, and Choi outlined what had happened. Minh ordered half his men ashore and spread the rest around as guards. The sampans landed without incident. Two returned, and Teewee and I got in the first one and Top and Hood in the second. We stepped onto the bank, and the post seemed deserted. It was completely dark now, and we used flashlights. *Granny* carried a giant searchlight rigged to 12-volt batteries, but Choi probably didn't want to attract attention.

"Over here, *bac si*," shouted someone. A light winked at me, and I hurried there.

A striker shined his light down on a man. The man was a Viet Cong and he was very dead. Cut-off black pajama pants, a torn black shirt, ammo belt, and Bata boots. I saw no gun. He was in his early twenties and lean. High cheekbones dropped sharply to a square jaw. I opened his shirt. Two small holes six inches apart. Such tiny holes. To kill someone.

Wheaty called, "Come here, Warren."

I stumbled through the darkness to the corner bunker, where Teewee pointed his light at a second body. The man wasn't dressed like the other. He wore pale green fatigues, leather boots, and a purple scarf over one shoulder, draped the way Boy Scouts wore them. Near his head was a brown beret.

I shined the light on his face. His skin was dark and his hair wavy. His face was broader and flatter than that of a Vietnamese.

"Cambodian," I said. "We're in a world of trouble if the Bodes are helping the VC."

Wheaty called Hood and Top over. After searching the man's clothes and equipment, Hood said, "He was a member of the KKK."

"No shit?" said Top.

"Look here," said Hood, holding up the man's left hand. He had no little finger. Only a stub to the second joint. "When men join the KKK, the end of their little finger is cut off. Not only does it test their sincerity—it forever marks them as a member."

Top said, "Goddamn. That's all we need. The fucking KKK and the VC working together."

We searched the post but found no more bodies or any guns. There was surprisingly little damage. More than likely, the soldiers and their families had abandoned Bac Lam as soon as the VC started shooting. The post's only heavy weapon, an old French sixty-millimeter mortar, was missing.

Top sent strikers to search outside the post, and we paddled back to *Granny*. Choi and Minh were planning several ambushes up and down the river in tenuous hopes of catching the Cong. As I started to check on Nha, there was a commotion on shore. Someone shouted that they had found a soldier hiding in the bushes.

They brought him aboard. He was a skinny old man whose camouflaged fatigues were too big for him. He was barefoot and trembling.

Choi said, "Relax. We're here. Tell us what happened."

The man stuttered for a moment, glancing from Choi to me and back again. Finally he got out, "The doctor who walks on water!" He made a sort of half curtsy. Choi was no help. The corners of his eyes wrinkled slightly in humor.

Feeling like a fool, I said, "It's all right. Go ahead and tell us."

"The Viet Cong attacked the post about an hour and a half before dark. They came from the south with many guns."

"How many?" asked Choi.

"Many," the man said. "Maybe forty soldiers or more." Mentally, I reduced that to twenty-five. "We held out as long as we could, and when we saw we could not stop them, we were driven out."

162

"You mean you left before they got inside?" asked Choi.

"Yes." The man swallowed and looked down.

"Where are the rest of your men?"

"We go in different directions." He paused. "To confuse the VC."

Mild panic, I translated.

"Was anyone injured?" questioned Choi.

"I did not see anyone hit."

Choi asked him about weapons. The man said most of the troops carried their own guns out, but no one picked up the mortar.

"And then you saw us arrive?"

"Oh, no! Then there was another attack."

"What?" said Choi. My ears perked up.

"Yes. I was hiding in the bushes. The VC had been inside maybe fifteen or twenty minutes, and I heard shooting from the east side of the camp. I thought it was you, but I look and see forty or fifty soldiers and I do not recognize them. They looked Khmer. And they wore funny-looking hats."

"The KKK!" said Hood, as excited as I had ever seen him.

The man went on. "They fought with the VC and finally drove them off. They went inside the post, and two carried off the mortar and some weapons. Then you come not long afterwards and fight with them."

Top began to laugh, and seconds later we were all laughing. The VC hit the post to get the mortar and were, in turn, attacked by the KKK, who also wanted the mortar.

The man stared at us as if we were crazy. Probably both the VC and the KKK had planned to attack the post and, by some incredible coincidence, picked the same night. And then we attacked the KKK. Somehow it made as much sense as everything else. Or as little. The VC wanted to free the South Vietnamese for the North Vietnamese government, although maybe as a side effect for the South Vietnamese. The KKK wanted to free South Vietnam for Cambodia. The U.S. Army wanted to free the South Vietnamese for the South Vietnamese government, and maybe as a side effect, for the South Vietnamese themselves. The Nungs wanted to free something because they were being paid four thousand piasters each a month. And all the South Vietnamese wanted was to grow a little rice.

Choi and Hood went on questioning the man for ten minutes, but we learned nothing more. Choi left thirty men to secure the post and round up the troops. We said good night to Minh and turned *Granny* around.

The Nungs and strikers were in good spirits. Talk ran back and forth along *Granny* like a buzz saw. Choi did not hoist sails, for the wind had died completely. A half-moon had risen and pale light sprinkled the water.

We relaxed. After the fiasco at Bac Lam there seemed little chance of an ambush. Lawn chairs and beer were brought from Choi's cabin, and we sat down around the wheel.

Choi said, "*Granny* gave us very good protection." He was fond of our nickname for his boat. "We have a few holes in the sails, but nothing serious."

I lit a cigarette and leaned back, my carbine in my lap.

"Yes, indeed. With *Granny* we can also take clothes and food and medicine to villages that do not have these things. *Granny* is a good ghost," he chuckled.

Choi was in a rare talkative mood.

"Maybe soon we can buy another *Granny*," he said.

"Is that so?" asked Top. "You'll have your own little Navy up here."

"Yes. If we had another boat, with a shallow draft like this one, we could keep one in the field all the time, not only selling clothes and food but as a military support vessel for our men. Like tonight."

Choi flipped the searchlight on briefly and checked the banks ahead of us. He said, "Our textile company has been very successful. We are employing thirty-two men and women from our village and a platoon of strikers. With the Nungs here, maybe even more of our men can help. Yes, Hoa Hao Unlimited Ltd. is very good for my people." Choi had a one-track mind tonight. I wondered what he was driving at. He went on, "Santee is a good man. Sometimes he's too impulsive and wants to move too quickly, but still a good man. Our stock is doing well too."

We were waiting for Choi to get to the point.

"Our sales of VC souvenirs are picking up, especially with more GIs in the delta," said Choi. His hands fiddled with something in his lap. Probably that awful pig's teat. "Maybe we should talk over what you told me yesterday, Sergeant Hood. Captain and Sergeant O'Hara, I haven't had time to tell you yet. This is a good time. Sergeant Hood—"

Hood cleared his throat. "Warren, you remember Captain Clow from MAAG? We ran into him that time in Chau An."

"Yes," I said.

Hood turned to Top and Wheaty. "He put out the word, and, as he guessed, my agents picked it up. He wants us to furnish him with intelligence from this area. Gave a big song and dance about how hard it is to get good intelligence about the VC up here, and anything we could forward along would naturally be classified and in strictest confidence. Remember he thinks we're with the CIA. What do you think?"

My first reaction was negative. "I don't see why we should give them anything."

O'Hara disagreed. "One of these days the Army's gonna find out we're still here and it ain't gonna hurt to have a few friends around. We don't lose anything by passing along what we know."

Choi turned on the searchlight to look for the Tri-Chlong canal, angling off to our right. With water still covering everything, our only guide would be a drooping banyan tree on a mound at the junction.

Hood said, "Warren touched on the main point, which is

why I think we should cooperate. If we don't supply intelligence, it's only a matter of time before MAAG moves in their own people to do it. That means a couple MAAG officers, probably working with the major here, some aides, then a few troops for security reasons and a landing strip to get in and out, and then a few hundred more troops to secure the landing strip. I sure as hell don't want all that, and I don't think you do either, Major Choi."

"I'm glad to hear you say that, Sergeant Hood," Choi paused and then continued, "We should supply a certain amount of intelligence to the MAAG officer. You and I will go over the reports very carefully."

It was settled.

The banyan tree appeared, and we turned right. Black on black. The tree, with its roots beginning above the ground, seemed like a giant hulking spider. The tree of Buddha's enlightenment.

Every minute took us farther from Cambodia. One of Choi's bodyguards brought more beer and a small lantern. Choi lit a Salem. He smoked only occasionally, usually during meetings with us or patrol briefings.

Exhaling, he said, "That brings up something I've been thinking about for some time. As you know, your government has sent in several divisions of soldiers. More will be coming. And soon they may be in this area. Maybe it is okay for soldiers to go where they are fighting many VC. In III Corps and I Corps. It is also true that if there are many American soldiers here, more VC will come and fight. The U.S. generals believe they should build large, stationary camps. Barricaded villages. The VC will surely attack. And more U.S. soldiers will come in. And more VC."

The major stopped a moment. This was what he'd been working up to all night.

Choi said, "My people are tired of fighting. We want freedom and we want to be left alone. We have been fighting for twenty-five years. I was thirteen years old when I killed my first man—a Japanese."

For a crazy moment I wanted to say, "*Beaucoup* Japanese, huh?"

"The Viet Cong are very bad. And the South Vietnamese government has treated us shamefully. If more Vietnamese troops and American soldiers and Viet Cong come in, it will be bad for my people."

I had never heard Choi talk so frankly before.

Still fiddling with his pig's teat, Choi said, "Among the Hoa Hao, I am a *trung tuong,* a lieutenant general. The other Hoa Hao generals and myself met last week to discuss this problem. We have about forty thousand soldiers, many trained by Special Forces. We will not let the Viet Cong take our land and our people. But we do not want our land and people destroyed by fighting, either. Not too long ago we tried to make our six provinces independent of the government and the Viet Cong. We were not successful. I don't think we would be successful now, although two of our generals favor this course. But I talk too much. What do you think?"

Top said, "It might not be as bad as all that. The VC may let this area alone. Hell, we're a lot better off than many camps. Besides, your people are more loyal to the Hoa Hao leaders than many Vietnamese are to the government. Few Hoa Hao have become Viet Cong."

"Thank you. But I see more fighting in the future." Choi sounded grim. "Like the one tonight. The Viet Cong and the KKK. We were caught in the middle. What will happen when a battalion of ARVN decides to sweep through this area? Many innocent people will die. Also, American planes are using chemicals to kill the trees in the jungles in Laos and Cambodia. They will poison the water and the land."

We, too, had heard that our planes wers using defoliants. Reluctantly I admitted the rumors were probably true. We had heard it too many times from too many different people.

Choi was silent a moment. Then he said, "Are you familiar with the yin and the yang? Some believe all aspects of this world and our life can be characterized as yin or yang. Yin represents the female principle, the negative, passive earthiness of darkness, cold, and death. Tonight has been mostly a yin night. Yang would represent the positive, active, productive, light, heat, and life. This is the difference between the East and West. The West thinks of dark as essentially evil and light as essentially good, but in yin and yang the two are independent and elementary parts of existence. The answer is not the triumph of light over dark, but the attainment of life in perfect balance between the two."

Hood asked, "What do you think the Hoa Hao should do?"

"I asked the generals to wait before deciding. There was talk of assisting the IV Corps general in assuming control of the government. I don't think that is the correct answer. There is a story about once when Confucius and Tze-loo were passing through a rugged and deserted mountain area in China and found an old woman weeping beside a grave. They asked about her grief. 'My husband's father,' she said, 'was killed here by a tiger, and my husband, also, and now my son has met the same fate.' When Confucius asked why she continued to live in so dangerous a place, she said, 'There is no oppressive government here.' "

We were silent. Choi peered off into the dark, trying to see the channel, to keep to the middle of the way.

Hood said, "I've got an idea. It might not make much sense. I have a brother-in-law who is a graduate of Harvard and who works for an outfit called the Rand Corporation in California. It's one of those think-tank companies that work on problems for the Army. For example, the Army might want to know what would happen if we invaded Rumania. The brains at Rand would sit down and feed a bunch of information into computers, which would project what different courses of action would cause. Most of their work is classified government work. Maybe we should contact them."

"Why would they be interested in us?" asked Choi.

"They would be, for a price. I could ask my brother-in-law if they can handle this. They're damn good."

"I don't understand how it works," said Choi.

"We would give them every bit of information that we know about the VC, the Hoa Hao, the Americans, the South Vietnamese government—troop strength, social values, religious beliefs, climate, local economy, health—everything we can think of. Then give them the problem: We don't want to be fucked with and we want to survive. What do we do? Rand would assign their top intellectuals and computers to work on it. And they would arrive at several alternate scenarios. For example, they might say a coup would be the best thing because in the long run X number of people will die as compared to Y number if the Hoa Hao tried to become independent. Or they might come up with something new."

Choi glanced at Teewee and me.

I said, "It might be worth a try. They're supposed to be the best."

Teewee said, "I don't know how they're going to analyze our situation here when they're in California."

Hood said, "I don't think we've got anything to lose. If we don't like what they recommend, we can forget it. At least, we won't be any worse off."

"You really think this is a good idea?" asked Choi.

"I could write my brother-in-law and ask if they'd be interested," he said.

"To be truthful," said Top, "in Laos once, we used a Rand scenario about what was going to happen to the government, and they hit it right on the head."

"Okay," said Choi. "We will try them."

High overhead, the wind hurried a cloud across the moon. A secret wink to someone.

15

WOMEN WERE carrying bowls of vegetables, meats, and fruits to the fifty-foot table set up beside the team house. Two assistant cooks, hand-picked by Lon, and four strikers were lifting a fat pig off the fire. Major Choi was directing where the last of some seventy-five potted plants were to be placed.

"So this is Tet," said Cranston. "Far fucking out."

"Their new year," I said. "A celebration of the coming of a new year and thanks for the harvest just ended. Choi says the harvest was one of the best in years."

"And the VC got very little this year, mostly because of *Granny's Ghost. Granny* was so heavy with that load that came in today that the decks were like inches above the water."

The harvest had started in early December, and *Granny* had been hauling rice back for the past seven weeks. It was now January 30. Choi paid good prices, fifty-five piasters per gia, which was a little more than forty-four pounds. A careful farmer could squeeze 1500 pounds of rice from an acre of land. In previous years the farmers had received about forty-five piasters; plus, they had had to carry the rice to Chau An by sicylo or on their backs. That, of course, invited the annual attempts by the Viet Cong to steal the rice.

Choi and Santee also were trying a scheme they thought would bring better prices. They were storing the rice in a rented warehouse in Chau An until after the harvest season. Their theory was that the price would then begin to rise and they could sell at higher prices. Tran Van Soai, the great Hoa Hao general in the early 1950s, had used this tactic successfully. In 1953 Soai had held in warehouses in Can Tho more than 10 per cent of the entire rice crop of the delta.

"How'd your patrol with the Nungs go?" I asked Cranston. He and Hood had returned late last night from a four-day patrol.

"No trouble at all. We went to Phu Hai, way the hell out in the middle of nowhere. I don't think there's been a half dozen white men to visit that village. My skin was sore from being stared at all day. We stayed two days and helped harvest rice. Let me tell you about a funny thing that happened. On the second night me and the village chief and some elders were drinking rice wine and talking and having a good time. They got into an argument about the fact that they didn't have a song and dance for the late-baby-rice-shoot planting."

"What?"

"You know the Vietnamese have songs and dances for nearly all their farming seasons, like the rice planting song and the we-need-more-rain song and the harvest dance. This year in Phu Hai they were trying a late crop of rice, using some hybrid seeds Top sent out to them. But they didn't have a traditional song and dance for it. I was feeling pretty good by that time, so I said, 'Look, we got a late-baby-rice-shoot planting song back in New York. Maybe you'd like to hear it?' They did and I spent the evening teaching them the Hora and the 'Hava N'gila.' "

"The what?"

" 'Hava N'gila.' The Jewish folk song," said Cranston, squatting down and jumping from one foot to the other in a circle. "Hey, hey, hey! Hava N'gila, gila, hey, hey, hey!"

I started laughing.

"It's true, man. Right now, out there in Phu Hai, at the end of nowhere, there's a whole village doing the old New York 'Hava N'gila' late-baby-rice-shoot planting song and dance. They liked the dance best of all."

The more I imagined the scene, the more I laughed. I pictured sociologists visiting Phu Hai ten years from now to study the mores of the Hoa Hao and being dumfounded by the "Hava N'gila." They might develop a whole new theory about the eleventh tribe of Israel going to Cochin China. I laughed even harder when I fancied them bumping into an old gray-haired black man named Santee, who claimed he was Oriental.

Top and Teewee shouted as they walked by that the meal was ready and to get our young asses over. I recognized most of the men: Choi and his staff, the commanding officers from each company, the police chief, Nan Phuc's elders, and several religious figures from Long Xuyen. Guards had been doubled around the camp.

The table was splendid: a dozen incense burners, long tapering purple and gold candles, flowers, altar trays, paper money to bribe the evil and greedy spirits, ice-cold Ba Muoi Bas, and in the middle of the table was the greasy pig with a rose between her ears.

I never did figure out that rose.

Vietnamese toasts come at the end of the meal, so without ado Choi asked Teewee to cut the pig. With his chrome-plated butcher knife and a smile that made him look twelve years old, Wheaty delivered sliced pig with charm and skill. I think it was the proudest moment of his life.

Plates of rice, river trout stewed in vegetable sauce, shredded banana stalk blended with cucumber and lotus

172

flowers, fried shrimp, squash, hog intestines soup, sweet potatoes, bindweed (which Hood told me was a species of morning glory), soya cheese, dried squid strips, bean sprouts, and the inevitable *nuoc man* were passed around the table. I was finally used to *nuoc man*, a black water sauce made from fish preserved in brine. It smelled and tasted like rotten fish. *Nuoc man* was more than a sauce to vary the rice; it was cheap and loaded with protein.

"Top, when do you think our rice information will get here?" asked Cranston.

"Probably in a week or so. We wrote—what was it?—about three weeks ago," said Top. "Why?"

"If we're to try a second crop, we should get on with it. At Phu Hai it's already in the ground."

With part of the profits from Hoa Hao Unlimited Ltd., we had hired a rice consultant at the School of Agriculture, University of Bangkok. The professor said he could not visit for several months, but told us to send him soil samples, rice specimens, and a report on the local agricultural habits. In this area the farmers grew a type of late-maturing rice, called floating rice. Seedlings were put in with the first monsoons. The rice grew rapidly, always keeping above the rising water. Supported by the water, it could grow eight or ten feet tall. By the time the floodwaters were receding, the plants were flowering. In most areas the ground was too dry during spring and summer for a second crop. Our Thai consultant said he would do what he could by mail. Which was better help than we had received. Several times Choi had asked the government to send us an agricultural expert. The one who had finally come, six months ago, was an AID official, who knew agriculture but nothing about the people. First, he spoke no Vietnamese, which we could have gotten around, but, second, he dogmatically dictated principles of farming with no mention of the phases of the moon or the prevailing winds. Which, as every Vietnamese knew, were rudimentary aspects of farming. When Top suggested that he do so, if only to humor local customs, he laughed.

Cranston was working on an automatic device for setting out rice seedlings. Now, as for the past two thousand years, it was back-breaking work: one had to bend over hundreds of times a day to set out seedlings. Cranston was building a funnel-shaped thing through which seedlings would be dropped.

The food was delicious and everyone seemed excited, if not from the holiday air, then from the Ba Muoi Bas. The harvest was good and the company was making money. Although the VC were very much alive, we had welcomed eight defectors since Christmas, four of them Hoa Hao. All said they had heard how prosperous the people were becoming. Choi was so pleased that he sent a report to GVN about Hoa Hao Unlimited Ltd. He did not mention the VC flags. GVN answered with a terse message: All captured enemy would be forwarded through command channels to the Chu Phoc rehabilitation center, and Major Choi was reminded to be alert for six Viet Cong disguised as Americans operating in this area.

Top was not as talkative as usual, but I attributed it to the relative formality of the occasion.

An hour and a half later we finished eating and the toasts and speeches began. Choi dedicated the pig to the past four generations of ancestors. A monk read passages from the *Sam Gian*, Huynh Phu So's book of oracles and prayers. Choi complimented the spirits of the water, the rice, the wind, and several more, the names of which I missed. And then in the finest tradition of military personnel everywhere, he began toasts to each level of the Army hierarchy, except that he began at the highest level with the IV Corps commander.

Finally he got to us. "And here's to Captain Wheaty, a brave officer who helped sink a Viet Cong gunboat and carves food very well.

"To Master Sergeant O'Hara, who is helping our people grow bigger and better vegetables."

"Bullshit," Top said under his breath.

"To First Sergeant Hood, who tells us what the VC are doing before they decide to do it.

"To Sergeant Santee, who, as executive vice-president of Hoa Hao Unlimited Ltd., is bringing prosperity and good luck to the Hoa Hao.

"To Sergeant Cranston, who is humble enough to work side by side with our farmers, as well as our soldiers."

"Far out," muttered Cranston.

"And to *than thanh bac si dao bao,* our favorite doctor who walks on water."

At last the dinner was over, and my stomach was bloated. When it looked like the Vietnamese were going to stay and drink, we began to wander off. It was their holiday.

As I started for the team house, Top called, "Hey, Phil. Hold up a second." I knew something was wrong. Top rarely called me Phil—usually shithead. He asked me to go to the dispensary with him.

"What's wrong, Top?"

"My goddamn back has popped out," he said, finally allowing himself to reach back and massage it. "I got a bad disk that's slipped out. It's got to be pushed back in."

"Has this happened before?" I opened the dispensary door.

"A couple times."

"When was the first time?"

"I don't remember. Years ago," Top grumbled.

"Why isn't there anything in your records?"

"Are you going to help me up on this fucking table or kill me with questions?" Top sat down but couldn't lift his feet. I raised them and told him to take his shirt off and turn over.

"How'd it happen?" I asked.

"Santee and I were moving a mortar and it slipped out,

slick as could be. About noon. Have you ever put a disk back in place?"

"No."

"Okay, do what I say. Feel along the lower part of my spine. It's the fourth or fifth disk from the bottom. It'll be about a quarter inch out of line."

I felt it immediately.

"Put the heel of one hand against it and put your other hand on top of that hand. Now push and push hard. Don't be a pussy. I'll holler, but go ahead."

Top's hands were white where he gripped the table. I pushed. Top shouted, a belly-deep sound of pain. The disk slid in perfectly. I ran my fingers along his spine.

"It's in," I said. Top lay there, unspeaking.

"Top?"

"I'm all right," he said through clenched jaws.

"Stay here awhile and let the muscles unwind. I'll rub some methyl salicylate in."

"You talked me into it, *bac si*. Hand me the rest of that tiger piss."

As I massaged his back, Top began to relax. In a few minutes he started talking. "I remember when we celebrated Tet at Hop Tac. Goddamn, but that was great. Miller got so drunk and fucked up that he stepped on one of our own punji stakes. He came staggering and hobbling into the team room holding up his foot and blood running all over the floor. Doc Worley looked at him and said, 'Damn, Miller. I'll bet that smarts something awful.' Goddamn, but that was funny. Did you ever know Worley?"

"No, I didn't." I couldn't have. Both Worley and Miller were captured the morning Hop Tac fell.

"And the next day Miller was trying to get Doc to sign a recommendation for the Purple Heart on account of his wound. Some great guys. I wonder where they are."

I tried changing the subject. "I hear the stock offering's going well."

"It don't seem right," said Top, working a cigarette out of his pack. "Us down here acting like a glorified Peace Corps and buying stock like it was Wall Street, and out there, with the lions, are Worley, Miller, Cauthen, and Green."

I gave him a light.

Top blew the smoke out. "We've been here over four months. You'd think the Army would be wondering where we are. But . . . fuck 'em if they can't take a joke. Besides, the water's dropping, and in a month or so we'll be able to get out on our own."

"Tell me, Top, how come Hood doesn't say much about his wife? He's the only one of us married."

"Peggy? They have a strange relationship. Me and Beth used to play pinochle with them, and I'm not sure I ever understood her. She was a good-looking piece but snotty. You knew right away that her shit didn't stink. In fact, she probably didn't even shit. Her old man was a big dairy farmer and politician in southern Arkansas. I gathered he felt his daughter married beneath her station. They don't have any kids, and I think that was touchy between them. They tried. And there's another thing. Hood thinks she's running around on him. It started when we got back from our last tour. She was acting funny, so he said, and he decided it was because somebody was backdooring him. And him being black makes it even worse."

"Who?"

"Hood."

"But he's not black," I said.

"No, but he thinks he is. Shit, if he's dumb enough to think that, he might as well be a nigger."

Just then Nha, the striker who'd been wounded on our run-in with the KKK, walked in for his checkup.

"Stay there, Top. This won't take long. *Chau,* Nha. *Bao nhieu canh tay ong?*"

"Okay." He grinned and threw me a mock jab. I removed the bandages. The wounds looked good. After the fight at Bac Lam I had solved the riddle of the strange exit hole. Nha had been firing his carbine; thus his left arm had been crooked. The bullet came in forward of the elbow, grazed the bone without breaking it, continued in a straight line through the inside of the elbow and straight out behind the upper arm. I had taken the stitches out two weeks ago. Nha left, delighted when I said bandages were no longer necessary.

After giving Top two APCs, I helped him down and suggested he lie on towels soaked in hot water. I figured the chances were fifty-fifty he would ignore me.

It was nearly dark, but the Tet celebration was still going strong. Inside the team house everyone except Cranston was there and in various stages of sobriety. Cranston and Lao were spending the evening with her foster parents. Hood was polishing his boots to remove a gray-green mold that had overrun them. Teewee was flipping through a textbook for his new private-investigator course. The book had a giant fingerprint on the cover and was titled "Evidence and How You Can Find It." Santee was laboriously filling out some form at the table.

"Hogjaw, what the fuck are you doing now?" said Top, pulling out a chair and slowly sitting down.

Santee said, "This is an application for an SBA-guaranteed loan to the tune of seventy-five thousand dollars."

"Run that by me again," said Top.

"Small Business Administration. It's a U.S. government agency that will either give you a loan or guarantee a bank loan for small businessmen. And we're a small business."

Top asked, "Why would they give us a loan? Here in Vietnam?"

"They have a special overseas division to help American

businessmen in foreign countries. I've also ordered brochures from the Murphy Manufacturing Company in Birmingham for those rolling machines you told me about. Choi and I decided we'll get one if this loan comes through. We'll be able to make aluminum piping for water and irrigation as well as for chairs and tables."

Top sighed. "What ever happened to the good old days when you knew who your enemy was and you went out and you shot him?"

"New wars. New times," said Santee. "We have to be ready to switch over to a peacetime economy when it comes. We can't go on making flags and AK-47s forever. Guns to plowshares and flags to bras."

"Peacetime economy," snorted Top. "Twenty-five thousand more GIs last month and you talk about a peacetime economy?"

Santee finished filling out a line and said, "All we can do is get our little corner of it right. Say, when it says, 'Other Product Lines Anticipated,' do you think I should mention Chinese carbines?"

So far, about sixty thousand shares of stock in Hoa Hao Unlimited Ltd. had been sold. That meant nearly thirty-three thousand dollars raised. The best sales had been here in the Nan Phuc area, where people could see the company in action and where, for the first time, some families were accumulating savings.

Forty men and women now worked full-time making VC flags, two lines of work clothes, ready-made bamboo roof sections, brassieres, AK-47s, and GI dog tags. The roof sections, Cranston's idea, were four-by-four woven bamboo strips and sold for only one hundred piasters each. For eight hundred piasters a family could put up a roof in thirty minutes. We bought the blank dog tags through a storekeeper in Chau An. Then we added fictitious names and strung the tags on chains. The tags were a new line for the VC and we

179

weren't sure how successful they would be. Linh, the ex-VC, was being trained by Santee as a salesman for the company and by Hood as a spy for us. Linh had made one contact with the VC. A week ago he had delivered a piece of true but inconsequential intelligence to the 485th's top NCOIC—Intelligence. Linh said he was runner for a secret VC intelligence squad operating in the Nam Phuc area. There were no questions raised. Unlike procedures in our army, small-unit military orders in the Viet Cong often came from the bottom up, from the people closest to the situation. The broad strategies came from the top down, but local units usually made their own specific, final decisions. This was especially true with the Viet Cong as opposed to the North Vietnamese regular army.

Hood's theory was that Linh would stay longer each time he visited the 485th, eventually working himself into a position of trust. There was no danger that anyone would recognize him. His original company had been moved from the 485th to the 232nd in the Seven Mountains area.

Choi spread the money around. I had ordered a Ritter portable X-ray machine. It would make diagnosis of tuberculosis, pneumonia, and a dozen other diseases much surer. But I needed no machines to tell me that An Hoac Tien, the old man who had tuberculosis, couldn't last much longer. He now weighed seventy-eight pounds and had begun to cough up blood. He had scarcely been able to talk when I'd visited him last. After I had been able again to obtain the drugs for TB, I had kept him on them, but it was too late.

Teewee interrupted my thoughts. "Did you guys know they can take pictures of the inside of your eyeball and that the inside of everyone's eyeball is different from everyone else's?"

"Everyone's dick is different from everyone else's, too," said Top. "Niggers' are longer, and some, mentioning no names, get leeches on them."

"What good is that?" asked Hood.

"A long dick?" I said. "They're good for—"

"No, what good are eyeball pictures?"

Teewee answered, "For police identification purposes."

"What are you going to do?" asked Top. "Point a camera at a bank robber and say, 'Stare at the camera. I need a picture of the inside of your eyeballs'?"

16

I BUNCHED the pillow of duck feathers behind my head and read Nina's letter again. She was returning to the States in three months for graduate work in English at the University of North Carolina. Her father, the colonel, had been reassigned as commander of the jump school at Fort Benning. She missed me and wanted to know when I'd be home.

Outside, the Tet festivities were continuing apace. I propped my feet on the cot railing and remembered a week we had had together before we both left. January, a little more than a year ago, on the isolated outer banks of North Carolina. By an almost empty ferry we went to the small island of Ocracoke, which had two hundred year-round inhabitants. It had been cold, rainy, windy, desolate, and beautiful. Wide-bottomed gray fishing boats floated, waiting and alone, in their winter moorings. Wild Spanish ponies, survivors of wrecks centuries ago, huddled among the sand dunes and sea oats. It was a time for holding close, for slow walks on foggy beaches, for throwing crackers to gulls. A time for playing and dreaming together in the soft moments after making love. A week that belonged to a time that was so far away. Another time, another me. This was my reality, and the emotions from that past were beautiful but dreamlike.

My discharge date was five months away, and even that was not real. I didn't want to leave my Hoa Hao. The idea of going to a movie in Chapel Hill while these people tried to survive in a war was too contradictory for me to accept. I chose not to think about leaving.

As if to punctuate that choice, gunfire shook me out of bed. I grabbed my guns and pinpointed the shooting as inside, northern end of camp. I nearly flattened Top on my way out.

"Whoa, there, Warren," he said. "It's only Major Choi and the boys celebrating Tet."

"Why didn't they tell us?" I said angrily.

"Choi did, a few minutes ago. I was going around to warn everybody." Another string of shots went off. "Hot damn! Like the Fourth of July," said Top.

I slung my carbine over my shoulder and walked outside. As I passed the mortar pit, it shouted, "Goddamn it!"

I looked in. Wheaty, loaded with his full-alert gear, was picking himself up.

"What's the matter, Lieutenant, fall in?" I asked, extending my hand.

"Captain. And what the hell is the shooting about?"

"They're celebrating Tet," I said.

Two of Choi's bodyguards slid to a halt and asked to use our mortar to fire illumination rounds.

"It's only five dollars a round and your ammunition," said Teewee.

At my machine-gun pit we perched on the sandbags to watch the show. The CIDG were setting off brilliant-white ground flares, one after the other in the middle of camp. All

183

four mortars were firing illumination rounds, which turned the rice fields into stark black-and-white. A few shocks of rice still stood, like tombstones in a graveyard.

Teewee and I flinched as someone exploded simulated artillery rounds, which were huge firecrackers used for training. We had no artillery, but the rounds were standard equipment for a CIDG camp, so we had them.

Major Choi and two company commanders, alabaster soldiers in the harsh light, climbed to the fifty caliber. Moments later that awesome *ack-ack-ack* started. Choi had loaded a belt of only tracers, and a stream of red dots sailed upward against the night. It's funny, I thought, the bullets seem to move so slowly. He swung the fifty back and forth, creating giant S's and O's in the black sky.

"Look over there." Teewee pointed toward the western border. Distant flares fell toward the tree line. Soon others lit the sky to the north and east. All the companies were joining in.

Far to the south pinpoints of light danced around the western side of the Seven Mountains. Even farther south and west of there, the sky flickered like a neon light. Outposts along the entire border were shooting flares.

"You know," said Teewee, lowering his voice an octave, "some of those fireworks could be the KKK or even the VC celebrating."

"I doubt they have extra ammunition to throw away."

And what they had, they were throwing our way. Our men had tangled with guerrillas a half dozen times during the past month, and with consistently larger forces than six months ago. Two strikers in D Company had been killed by a sniper, and five had been wounded in assorted incidents. Intelligence reported a new North Vietnamese Army battalion at Kompong Cheu. Clow's reports confirmed ours. We now supplied the captain with some intelligence. That portion of it about the Viet Cong was correct; however, Choi and Hood were more cautious about our own troops. For example, we hinted that the Nungs were part of a secret CIA scheme. Clow would find that easier to believe.

Elsewhere in the delta the Viet Cong were busy. Four village officials near Chau An had been kidnaped a week ago. A civilian bus hit a mine near Can Tho and nine people died.

A battalion of U.S. ground troops had arrived in Can Tho, and it was rumored that more would follow. Word of an amazing statement had come to us several days ago. It seemed that after our own Air Forces planes had obliterated a coastal hamlet, the major in charge said, "We had to destroy the village in order to save it."

I think if we had not heard the news over Armed Forces Radio, we would have called it VC propaganda. The comment was dangerously close to those lines from *1984:* "War is peace! Freedom is slavery! Ignorance is strength!"

A few minutes later the fifty stopped, and on his way back Choi paused before us. He waved his arm at the camp. "The VC will believe we have many men here, no?"

We nodded.

"I am very proud of our men. We are luckier than some other people in Vietnam. But it may not last. There are clouds gathering, but none are in the sky." His voice and words were suddenly distant. "There is an old Vietnamese saying, 'There is no shame to avoid standing in the way of an elephant.' "

He shook his head, as if at himself. "But today is Tet. We celebrate. Did you enjoy your meal?"

We said we did.

"I hope it pleased our ancestors as much as it pleased everyone today," he said. "Someday we too will be ancestors and our children's children should have cause to honor and respect us." He started to go, but added, "Perhaps we'll soon see what the Rand people have to say about our situation." Choi wished us a good evening and left.

Hood's brother-in-law had answered that Rand would

attempt a "profile of alternate eventualities," as he called it. Apparently their normal procedure was to send in their own research team, but because of the time and distance we did the legwork. Also, according to the letter, Rand had done a number of studies on Vietnam and thus already had a good amount of information. They had requested volumes of statistics about the Hoa Hao. Working day and night, we had prepared the answers and shipped them back within a week. No one had said exactly what the cost was, but, based on several remarks, I suspected the figure ten thousand dollars would be close.

Teewee and I chatted until after midnight, when the noise and excitement began to taper off.

I was up early the next morning. Today was payday for the companies, and Cranston and I were going with Choi and a Nung platoon as far as E Company. The two of us were then splitting off for an overnight patrol with the Popular Force soldiers at Doc Gia. At least once a week somebody from the team would go on patrols with the PF-ers. Although on paper they were under the province chief, in this area they took orders from Choi. The only difference between the SDC posts (which were under our direct command) and the PF posts was the name. I suppose it made someone happy in Saigon—another color for the maps. We ran periodic classes for the PF-ers, and this was the best way to see what they had learned and what needed to be taught.

As we left we passed through Nan Phuc, where the effects of Hoa Hao Unlimited Ltd. were becoming apparent. A half dozen houses displayed new paint—bright yellows, blues, or reds. Several sampans were being built, and more than one kid wore a new T-shirt. Most rural Vietnamese children ran around naked until they were six or seven. If clothing was worn, such as now, in the winter, it was usually a shirt. The disadvantages were hookworm, malaria, and dysentery, to name a few, but the advantages were no diapers to change, wash, or worry about.

The water was falling fast—it was down six feet from the peak—and we made good time along the banks. We reached E at noon without trouble. E's headquarters occupied an orange grove a few hundred yards outside Hiep Phung, the village the VC and their gunboat had destroyed seven months ago. Half of the huts had been repaired.

Choi borrowed a wooden table from the village chief, set up his ever-present lawn chair, and began paying. The soldiers were excited not only because of Tet, but because Choi was giving his annual 10 per cent Tet bonus. That was Hoa Hao money, not American. For the average private who earned twenty-five dollars a month, that meant enough food for three or four days.

Cranston and I wandered off and found the village sassy stand. However small the hamlet, someone managed to have a sassy stand. Here, it was a wooden box on a front porch with six hot Cambodian root beers, several packs of cigarettes, a dozen rice balls, and two jars of Tiger Balm.

We bought rice and root beers and sprawled out under a nearby tree. Looking at the houses, up on their fragile stilts, I finally remembered what they reminded me of: the playhouses I used to build as a kid. The huts were tiny to begin with, at the most twenty feet by twenty feet, and constructed of bamboo, leaves, and an occasional piece of tin. The war was making its inevitable contribution. Over there was a step made from an ammo box, and two roofs were patched with ponchos. Behind one house a Hoa Hao Unlimited Ltd. brassiere was drying in the sun.

Because this was Tet, the spirit houses were smothered under flowers and fruit. No matter how poor the family, they always built a spirit house on a small platform in front of the house. The spirit house, styled after a Vietnamese house and about two feet square, was connected to the front porch by a long board. During holidays or on family occasions, the family honored the spirits with flowers, incense, and small pieces of food. Spirits meant not only the "animate" spirits of this world but the spirits of a family's ancestors.

The typical Hoa Hao house had a porch and a front room and a back room, the rooms separated by a blanket or, rarely, a bamboo wall. The front room was a religious room, living room, and spare bedroom. It was usually bare except for a bamboo mat and a small stool before the simple family altar. Hoa Hao religious ceremonies were quiet, informal, and family oriented. One of So's teachings was, "It is better to pray with a pure heart before the family altar than to perform elaborate ceremonies in a pagoda clad in the robes of an unworthy priest."

The back room was a combination bedroom and kitchen. The bed was a low, solid wood structure with a thin woven bamboo mat for a mattress. Stoves were stone hibachis.

No closets, no bathrooms, no doors, no lights, no sinks, no refrigerators, no windows, and no television. I was used to it, and now I didn't miss or want the extras. I understood Cranston's infatuation.

After pok time six soldiers from E accompanied Cranston and me to Doc Gia. We arrived there before dark and in time for another Tet supper. Compared to the meal yesterday, Doc Gia's was poor indeed. There was only enough food for a few pieces of rat, which tasted like well-cooked squirrel, a banana, a spoonful of rice, and a cup of thin soup for each of us. But "poor" was only our term. The adults and children of Doc Gia enjoyed the meal.

At 1900 hours we and eight PF-ers slipped out of camp to our ambush site near a hamlet two miles east. The post commander said that three nights ago four Viet Cong had entered the hamlet and forced the people to dig two trenches across a trail. The trenches were of no practical value—the trail was only a footpath. It was psychological harassment. In the same sense, our ambush was psychological. We wanted to let the people know we could be here some of the time.

We spread the men out, five feet apart in the brush beside the trail, and settled down. Cranston and I leaned against a tree. The night was quiet; the only noises were tree frogs, crickets, and leaves rustling gently.

The excitement of an ambush subsided into boredom after several hours, and we began to talk softly.

"I heard from Nina the other day," I said.

"How is she doing?"

"Okay. She'll be going home in a couple months. She's returning to school and asked me to meet her there."

"What are you going to do?" Cranston asked.

"To tell you the truth, I thought we'd be out of here by now. What about you?"

"I'm going to stay here," said Cranston.

"No shit?" I said, surprised. "For sure?"

"Yes. I haven't said anything to Top yet. Lao and I are going to be married and grow some rice and some booje. If the war gets real bad, we might go to Cambodia or Thailand. I've already asked her to marry me and she said yes." He plucked a guava from a nearby bush and picked at the skin. "Phil, what did the doctor in Can Tho say about her eye that time?"

"He said he needed to look at it. It might take several operations, probably in Saigon, and they might work."

Cranston touched his tongue to the inner part of the fruit. I asked, "Why don't you take her to Can Tho to see him?"

"She's shy and embarrassed. She doesn't think they can do anything. And she hasn't had the money before to afford operations. When we get married, I think I can talk her into it."

"Is it a bad thing for you?" I asked.

"No. I don't notice it any more at all. But she's so self-conscious that it would be good for her to get it fixed. It would help her see better, too. She has little depth perception.

But, then, nobody's going to Can Tho for a while. The river's still blockaded by the VC."

"Did you know Choi was in Long Xuyen with the other Hoa Hao generals when you were on patrol?"

"No. What's happening?"

"I heard they're talking about supporting a coup attempt with the IV Corps general. Choi is holding out, because he thinks they don't have enough support, and if it fails, there would be reprisals against the Hoa Hao."

The night passed slowly, marked by a rising pile of guava shells and discarded bits of conversation. Once, about 0230 hours, there was distant machine-gun fire, far to the west. Sometime toward dawn Cranston crawled off to check out the men. The night was chilly, and I made a routine of flexing muscles to keep them warm and awake. Thirty minutes after Cranston left, I heard what sounded like someone stepping on twigs. It stopped. Could have been the wind or an animal. I scrounged around on the ground and found a twig to chew on to relieve the craving for a cigarette.

Time passed and the false dawn faded the eastern sky to a dirty pink. Cranston should have been back by now.

Suddenly shooting broke out. Two bursts of about six each. I saw nothing on the trail. Another shot and then silence hung in the air, as oppressive as the shooting had been. Men started talking and I recognized the voices. Whatever had happened was over.

I pushed my way through vines and limbs. The soldiers and Cranston were standing in a circle on the trail. When he saw me, Cranston gave a helpless shrug and shook his head. I walked up. They were looking down at a dead pig, riddled with bullet holes.

"Cranston, did you shoot a pig?" I said.

"Jesus, I didn't know it was a pig."

"It looks like a pig. It has four legs and is not in uniform. And I don't see a weapon around," I said.

I asked the soldiers in Vietnamese, "Was this pig carrying a gun?"

They cracked up.

"Oh, good grief, Warren. Look, we were laying there when I heard shuffling around in the bushes. I thought at first it was a VC, then I decided it was an animal. But it went on and on. Little noises. It began to sound like it was a whole company of VC crawling through the jungle. The more I listened, the more convinced I was that it was at least a company, maybe a battalion, slipping by. Then it started getting light. Finally I made out a shadow moving toward me, slowly. It got closer and closer, and I knew it was a VC coming straight at me. So I opened up."

"We can report no friendly casualties, one pig, suspected VC, KIA. Let's go back," I said. I was joking, but Cranston and I both knew how easily it could have been a villager. Or a child. Or a Viet Cong.

The troops were elated. They tied the pig's feet together and slung it under a rifle. At least it would feed the post for a couple days.

17

TWO WEEKS later, Monday, February 15, the Rand report came and, as Top said, it was the hottest thing since buttered popcorn. I had just finished a class on how to treat broken arms and had walked back to the team house for a cup of coffee.

Wheaty, Top, and Hood were sitting around the table reading the report.

"Here, shithead," said Top, throwing a mass of papers at me. "You're the college graduate. Maybe you can figure out what these eggheads are saying."

I poured a cup of coffee and sat down. An hour and four cups later, I was excited, and not from the caffeine. Rand recommended our cooperating with *both* the Viet Cong and the government of South Vietnam. Rather than explain all the details, I'll run through key sections from the report.

The first "alternate eventuality," as Rand called it, was what would happen if the six Hoa Hao provinces declared military and political independence from South Vietnam.

Rand said chances were the Cao Dai would support the move, that the Hoa Hao needed a standing army of 70,000, and that two more naval vessels must be purchased. Even so, the chances of success were a slim 5.7 per cent.

The second eventuality was what would happen if the Hoa Hao joined with other political factions to overthrow the government of South Vietnam. I was frankly surprised that those groups which Rand predicted would join in such a cabal included the Cao Dai, the Vietnamese Special Forces, the 32nd Air Wing of the South Vietnamese Air Force, and six members of the Vietnamese National Security Council. Even more surprising were the ones who would remain neutral during the coup: the CIA, the I and II Corps commanders, most of the South Vietnamese Navy, and three Wings of the Air Force. Rand said this possibility had a 35.5 per cent chance of succeeding. However, the problem was that another coup would probably occur within a year and also that the Hoa Hao would have to side with so many other factions that their power to make any real decisions would be limited. So this alternative was rejected.

The third eventuality was what would happen if things continued as they were—that is, the Hoa Hao cooperating with the South Vietnamese government. Rand predicted there would be a loss of local autonomy within six years, that military activities would be stepped up by both sides, that taxation and the drafting of young men would increase, that protective compounds would be introduced, and that the Hoa Hao would "disappear as a cohesive political, religious, and social group within ten years." Rand rejected this alternative, too.

The fourth eventuality was what would happen if the Hoa Hao secretly cooperated with the Viet Cong. Rand said first the Hoa Hao would have to get rid of the Americans (us!). What would happen then would be an increase in military operations by both sides; a loss of local autonomy within five years; increased taxation and drafting; Hoa Hao Unlimited Ltd. would be taken over by the VC; and there would be the "demise of the Hoa Hao as a cohesive . . . group within nine years." Rand added that even though their projections gave the war to the Viet Cong within eighteen years, the VC would tolerate no minority as strong as the Hoa Hao, even if they had cooperated.

I thought one footnote from this section was especially telling:

> We confirm that the over-all chances of success for both eventualities, cooperation with the Viet Cong, and cooperation with GVN, are identical at 17.8 per cent. This was so unusual that Rand technicians reprogrammed our computers three times, and yet, strange as it may seem, it appears that cooperation with either the Viet Cong or the GVN would have the same level of destruction on the Hoa Hao society. (The chances of two alternate eventualities producing the same probability are 1 in 539,950,000. A report on this unusual correlation is being prepared for the annual convention of the American Association of Statisticians in Chicago in August.)

The eventuality rated as having the best chance to succeed (69.3 per cent) was if the Hoa Hao appeared to cooperate with both the Viet Cong and the South Vietnamese government. There would be real cooperation, up to a point, and each side would believe it was winning the allegiance of the Hoa Hao. Specifically, here's what Rand said would take place:

> —Chances are slim, less than 10 per cent, that there will be relocation of a significant number of Hoa Hao civilians.
> —There will be little or no loss of local autonomy for a minimum of fifteen years.

194

—The chances are fair (19 per cent) that Hoa Hao Unlimited Ltd. will be accidentally destroyed by U.S. aircraft bombing or MAAG operations.

—There is little chance of increased Viet Cong terrorism or assassination of Hoa Hao civilians.

—The chances of conscription, or increased taxation, by either side are insignificant.

—There will be the eventual demise of the Hoa Hao as a cohesive . . . group within twenty years.

Here are some of Rand's comments on this eventuality:

As long as each side is confident that it is winning, or has won, control of the Hoa Hao provinces, it will do little to interfere. The plan involves more than apparent cooperation: Each side must not only be convinced the area is under their complete control, but that a highly classified operation is being conducted and that regular or guerrilla troops are forbidden.

As noted before, we believe the war will last at least fifteen years and that the chances are 61 per cent the Viet Cong will ultimately win the war. As you know, the accuracy of a prediction of this nature declines by a minimum of 2 per cent for each year into the future that probability must extend. With that in mind, our projection is that a negotiated settlement will be signed in eighteen years and it will provide for a government made up of Viet Cong, South Vietnamese, and representatives of the United Nations, Laos, and/or Cambodia. But we also predict it will be at least twenty-five years before the Viet Cong so consolidate their strength as to dominate the government.

As with the other eventualities, there will be an

inevitable decline in the solidarity and autonomy of the Hoa Hao. But, unlike the other alternatives, it will not begin to occur for at least fifteen years and perhaps as much as twenty-three years.

To fill you in on exactly how Rand said we should accomplish this ambitious plan, here are several sections from Appendix V, which gave instructions on carrying it out:

In spite of its simplicity, the chances are good that each side will believe the plan. Both sides are, in fact, conducting many secret operations not necessarily known to all its military branches. Both sides would like to believe they are winning the "hearts and minds" of the people. Naturally, neither antagonist will accept such reports without physical inspection, but Sections C and D below offer proposals to handle this.

There are several important keys to the achievement of this plan: A. Complete cooperation from all segments of the Hoa Hao population: Judging from the Hoa Hao ability to survive World War II and the Indochina War, thus far (See Section II, background), we feel this can be accomplished. B. Secrecy: Already a good start has been made. The infiltration of former Viet Cong Nguyen Van Linh back into the VC infrastructure should create additionally the appearance that he is a member of the Con Mat, which is conducting a "classified operation" involving the Hoa Hao provinces. The "operation" must be carried out in utmost secrecy without involvement of, or interference by, regular or guerrilla forces. Viet Cong communications between Hanoi and IV Corps military units are tenuous, and there is often confusion about assignments between, on one hand, the regular and guerrilla forces, and, on the other hand, the several secret commando units, of which the Con Mat is the most dreaded.

As for GVN and MAAG, a similar situation also exists. MAAG's only intelligence about the Hoa Hao is channeled through the provincial intelligence officer, Captain Ervin Clow in Can Tho. Camp Nan Phuc has established a communications line with Clow. As long as a sufficient volume of credible intelligence—we estimate the U.S. Army would consider three to four double-spaced typed pages per week sufficient volume—is maintained, MAAG will not insist on further physical involvement of MAAG advisory personnel. Clow already believes there is a team of U.S. Army personnel operating under Central Intelligence Agency orders in the Nan Phuc area. Since the CIA is historically reluctant to advise branches of the Armed services of its activities, Clow will delay questioning your "orders" for as long as possible.

A similar approach should be taken with GVN. Major Choi will report through proper channels that the CIA is conducting a secret operation in the area. Chances of GVN accepting this without question are 83.7 per cent, since the CIA did, in fact, operate in this area until nine months ago.

As long as the Viet Cong, GVN, and MAAG are convinced there is a highly classified operation being conducted, their impetus is not to become involved. Not only will they probably adopt a hands-off policy; they will welcome the chance to use their troops in other areas. It will be satisfying to the egos of the respective military commands to believe that their war effort has evolved to the point of highly secret operations.

C: Establishment of liaison officers: Since the respective antagonists will insist on physical inspections, you should establish, as soon as possible, liaison intelligence officers to whom the Viet Cong, MAAG, and GVN should direct all questions and inquiries. This is not only the correct military procedure; it is psychologically satisfying by appearing to relieve the respective commanders of any responsibility for what happens in the area. . . .

By forcing communications to cut across military branches, you add to the confusion and, paradoxically, to the plausibility of the plan.

In all cases, it would be best to approve on-site inspections and visits whenever possible to allay any suspicions the various commands may have. By giving personal attention and yet, at the same time, warning the officers of the highly secret nature of the "operation," you will enlist their support by appealing to their military psyche.

D. Confusion: If the primary key to success is secrecy, confusion is oil on the hinges. Intelligence reports, briefings, after-action reports, etc., must be couched in oblique and obscure terms. This is acceptable to the various commands as it allows an officer to read into the report any information which supports his prior opinions, gives eloquence to his position and hastens his own promotion, and which requires no decision from him.

That gives you an idea of the Rand report. It was 135 pages long and at least half of that was in multisyllable words. I laid the report down and looked around the table.

"They got balls, all right," said Hood. "The question is, 'Do we?' "

18

"WELL, *bac si*, what do you think of it?" said Hood, counting out three tablespoons of sugar in his coffee. He and I were alone. Lon was preparing lunch in the kitchen.

"I don't even know where to begin. Has Choi seen it?"

"It came in the mail this morning from Phnom Penh. Choi gave us a copy, went into his room, and locked the door. Two hours later he made four radio calls and left for Long Xuyen. He didn't say anything."

I flipped through the report. "First, the detail amazes me. They make recommendations right down to what caliber machine gun is best suited for *Granny's Ghost*. There's stuff in here about the Hoa Hao that I didn't even know."

"That's their job," said Hood, adding still another tablespoon of sugar to his coffee. The man must have the taste buds of a rock.

"Apparently they think our best chance is to fool the VC and MAAG with this plan and, hopefully, everybody will leave us alone. Do you think the VC will believe it?"

"They might. Rand is right about the Con Mat being the most feared and most secret of the VC secret units. In South Vietnam they are the special assassination and terrorist squads. In North Vietnam the Con Mat serves as an anti-coup force and bodyguard for Uncle Ho and General Giap. Like the Gestapo."

From the hall loud voices, hot in disagreement, interrupted us.

"—never eaten a pussy?" Top was saying with astonishment.

"Of course not. They're nasty," answered Wheaty as they walked into the team room.

"No wonder your wife left you," said Top, sitting down.

"Ease off," said Wheaty, his face reddening at the uncertainty of whether or not Top was pulling his leg or making fun of him. "Doesn't the hair get in your mouth?"

"Sir, the greatest thing in the world is brushing hair out of your teeth. If we ever get back to Saigon, I'll show you how it's done." Top smacked his lips.

From the kitchen Lon called, "Eat pussy? Pussy good."

"See," said Top, pointing. "Even old Lon eats pussy."

I handed the Rand report to Top. He grinned at me. "Ain't this some shit, though? It's like that old TV program, Herb somebody. Where he's a spy for both sides. What was the name of that?"

"*I Led Three Lives*," said Hood.

"That's it. This is about the goddamnedest harebrained scheme I've ever heard. I'd like an 'alternate eventuality' on killing some VC," said Top.

Santee walked in. "Did you all read the suggestions for improving the company? Stock option plans—profit sharing—convertible debentures—a holding company!"

"Hogjaw," said Top, "can't you think about anything but that fucking company? We got a war going on here, in case you hadn't noticed."

Santee rapped on the table with one finger. "Top, our company might win this war for us yet. Why do you think those VC are defecting to us and not to one of the other camps? These people are getting a decent, fair salary for their work. We're helping them. They're helping us. One for one. A fair trade."

Santee made a good point. Since Tet, thirteen more Viet Cong, four of them Hoa Hao, had defected. All had mentioned Hoa Hao Unlimited Ltd. Its fame was running faster than its reality. They wanted jobs in the "place where everyone gets rich."

"One well-placed mortar and where would you be?" asked Top.

Santee slapped the Rand report with the back of his hand. "That's why this makes good sense. If our bank loan comes through, Rand thinks we can float some bonds in Thailand—"

"Lord!" Top rolled his eyes upward. "The man's not a soldier. He's a stockbroker."

Through the door walked Cranston, wearing his usual farmer's black pajamas and rubber sandals. Motioning toward the report, he said, "Far fucking out, isn't it?"

"How's the old married man?" asked Top. "Getting much?"

Cranston sat down with a weary sigh. He and Lao had gotten married last week and we had seen little of him since. It had been a simple and beautiful ceremony. Since Cranston's parents were not here and Lao's were dead, they had not waited the traditional six months between the engagement announcement and the wedding.

As it was, the wedding had been delayed four days, on advice from the local astrologer, so that the moon would be in favorable alignment with the sun. The wedding had been in the late afternoon. Top, much to his embarrassment, and Major Choi, much to his pleasure, led the formal procession from the camp to Lao's home. I think what flustered Top was that he had to carry a small brass box with a betel nut in it. Choi carried a similar box filled with incense. Lao looked lovely. Her deep brown skin and black hair were exciting contrasts to her pure white *ao dai*. Cranston, unable to find a tie, wore black pants and a white shirt buttoned to the neck.

We had walked slowly to Lao's home where Choi and Top placed their "burdens" on the ancestral altar. Green tea was served, and Lao's foster parents began a long ritual of informing her ancestors that she was getting married and that her husband was intelligent, handsome, and healthy. Then Lao bowed low before the altar three times. Cranston followed. The ritual was repeated with Major Choi telling Cranston's ancestors about Lao. Luc, the interpreter, whispered that this part would normally have been done by Cranston's family.

The couple walked to the spirit house outside and repeated the ceremony, informing the god of love that they were getting married. The spirit house was barely visible under offerings of chicken, rice, alcohol, betel, tea, flowers, and wine.

After that, we got down to serious partying and drinking. At one point in the evening Top and I were drinking on the porch and he said, "She ain't a bad-looking girl. You could always throw a pillow over that one eye."

The ceremony had not been necessary. The Hoa Hao had accepted Cranston and it was open knowledge he and Lao were sleeping together. Premarital intercourse, while not condoned, at least was tolerated in a couple so clearly in love. I think Cranston, especially, wanted the traditional rites as tangible and public proof that he loved Lao.

Now Teewee asked Cranston, "Have you read the report?"

"Yes. It's crazy, but it's crazy enough to work. I believe the people will go for it."

To Hood I said, "You're the intelligence man. What about infiltrating the VC? Will they believe this secret operation stuff?"

"Maybe. As you know, ex-VC Linh has been into the 485th headquarters on four occasions now. He said there was no trouble at all. It all really depends on Choi and the Hoa Hao generals. They have the real clout in this area. If they want something to work, they can get the people behind them. I think there's a chance."

Top spoke, dropping his voice. "What I want to know is what you all think about this sentence about 'silencing the Americans.' You know that means us, and you know the Hoa Hao would do it and not bat an eye."

Hood said, "That was suggested in the section about the Hoa Hao cooperating with the Viet Cong, and I think that was one of the few places where Rand miscalculated. I don't think the Hoa Hao would ever cooperate with the Cong to the point of letting them run the show. Rand underestimated how much the Hoa Hao hate the Cong."

"I agree, but, between us, everyone keep a tight asshole and stay packed. If it comes to it, we'll bust out together. I don't know about you all, but I'm looking out for number one." Top put out a cigarette and added, "Anyway, we're pissing in the dark. We don't know if the generals will buy this report or not."

Wheaty, scratching the top of his head, said, "It's a pretty good report. But somehow I like having American infantry back there if we need them. What if the VC don't buy this and decide to pay us a visit one night?"

"That's the beauty of this," said Hood. "We're in no worse shape than we are now. If we call for help, we'll get it. If MAAG thinks we're CIA, they'll send reinforcements in a hurry. If MAAG doesn't buy the idea, they'll still send in troops because we're a CIDG camp."

Lon sat bowls of steaming soup before us. Lunch was the most spirited it had been in weeks. Cranston rarely ate with us any more. Technically, he was still on the team, but he was moving quickly into his new life. Each of us had held private doubts about his marriage to Lao, but his happiness, so far, was dispelling them.

We talked some more about the Rand report. Hood was cautious, Teewee noncommittal. Santee was excited about the potential Rand saw for Hoa Hao Unlimited Ltd. Cranston and I liked it and Top didn't trust it. At least it was something we discussed. We had been here eleven months, and it was beginning to gnaw at most of us. Cranston and Santee, of course, were carving out their own niche here. For the rest of us, it wasn't so easy. More and more I found myself thinking about Nina and going to medical school.

After lunch I started toward the dispensary. Halfway there, I noticed a foul odor coming from my machine-gun pit. Underneath my M-30 and its tarpaulin I found two dozen dead rats in a box. I almost gagged at the rotten smell. Someone was caching their rats in my pit.

"*An*," I shouted at a striker walking by. "*An muon chuot cong mot?*"

He leaped over the sandbags and grabbed the box like it was full of piasters. Actually, it was worth more than that. He would get two or three days' leave from that box. Rats had gotten so bad in the camp that Choi had offered a bounty: for every ten rats, one day of leave.

Strikers were staying up all night with sticks, crossbows, and rocks, looking for rats. Teewee had been knocked out of his bunk two nights ago when two strikers who were chasing a rat crashed headlong into the team house. There had been five fights that I knew about between the troops over rats. Lately the supply in camp had run low and the men had taken to sneaking into Nan Phuc on their hunts.

I, too, was involved in the great rat war. Two weeks ago a giant rat had begun terrorizing me. I slept beside the supply room, and it was clear that this one rat had decided my bed was the freeway to the supplies. He would run across a rafter until it stopped directly over my bed. Then he jumped to the metal rod at the foot of my cot that held the mosquito netting up. He ran along the netting, up the wall, and into the supply room. The bed would shake when he hit that rod. I had tried everything. I threw boots at him, set rat traps, devised a safe-fall, and one night I stole Teewee's crossbow and tried to shoot him. He was too smart. If I sat up waiting for him, he would outwait me. And five minutes after I sacked out—*ca-whomp!*—he would land on the bed.

So I finally said, "The hell with it. It's all-out war. God has seen fit that this is my test. And the struggle must be face to face, hand to claw." That night—it was a week ago—I had sharpened my Air Force K-Bar knife to a fine edge. Leaving my fatigue pants on, I crawled into bed. Ten minutes later he was on the rafter. I think he, too, knew it was tonight. He sat on that board for fifteen long minutes, never once taking his eyes off mine. His tail hung down, more than a foot long, twitching back and forth like a metronome.

Hemingway, where were you when I needed you? He jumped to the rod and paused. I didn't move. Not yet. My hands were sweaty. Then he started across the netting.

"Ahhhhheeee!" I screamed and lunged. The knife tore through the netting. The rat screamed. I missed him. He lost his balance and fell. As I tumbled head first off the end of the cot, dragging the netting with me, I saw the rat, upside down and scrambling in the middle of my bed. I ripped through the netting, getting my arms and head free. The rat leaped over the side of the bunk and disappeared. I hobbled, as fast as one can hobble on one's knees and dragging twenty square yards of mosquito netting, around to the side of the bed. I had him trapped. There was no exit behind the bed.

I knelt and spread my arms wide apart. I moved my right hand, which was holding the knife, under the cot in short, jerky motions. Suddenly a blur of gray. The rat jumped out and landed for an instant on my left wrist. I stabbed! "Ahhhhheeee!" A sharp, piercing pain sunk into my wrist.

The rat was gone and the knife was in my arm. Goddamn! I pulled the knife out and immediately blood spurted three feet high. Goddamn again! I had hit an artery. In fact, the main artery in my left arm. It spurted three times, blood arcing up and over my bunk before I got my wits together to put my thumb on it. By that time the rest of the team had heard the noise and were crowding in. I was sitting on the floor, half naked, draped in a ripped mosquito net and trying to stop a punctured artery.

Top said, "Goddamn, *bac si*, if you look that bad, I'd hate to see him."

Although Santee had been slightly cross-trained as a medic, I was worried. Standard treatment for most large artery punctures is suturing. But with only one good hand and no other medic around, I did the only thing I could. I held my thumb on it for the next two hours. It worked.

The next night the rat came bounding back on the rafter and stopped. I lay there, feeling the pressure bandage on my wrist. "It's okay, my friend," I said. "There's enough rice for both of us."

His tail flicked and he jumped down. As he passed by, his lips curled upward, ever so slightly.

Choi's idea of a bounty was creating havoc, but as a medic I had to admit it was getting rid of the rats in camp.

The striker carried away the box of rats and I went in to my dispensary. Several hours later, as sick call was beginning, Top came in. He often sat through sick call to chat with the strikers and to watch my treatments.

The woman and the baby were standing third in line. A striker behind her explained that she was his cousin. She was about twenty years old and lovely. Autumn skin and straight black hair around a flawless complexion. She clutched a baby, who looked seven or eight months old, in her arms. She told me she had a stomach ache. After receiving vague replies to my questions, I decided that whatever she had wasn't serious. Then she said, rather quickly and nervously, that the baby, her sister's baby, was hurting.

That was the real reason she was here.

She unwound the maroon cloth the baby was wrapped in and held out the child's small, frail arm. A fresh bamboo leaf was tied below the baby's shoulder. I snipped the vines and pulled the leaf off. There was a large, ugly hole. Fairly fresh. A home remedy of dirt and betel nut juice was caked around it.

Top peered over my shoulder.

The sore turned out to be a gash across the baby's upper arm, going deep, nearly to the bone. I asked her about it. She was from a small hamlet far to the south, on the outskirts of Chau An. She was Hoa Hao and had been working in the rice fields yesterday with her sister and her husband and several other family members. Suddenly a "lot of soldiers" came by. She hadn't recognized them, but from her description it could only have been GVN troops. The soldiers had shouted something at the family in the field. She said she didn't understand what they said. A moment later they opened fire on them. She fell to the ground, but one of the first shots killed her sister and hit the baby carried on her back.

I asked her why she'd come here instead of a dispensary in Chau An. She said she was afraid and also that she knew Major Choi and trusted him.

Top asked if she had told anyone of the incident. She said she had been afraid to.

Too much time had passed for me to suture the wound. I cleaned it and used butterfly bandages to pull the edges together. The woman told me the baby was a year old. It couldn't have weighed more than ten pounds. I measured out a dozen baby-size doses of Penicillin G. Since she couldn't walk back here every day, I gave her tape, scissors, peroxide, and Bacitracin-Neomycin ointment and showed her how to clean the wound and cut butterfly bandages. It was the best I could do. I told her to come back if the wound became red or swollen.

She thanked me, bowed, and left.

Top said, "The shit is going to hit the fan when Major Choi hears about this."

"You want a report?" I said.

"Write down everything she said and I'll sign it and we'll give it to Choi. He should be back tomorrow." Top walked to the door and stared out. Softly he said, "Crazy goddamn soldiers. Shooting at people in a field because they couldn't hear what they said. Even if they had heard, it might not have made any difference."

He shook his head and walked out.

19

WEDNESDAY AFTERNOON Choi told us the Hoa Hao command had voted for Rand Alternate 5: cooperation with both the Viet Cong and the government of South Vietnam. We met in his office after pok time. Without preamble, he said, "We discussed the Rand report for a long time. Several generals did not place much faith in—uh—"

"Americans?" supplied Top.

Choi answered with a marginal smile, "Those who prepared the report. Nevertheless, much of it was good thinking. We will give Alternate 5 a trial period. It is a narrow path to walk between the Viet Cong and GVN, but tigers wait on both sides. We have walked the middle path before."

Hood said, "I'm curious, Major, which recommendation came in second?"

"Our supporting a coup against the government. The generals felt we have more support than the Rand report indicated." Choi absent-mindedly pulled out his bizarre pig's teat and rubbed the leatherlike nipple with his thumb. Maybe we should make artificial pigs' teats and sell them as worry tits.

"We will start Alternate 5 in our district, Nan Phuc. If it seems to work, we'll expand it to the other Hoa Hao provinces."

Choi asked for our opinions on Alternate 5. Only Top had reservations about the plan.

"It seems pretty risky. So far, at least a dozen people know about it, and according to Rand, we've got to tell civilians. I'll be damned if I see how you can keep it a secret."

Choi said, "Sergeant O'Hara, if you were a Viet Cong and you heard an entire population in a military zone was cooperating with both you and the government of South Vietnam, would you believe it? Especially when you were invited to tour the area?"

"Maybe," said Top, a question still in his voice. "I tell you what, this is all new to us. Let us think about it, and tomorrow we'll get back together."

"That is all right," said Choi. "By the way, Sergeant O'Hara, I received your report about the woman and the baby who was shot. In Long Xuyen we received the same report. We told provincial headquarters that this sort. of stupidity will not be tolerated. The soldiers were GVN troops on a sweeping operation. General Ba reported a similar incident in his district where a family was accidentally killed by mortars fired by GVN troops. The Viet Cong also have kidnaped two village chiefs in Ba's district. It seems both the government and the VC have decided to increase their operations in and around our territory. I tell you these things so you may understand why we chose Rand Alternate 5."

Minutes later we were seated around the table in our team room. Top said, "I admit Alternate 5 is the plan that makes the best sense from Choi's point of view. What I called you in here for is to see if you all wanted to be part of it or not. I don't know if it's exactly treason or not, but I don't like the idea of cooperating with the lions. We were sent out here to teach these men how to fight the Viet Cong and to get them to go

210

along with the government. And while there's no love lost between us and the government, the idea of cooperating with the Cong doesn't sit right with me."

Hood spoke up. "We wouldn't be really helping the VC, Top. If the plan works, there won't be any VC in here. They won't be taking over control of anything, and the intelligence reports we feed them will be faked. Enough will be true to be believed, but still faked."

Wheaty said, "I guess what you're asking, Top, is if any of us object enough to the plan to want out?"

Teewee forgot to lower his voice. Or perhaps he didn't forget. I remembered Top's words when Wheaty first joined the team: "We'll make a goddamned officer out of that boy or kill him trying."

"That's it, sir," said Top.

Wheaty looked around. "From everything I've heard, we're all willing to give it a try. Especially since there's no way to get out of here yet."

Top answered, "The water's getting on down, but we can't walk to Can Tho yet. In a month or six weeks, for sure. The VC still have the Bassac cut off, and you heard what Choi said about Ba's district below Chau An. I figure as soon as we can—on the ground or on the water—we ought to make a run for it. How do the rest of you feel about that?"

Wheaty spoke first. "Any time. We've been here a year, and that's enough time in grade, at least, for me to make first lieutenant."

Cranston cleared his throat and said, "Top, you know I'm staying on with my wife. I'm not going back."

"Cranston, the Army will probably okay your marriage, and after the formalities you can come back," said Top. But his tone said that he and Cranston had been through this before and Top had lost then, too.

"I'm taking no chances. I'd like it if you said I was captured or lost on a patrol, but if you feel you've got to tell them

I'm here, I'll understand. My ETS was three weeks ago."

"Well," said Top, "if you're crazy enough to stay here, I'm not going to fuck it up for you. Warren?"

"I'll go whenever you think we can make it. My ETS is in June and I'm going to medical school." I surprised myself. It's funny. You suddenly say something that's been on your mind, but it sounds all different. Solid. Decided.

Top looked at Santee. He was drawing circles on paper.

"Well," he drawled, "I reckon I'm going to stay here, too. You know this little factory is a big part of me. We're going to sell some bonds in Thailand in a month. Uncle Sugar gave Thailand a fifty-million-dollar loan and that should make the rate a little lower. These are my people, Top. No offense, but there ain't nothing for me to go back to. I'd appreciate it if you reported that I was killed. It would mean my mother would get a nice hunk of insurance, plus payments from the Army."

We all had suspected Santee would remain here, but it was the first time he'd made it public.

"Have you thought about this?" asked Top.

"There's no changing my mind."

"You got no more sense than Cranston," mumbled Top. "Have you two talked with Choi about becoming natives?"

They said Choi had given his blessings.

Top turned to Hood. "I suppose you're going to stay?"

"No. I've been in the Army too long. Besides, I told you once I'd make sergeant major before you."

Top said, "Okay. Are we agreed then? We'll give this crazy goddamn plan a try, and whether or not it works, we—at least four of us—are cutting out as soon as the water's down."

We were agreed.

Tien died that night at 2130 hours with his family around him. It had been only a matter of time; still, it surprised me when Lao came for me after supper.

"You must come, *bac si*. Tien is very sick."

My resumption of the proper treatment had been too late. Chest complications had set in ten days ago, and there was little I could do. I had been giving Tien codeine to ease the pain of the constant coughing. Yesterday he had said he wanted no more medicine, and I'd noticed his relatives were beginning to arrive. He had called for them.

Lao and I walked hurriedly through the twilight to Tien's house at the edge of town on the Tran Tri Canal. Two children—Tien's grandchildren—were sitting on the porch making toy boats from bamboo leaves. We went inside.

Tien was in bed, surrounded by his wife, his son and daughter-in-law, two brothers and their wives, and Cranston. Pale and shrunken, he seemed only bones. I remembered a line from an old Irish ballad, "Low on flesh, high on bone. Ach, Johnny, I hardly knew you."

Candles flickered on the bamboo-slatted floor, making long shadows of us all. The air was thick with incense and sickness.

Kneeling, I said, "*Chao*, Tien."

He started to smile, but it turned into a coughing spasm. His right hand held a crumpled brassiere—one from our new line of Aristobras—and he spat bright red sputum into it. He closed his eyes.

"Tien," I said in Vietnamese, "your children are gathered around you and honor you greatly. We have much respect for you. I am sorry my medicine—"

His eyes opened, and he laid a small, fevered hand on mine. "Do not apologize, *bac si*. When I was young, I could forgive a man anything if he was intelligent." Another coughing fit shook his frame, and he spat again into the bra. "When I was older, I could forgive a man anything if he had a sense of humor. And when I grew old and weak, I could forgive a man anything if he would come and sit and talk with me. And you have done that." His fragile chest struggled with efforts to breathe. "I have made my coffin and I will rest with my father and my father's father in the family area."

His wife gave out a large sob and fell across Tien. From his gasping I realized that he could hardly breathe, and I gently pulled her shoulders back. Tien tried to reach her forehead with his hand but could not.

I moved back among the relatives. Tien's son, Den, knelt beside the bed. Tien shakily removed a small stack of papers from the inside of his shirt. Among them, I recognized several stock certificates in Hoa Hao Unlimited Ltd. Tien whispered weakly to his son. He was passing his documents on to Den, who would now become the head of the family.

Everyone, except Den and his wife, began moving to the front room. I realized the social custom must be to leave Tien with his immediate family now.

A neighbor had brought over a pot of tea, and while Lao poured for the family, Cranston and I stepped onto the porch. The grandchildren had gone inside.

Music began playing, coming from the house of the community mourner in the village. One man, who unfortunately lived on the same side of the village as our camp, owned an old French wind-up record player and one record of Vietnamese music. For five piasters an hour he would play the record for any and all occasions. Whenever we heard it, we knew someone was dying or sick, had died, gotten married, or had been born. Even today I know the record, note by agonizing note.

"Tien was a good man," said Cranston, staring at the yellow lights from our camp. "He was the best carpenter the camp ever had."

Lao brought us tea and went back inside. Sipping the hot tea reminded me of the Aristocrat's mother sitting on the veranda of her fallen-down mansion in the hills of North Carolina. Sitting and sipping her marijuana tea and rocking. Biding her time.

Cranston said, "Did you know I burned down a house once?"

214

That didn't fit in with the Cranston I knew. "No. When? Why?"

"It was stupid, but it seemed like a good idea at the time. It was in College Park, Maryland, when I was going to the university. A friend had a party in an old empty house his father owned. The party was one drunken brawl. Very late in the evening my friend made the mistake of saying the house was insured for more than it was worth, so I got the bright idea of burning it down to help his father. It came to me while I was pissing. So I set fire to the shower curtains. But somebody put that one out. I finally got the blaze going when I lit a bunch of newspapers under a staircase. Nobody was hurt or even scared and there were no houses close by. We cheered the fire department on, but they couldn't save it. When I sobered up the next day, I was really scared. It was a crazy thing to do. I'd never done anything like that before in my life."

Cranston stopped a moment. There was more to come.

"I don't think I've had more than a half dozen drinks since then. The nice thing about grass is that I've never done anything like that, or ever wanted to, when I've been smoking dope. That sounds like an excuse and maybe it is."

Probably a grain of truth under a shell of rationalization. "Maybe," I said, "but maybe it's true. Whether or not it's a copout isn't the point. It's that you got away from one bad thing and, for you, at least, dope isn't bad."

"I've never used it as much as some of the kids back home. Maybe once or twice a week. To relax. Like some people drink, I guess."

Each to his own private superstitions. Ways to make it through the night. I sipped more tea. "How are you and Lao doing?" I had more than a hunch that they were doing fine. Lao had been half simple with happiness since the wedding.

Cranston smiled. "Beautiful. Really beautiful, Phil. For the first time in my life I'm not trying to prove anything to anybody. Lao and I have a great thing going. It's called living.

Day to day. We're working on our house, and my foster father-in-law is letting me work part of his paddy."

I had been out several times to help them on their home. They were building a house, because Vietnamese tradition called for the oldest son to live at home with his parents. The family unit most favored by the gods was made up of four generations: the parents, one or two grandparents, the oldest son and his wife and their small children. Other brothers and sisters could live at home, but they usually moved away as soon as possible. Since Lao's foster parents already had a son, although unmarried, at home, she and Cranston were building their own home.

There was no such thing as a deed, so Cranston and Lao had selected an unused acre near the Bassac and told the neighbors they would like to build a home and live there. The neighbors talked it over and said that so long as they lived there and took care of the land, it was theirs.

With the help of the local astrologer, they built the spirit house in front and then Cranston strung a hammock between two papaya trees. Now the stilts were in the ground, the flooring laid, and a large front porch completed, facing the river. Idyllic.

Cranston was saying, "There's no rat race, no impressing people, no struggling to be something you're not. You raise some rice and you sit around the fire at night and talk. Calm. That's what it is. Calm. I don't worry about some kid in the alley knifing me, or having to get a job selling Bibles door-to-door, or where I'm going to raise the next payment on my Chevrolet."

I started to mention the Viet Cong but didn't. Cranston understood as well as I.

Loud wailing from inside the house interrupted us, and we knew Tien was dead.

20

THE MEN dug four graves before they found one dry enough for the coffin. Even so, muddy water was rising in the bottom. Tien's coffin was a simple rectangular box made of teak. The only decorations were large, petaled flowers carved in the ends and on the top. Splattered on the lid, like giant bloodstains, were wax drippings from red candles that had burned since Tien had died last night.

The local mortician, who was the same man who owned the record player and the single ceremonial record, had washed Tien's body, splashed on various perfumes, which not only kept evil spirits away but helped cover any smells that might develop, and wrapped the body in bamboo mats. The inside of the coffin was waterproofed with candle wax and soap.

We stood, sweating and waiting. The noon sun drew the shadows of the several dozen mourners in sharp relief on the ground. The graveyard was a raised mound, high enough not to be flooded, and contained fifty graves, the kinsmen of Tien.

Short, green grass and colorful flowers gave evidence that this family burial land was meticulously kept.

During his lifetime Tien had cared for his ancestral land well, and now it was his son's obligation. It wasn't so much a duty to the land as to the family. And the family not only meant the living members but past and future generations as well. Those alive were the link between their ancestors, to whom they owed an unending duty, and their unborn progeny. By fulfilling his obligations to his ancestors, through such things as maintaining their graves and sacrifices of food and incense, a man assured himself that he would be well treated after his own death and would not be condemned to eternity as a wandering spirit without food and care from anyone.

This filial piety and perpetuation of the family were much stronger among the rural Vietnamese, such as the Hoa Hao, than among the urban Vietnamese. And I suspected this was a key factor in the failure of the many resettlement schemes dreamed up by the government. To leave the family tombs and ancestral villages would be an extremely serious step. If the family disintegrated, left its home, and failed to carry out its duty to its ancestors, those spirits would be lost and alone through all eternity.

The ceremony itself was simple, practical, and brief. Major Choi was mumbling a few words, which I couldn't hear; Tien's widow moaned loudly in her grief; and in the background the record played in Nan Phuc.

The last time I had attended a funeral had been after the Viet Cong attack at Hiep Phung. Six coffins. Then, however, it was midsummer and the temperature was between 90 and 100 degrees every day. Two of the dead were from Chau An, and although we tried to keep the coffins cool until their families arrived, we couldn't. On the third day both coffins began leaking an awful, malodorous brown liquid. Fortunately, a distant cousin who knew both families was located in Nan Phuc, and that afternoon we had buried them.

That had been the first time I had seen men violently killed by other men. Death was no stranger to me, for my first real job had been as a photographer of automobile wrecks for the Hickory *Daily News*. But seeing those six bodies had closed a circuit in my mind, and I understood at last a recurring dream I had had a half dozen times, the earliest when I was eight years old. The dream was that I would go into our back yard with a great sense of dread and apprehension. In the yard would be our wooden lawn chair with its back to me. I would step in front of it, and there, staring straight ahead, would be my grandfather, sitting upright, pale and dead. That was when I always woke up screaming. When those six dead men were brought into my dispensary, I finally understood that the dream signaled my self's awareness, but not acceptance, of my own mortality. That I, too, would die someday.

Top nudged me. "Tien's son asked you to say a few words."

"Why me?" I muttered.

"As the doctor who walks saint-like on water." Top leered.

Do you suppose that's how it all got started? One day Jesus was waterskiing on the Sea of Galilee and the next day He was the carpenter who walked on water.

I stepped forward and bowed to Tien's widow and son. I didn't know what to say, but I began speaking about how well the family had paid their respects and added that Den would continue to honor the ancestors admirably. That sort of thing.

Out of the corner of my eye I spotted some unusual plants outside the graveyard at the edge of a paddy. The plants seemed familiar. They were six feet tall with long, sharply serrated leaves. Of course! It was Cranston's marijuana crop. They were a handsome set of plants. No doubt this was the first crop of aristograss coming up.

A loud wail reminded me that my last sentence had trailed

off into silence. I concluded with the hope that Tien's spirit would be forever happy. The family lowered the coffin into the grave. It settled down through the water, nearly disappearing under it. Tien's son, in an act like our own, threw in the first handful of dirt.

An hour later we were back in the team room preparing to meet with Choi about the Rand plan. Top opened the discussion. "According to this plan, we're to set up an American liaison officer who is supposed to okay troop movements, and so forth, in this area. Now, since all of us, except Cranston and Santee, are going back in a month or two, it's got to be one of them."

Cranston and Santee exchanged glances. That hadn't occurred to me either.

Top said, "You both speak Vietnamese pretty good. Santee, you're a nigger, but if we're going to have a nigger in the woodpile it might as well be a real one. Cranston's a little strange and married. The fact that he's married might get back to Clow."

Cranston said, "I'd as soon stay in the background as much as possible, Top. Lao and I want to have a child soon."

Top looked at Santee.

Santee said, "I'll be glad to try it, but it sounds risky. One mistake and I could blow it all."

Top said, "I tell you a little secret about people. If they back you against the wall, rush 'em. Once in Nashville I was at a buddy's house drinking of a Saturday afternoon. This fellow dropped by and got in an argument with my buddy. I didn't know who the hell he was, and I got the feeling my friend didn't know him very well, either. We were standing outside, and all of a sudden the guy pulled a Luger out and said to my friend, 'I think I'm going to shoot you.' Not having good sense, I walked over to his car and said, 'There's no need to do all that.' And he said, 'Say, I think I'll shoot you, too, if you don't get your hands off my car.' Well, goddamn, that pissed me off, so I jumped up on his hood and proceeded to stomp his car in. He was so amazed at a man jumping up and down on his car that he put up the gun and left."

So now all Santee had to do was jump up and down on top of any helicopters that landed and he had it made.

We went to Choi's office. As usual, he was alone. He liked the strength, the secrecy, and the responsibility of making his own decisions. No advisers to hide behind. Top outlined our reasoning about Santee, and Choi accepted the idea. Santee, U.S. Army sergeant and son of a Negro garbage collector from Georgia, was now Mr. Leroy Santee, an American liaison officer from the Central Intelligence Agency attached to the U.S. Army, IV CTZ, Special Operations, with the temporary rank of brigadier general. Choi selected his right-hand man, Captain Danh Van Mieng, to be the Con Mat's liaison officer, also a general.

Rand had given us a number of "alternate" ideas about what sort of secret operation we should claim to have under way. They ranged from underground missile silos to secret airfields. Whatever we decided the operation would be, said Rand, the same story should be told to both sides to lessen the danger if either side intercepted the other's messages.

Three hours later we concluded the best plan seemed to be to tell each side one half of the Rand plan itself. In other words, we would tell the Viet Cong that the secret plan was that we were attempting to deceive GVN into believing we were cooperating with them. And we would tell GVN that the secret plan was that we were attempting to deceive the Viet Cong into believing we were cooperating with them. Maybe half the truth would make us free. Also, it seemed to be the most confusing plan we could think of.

Additionally, both sides would be ordered to reduce military operations to a minimum, since "pending discussions were under way" with Hoa Hao leaders about the plan.

One problem was to explain to the VC why their lifelong

221

enemies, the Hoa Hao, would now be cooperating with them. We decided to tell them that the Hoa Hao leaders were disgusted with the government of South Vietnam and were tired of being oppressed. Choi convinced us that, to add to the plausibility of this, he would spread the word that the Hoa Hao were really cooperating with the Viet Cong in hopes of securing autonomous control of their provinces after the Viet Cong won. And, while the Viet Cong would do no such thing, they would be willing to allow the Hoa Hao leaders to believe that, in order to gain their support.

The idea was not as farfetched as it sounded. Last year in the Chaîne Annamitique the VC had curtailed their operations for nearly a full year against the Montagnards when the VC sensed the deep dissatisfaction the Yards had against the government. If anything, the Yards were more oppressed than the Hoa Hao. Until their rebellion last fall, no Montagnard could be an officer in the Vietnamese army. Schooling was unknown. The lowland Vietnamese, including the Hoa Hao, referred to the Yards, even in their dictionaries and newspapers, as *mois*, savages. The urban Vietnamese thought the Yards ate their children, killed animals for sacrifices (which was true), and were only a half step out of caves. They also thought the Yards were dumb and looked funny. The Montagnards, according to Hood, had their own prejudices. They felt the lowlanders were callous, liars, thieves, and fast-talking.

From the Rand Appendix about the Montagnards and from what we had heard through the grapevine, we had been able to get a pretty good picture of what happened up there last year. The first place the CIA sent Special Forces teams was into the highlands during the early 1960s. Last fall, on September 21, the Yards revolted. They captured Ban Me Thout, the provincial capital. They demanded that their men be allowed to attend OCS, that schools be provided, that they be allowed to form an independent nation, and that they be

222

allowed to hold governmental positions on the district and provincial levels.

The revolt ended two months later and with little violence, primarily because of the intervention of several high-ranking Special Forces officers and the CIA.

The mountain people were granted most of their demands. According to Rand, last November two Montagnard boys began attending the high school in Pleiku, the first ever to do so.

The interesting thing about the revolt, which no doubt justified, unfortunately, to Westmoreland his insistence on assuming command of Special Forces, was the mountain of circumstantial evidence that Special Forces men had known of the revolt ahead of time, condoned it, and perhaps even assisted the Yards in planning it. For example, the three thousand Montagnards who began the rebellion came from six Special Forces camps. Secondly, one of the Yards' demands was that they be allowed to raise a fifty-thousand-man army to be trained by Special Forces. MAAG was specifically excluded. Third, it was suspicious, to say the least, that in not a single camp were the Americans able to "free" themselves and attempt to stop the rebellion. We heard that in one case an entire twelve-man team of Green Berets was held "prisoner" for weeks by one Montagnard man, armed with a pistol.

Our motto was "Liberators of the Oppressed," after all.

Choi's words brought me back from my musings. "We will also include in the set of orders to the VC that this is an experimental program to win the Hoa Hao and that the success of the plan depends on their complete cooperation. Which is true. Also, I think it is a good idea to begin regular intelligence reports to the VC. Maybe we should include with this first set of orders an account of the sinking of the Vietnamese Navy junk by our soldiers south of Chau An and several GVN troop locations."

Wheaty objected, "But, Major, wouldn't that be giving them intelligence that they can use?"

Choi said, "Not really, Captain. The junk was sunk in broad daylight. You can be sure the VC already know exactly what happened. And the same is true of major troop locations. The VC are not fools. They know two new battalions of GVN soldiers are operational north of Can Tho. They already know how many latrines have been installed. But giving them information they know to be true increases our credibility."

Encoding the message to the Cong would be no problem. Hood's agents had intercepted several Con Mat messages in the past, so we knew the general format and could duplicate the paper. The most recent had been two weeks ago, when one of our agents in Moc Hap had captured a Con Mat messenger who had contacted our man—not knowing he was an agent—about buying some stock in Hoa Hao Unlimited Ltd. Our agent began to suspect the man when he dropped several North Vietnamese piasters while paying for the stock. We broke the code and sent the message on to the VC with Linh acting as the messenger. As long as the code hadn't been changed we were safe.

The message had been that the Con Mat was planning to assassinate several village chiefs in the Nac Nghia district near Can Tho. We had notified those men.

21

TEEWEE JERKED his hand away. "Jesus, *bac si*, that stings."

"Peroxide is supposed to sting. That means it's getting deep inside and bubbling out germs. Once more," I said. I filled the needleless syringe again, poked it inside the bright pink hole between Teewee's thumb and forefinger, and squeezed.

Wheaty's gunshot wound was healing nicely. He complained of stiffness in his thumb, and I had him exercising his hand daily. It would leave a nasty white scar, but I had a feeling that Teewee's scar, like good wine, would improve with age, especially if he never told the truth.

It had happened a week ago, on April 5. He and Santee were on an overnight patrol with the Nungs in the Giap Phang. About 0300 hours Wheaty decided to take a short nap. Santee said fine, he would stay awake. They were ten feet apart, hidden in the brush beside a trail. At 0420 hours a single pistol shot rang out. Santee found a shaking Wheaty, holding a bleeding left hand. It turned out that the lieutenant fell asleep with his head on his left arm. About 0415 something—a bird, a wild pig, or a VC—woke him up. The night was deep black. Teewee raised his head, listening for the noise. He wasn't aware that his left arm had gone to sleep. Completely numb. Convinced that the Cong were creeping about, he reached out with his right hand to get his carbine. And then he touched a hand. A human hand. Very slowly, he slid his right hand down, pulled his forty-five pistol, and carefully shot a hole in his left hand.

I finished and Teewee left. After washing the instruments, I walked over to look at the X-rays strung across the open-air window of the dispensary. Our Ritter portable X-ray unit had arrived via a Cambodian fisherman four days ago. As per our instructions, Ritter had shipped it in a crate marked "USIS Electrical Fans." It had worked. I had immediately X-rayed the team for practice and to check for tuberculosis.

There was no doubt about it. Something was in Top's right lung. It showed up twice. A mottled cloud of gray-white the size of a dime floated high in his upper lobe. When the spot appeared on the first negative, I had attributed it to my inexperience. Although Ritter sent a fifty-page booklet on how to use the PX-304Y, I found it difficult to see exactly what I was supposed to see. I told Top I had overdeveloped his negative and had to shoot another. Maybe he had had an unreported case of TB as a child and this was a scar. Maybe it was shrapnel from some wound, not in his medical records. Maybe it was a straw and I was clutching at it.

Top would want to know how the X-ray came out. I looked at my watch—1000 hours. Phu would be coming shortly for his lesson on the X-ray unit. I would talk with Top later.

Nguyen Van Phu had been C Company's chief medic until a month ago, when the Rand plan had officially gone into effect and when I had talked Choi into letting me train a Hoa Hao medic to run the dispensary. I would be leaving soon and a Vietnamese should be running the dispensary anyway.

Phu was the brightest and quickest of my medics. Even so, I

226

did not know how poor he was at reading and writing until one day when I was teaching him the importance of correct and detailed medical records. I asked him to pretend I was a patient. How would he obtain my medical history? He asked the right questions, but he held his pencil with a clenched fist. The pencil was gripped like it was an attacker, to be met and grappled with. Phu slowly formed the words, letter by nervous letter. So I had asked Luc to give Phu reading and writing lessons, and Phu was making good progress.

Our new X-ray machine was not the only tangible sign that both Hoa Hao Unlimited Ltd. and the Rand Alternate 5 were succeeding beyond anyone's expectations. The latest mail from Phnom Penh brought word from the Small Business Administration office in Atlanta that a loan for forty thousand dollars would be forthcoming from the Atlanta Bank and Trust Co., guaranteed by the SBA. We had also received thirty thousand dollars from our sale of convertible debentures to an underwriting syndicate in Bangkok. Santee's gamble had paid off. When he had made arrangements for the underwriting, he had neglected to inform the syndicate the SBA loan had not been approved at that time. And when he applied for the SBA loan, he had indicated cash on hand included thirty thousand dollars net proceeds from a bond sale. Which had not been held yet. The common stock offering was nearly sold out. So far, seventy-eight thousand shares had been sold for a total income of fifty-one thousand dollars.

Teewee had been working nights trying to keep track of the money pouring in. He was changing our entire bookkeeping system. Santee had decided to take Rand's advice and switch from first-in, first-out accounting to a weighted average system. Rand said this was more realistic and would give an accurate representation, even in the inflationary times that were upon us. Another change, also suggested by Rand, was accelerated depreciation. Having performed a study of the tax structure in Vietnam for U.S. AID, Rand knew the situation intimately and said the faster write-off would lower taxes initially and help us keep abreast of inflation.

The first thing Choi and Santee bought was a fireproof, bombproof, solid steel safe. There were no banks around.

The second thing we did was to make a down payment on an aluminum rolling machine. I suspected Choi envisioned the entire population of the delta sitting around in the late afternoon in plastic-webbed lawn chairs and wearing Hoa Hao Unlimited Ltd. bras. We ordered the machine from the Murphy Manufacturing Company in Birmingham and were told that they bought their machines from Japan, so ours should arrive within thirty days.

The third thing the money was spent on was two things: new boats. Both were in Nan Phuc being refinished, and they were nearly as beautiful as *Granny*. One was a World War II U.S. armored light patrol boat. It had been captured by North Korea in 1951, was given by the Red Chinese to North Vietnam, was captured by U.S. Marines near Danang, and then, mysteriously, had found its way into private hands. Choi's agent had paid ten thousand dollars for the boat to a Special Forces sergeant major, who ran the PXs in Danang. The boat was being outfitted as a fighting vessel. The other boat was a beautifully dilapidated junk, acquired from an Indian book-store operator in Saigon. The junk and *Granny* would be the trading and cargo boats.

While the junk, like *Granny*, drew only a few feet of water, the patrol boat needed at least six feet. During flood season this would be no problem, but the rest of the year the smaller canals were only four or five feet deep. Since the French left, many canals in the delta had fallen into disrepair.

Not only was the siltation hazardous to our patrol boat, it was hurting the rice crops. Our rice consultant from Bangkok University said we could increase the harvest by 10 per cent simply by cleaning and deepening the canals. He had arrived a few days ago, having survived a terrifying trip down the Bassac from Phnom Penh. Unwittingly, he had caught a boat ride with a well-known smuggler. A few hours south of the Cambodian capital the smuggler was attacked by a rival gang. The smuggler's men managed to beat the attackers off only to have two American jets from Thailand strafe the boat several hours later, probably thinking it was Viet Cong. To make the consultant's day complete, our own men had fired on the boat as it crossed the border into Vietnam.

Our consultant's name was Subchai Konchanart, and he was young and serious about his work. More important, he knew rice and he knew how to talk to farmers. Subchai was optimistic that our soil could handle a second crop of fast-growing, early-maturing rice, which could be planted immediately after the first harvest. He was also highly complimentary of Top's demonstration garden, which was now a showplace in Nan Phuc. Farmers came from as far downriver as the Xuyen Song Doa canal to inspect Top's crops and talk with him about his techniques.

Subchai and Cranston hit it off right away. Subchai spoke only Thai and English, so Cranston acted as interpreter most of the time. Subchai was intrigued with the automatic rice-seedling setter-outer that Cranston had developed. It was four feet long and funnel shaped. At the bottom the funnel came to a sharp point, which was hinged into two sections. You stuck the funnel two or three inches into the ground, squeezed a grip which opened the tip and at the same time made a hole. Then you dropped the seedling, root first, down the funnel, pulled the funnel out, and stepped around the plant. If it tested all right, Choi was planning to mass produce the funnel.

It looked like Choi's scheme to warehouse the rice until the market rose was going to work. Prices in Can Tho had reached sixty-five piasters per gia last week, and rumor was that the price would go much higher. Choi and Santee were planning to hold their fifteen thousand tons one more month and then begin selling.

Naturally, much of the money we were making went back into Hoa Hao Unlimited Ltd. At last count there were forty-eight men and women working in the factory itself, and they were producing six different lines of work clothes, bras, GI dog tags, bamboo roof sections, pottery and kitchen utensils, crossbows, fake AK-47s, and VC flags. Our biggest lines were still the VC flags and bras, but the work clothes were narrowing the gap.

Our ex-VC, Linh, was turning into quite a salesman. Besides the flags, the best-selling item to the VC was the GI dog tags. Linh said the Cong used the tags as evidence of Americans killed. Like Major Choi and the rats, the VC had a system of so-many-GIs-killed, so-much-leave-time.

The biggest success in the last four weeks had been the Rand plan. We had delivered our instructions to Captain Clow, informing him of our new secret operation. Word came back immediately that he would fully cooperate and would forward all future communications to Mr. Santee. There had been no GVN operations in our area since the communiqué. Whether that was by chance or because of the Rand plan remained to be seen. But it was a damned good sign.

Ex-VC Linh had carried the handwritten set of orders to General Phat. Choi had even sealed them with a Viet Cong signature ring we had captured several months ago. Linh returned with a terse note from Phat, saying he would visit Nan Phuc within the month to discuss the plan further. He said nothing about curtailing VC operations in our area, but clearly he had. Viet Cong activity had virtually ceased, except for several isolated incidents of sniping and taxation on the far eastern fringe of our territory.

Right after the Hoa Hao generals approved the plan, Choi and the leaders of the Dan Xa, the Hoa Hao political arm, traveled throughout the area, meeting with village chiefs, elders, soldiers, and farmers. At first there had been little reaction from the people. In Vietnam the only thing cheaper than bullets were words. But in the last few weeks I had seen hesitant optimism, a cautious smile, an expression of hope in the faces of the Hoa Hao. Maybe these words would work.

During the past month eighteen Viet Cong, three of them Hoa Hao, had turned themselves in to us. Their reasons could be boiled down to these: They had heard of the prosperity of the company, the fighting was dying down in this area, and we treated prisoners well.

Fifty thousand more combat American troops had arrived in Vietnam. We understood they were being deployed in II and III Corps, to protect Saigon and to stop the Cong from cutting the country in half at Pleiku, Kontum, and Qui Nhon. Things were definitely getting rougher. During Tet—we didn't hear about it for three weeks—the Cong blew up the Americana Hotel in downtown Saigon. It had been one of the special hotels reserved for American officers. Twenty-five Americans and Vietnamese had been killed in the explosion.

U.S. Air Force raids over North Vietnam were becoming a daily affair. I still didn't understand that. I supposed that if you dropped enough bombs, you could kill all the guerrillas. I didn't trust the jets for any accuracy. They were too damned fast. Over Armed Forces radio we had heard last night that one of our jets had accidentally dropped a five-hundred-pound bomb on an American patrol, killing seven GIs.

I was rereading the operations section of my Ritter booklet when Phu walked in.

Two hours later I finished the general rundown of how the X-ray unit worked and was explaining how to read negatives. It would take many more sessions for Phu to learn everything. Luc was translating the pamphlet into Vietnamese, and that would be a big help. Although this particular model was nearly foolproof—there were numerous fail-safe devices to prevent overexposure to patients or the operator—I didn't want to take any chances.

I placed the negatives of Cranston and Top side by side in front of the window and asked Phu to compare them. I watched the progress of his finger. It slid by the misty area on Top's lung, but only for a moment. He backtracked and looked from the left lung to the right lung. He glanced at me. I didn't change my expression.

"There is something wrong here," he said, pointing to the suspected lesion.

"What about the rest of the lung? Never assume the first thing you find is all that there is. What if there are more of these things? Make sure you aren't overlooking anything."

He went over both negatives, inch by inch. "I think that is all."

"Very good, Phu. This irregular dull gray-white area means there is something wrong. This tissue is not healthy. It shouldn't look this way. Something is not letting the light go through, and it is showing up as a cloudy area. It could be many things, and unless you are absolutely certain, and I mean absolutely, send the patient and his negative to the hospital in Can Tho. It could be a piece of shrapnel or a bullet, although they would probably be darker and more defined. It could be an old tuberculosis scar, but that should be whiter. It could be a new, active lesion. It could be cancer. In this case, it is Sergeant O'Hara's lung, so first you would go over his medical history. Find out if he ever had tuberculosis or any—"

"No. Not yet, anyway," said Top behind me.

I turned around. Top was grinning at me.

"That's all for today, Phu. Thank you. See you at sick call."

Phu looked from me to Top and back and left in a hurry. Phu spoke little English, but tones are universal.

Top sat down on the operating table.

I had to say something. "I was going to tell you after lunch, Top. Now don't get worried. It could be a lot of stuff."

"You didn't overdevelop that first negative, did you?"

"No," I said, going to my desk and digging out Top's medical records. "Did you ever have TB as a child? This could be a scar."

"No. And I've never been shot in the chest either. About everywhere else though."

"Have you lost any weight lately?"

"Not that I know of. And I haven't had any trouble sleeping, beyond the usual in Vietnam. And no night sweats. I've had this cough for a good five, ten years. Smoker's cough."

"Okay, so you know the signs of TB. Top, you've got to go to a real doctor and get him to check this out."

"Sure, I'll hop on the next bus south."

"We could claim some sort of emergency, maybe a VC attack or something, and get a helicopter up here."

Top hopped off the table. "We all gotta go someday. If you can't tell smallpox from chicken pox, how do I know you can read those things?"

"If this is TB or cancer, it's early. We all had X-rays last year before we came over and nothing showed up. So whatever it is is new. And, shit, you might be right. It could be something I'm doing wrong with the machine. It might not be anything."

"Warren"—Top said "Warren" only when he was serious— "you did your duty. You told me. We're all going out in two or three weeks anyway. I ain't going to leave another goddamn team out here in the boonies. Either what I got is serious . . . or . . . it isn't. Don't say anything to the rest of the team. Let's eat." He walked out.

Stubborn, stupid man, I thought, slamming his file back in the drawer.

If anything, Top told more jokes and laughed harder than

usual at lunch. I wasn't terribly hungry. Santee, who now ate with his own engraved ivory chopsticks, was excited over his latest idea: making colored mosquito netting with pockets on the inside. He thought that dyeing the white nets the Hoa Hao colors would increase sales, and he could use the Cao Dai colors to dye netting for sale to them. The pockets, he said, would be handy for cigarettes or bibles or whatever.

"I like the pockets idea," said Cranston, who was making one of his rare appearances with us today, "but the color thing is completely unnecessary. Who needs colors? That's a luxury. Why not make something people can use?"

Cranston seemed happier every day. He thought Lao was pregnant, and he was already beaming like a new father. Not content with being a soldier, rice and grass farmer, and potential father, he had borrowed the Wish Book and had ordered a deluxe beekeeper's outfit, which included enough bees and queens for two hives, the hives, combs, gloves, hat, spray gun, and a book on "How to Raise Bees."

"You're right, Lance. I was getting carried away," said Santee, deftly picking up a heaping tablespoonful of rice on his sticks.

Wheaty said, to no one in particular, "Have you all noticed how little crime there is in Vietnam? I keep wanting to test out some new techniques of crime detection and nothing ever happens around here."

Cranston said, "Crime? People are getting shot, kidnaped, bombed, and grenaded daily."

"No," said Teewee, "I mean real crime. Mugging, stealing, and assault. That sort of crime."

Top spoke wearily. "Lieutenant, there is a war going on here. People don't have time for crime. Besides, if anyone should be arrested, I know an officer who tried to assault himself. Shot himself right in the hand. Hard as it is to believe, it's true."

234

That night on guard duty, I decided to talk with Hood about Top. If anyone could get through to him, Hood could. I told him about the X-rays.

Hood said, "Have you ever known Top to do anything anyone told him to do if he didn't want to do it?"

"But this is different," I protested.

"Let me tell you something about O'Hara. You know that bad back of his? Has he ever told you about it?"

"No. The first I knew was the day at Tet when a vertebra slipped out."

"Is there anything in his medical records about his back?"

"No. Only what I just entered."

"He first hurt his back not long after he joined Special Forces. His chute tangled in a pine tree on a night jump and he hit the ground upside down. He conned the medic out of some codeine with a story about migraine headaches and finished the exercise. Later the Army doctor said he had slipped a disk and that he wouldn't be able to do any more jumping. That meant leaving Special Forces. Somehow that report disappeared from Top's records. And he began going to a private physician in Fayetteville, paying the bills himself, so the Army wouldn't find out. I don't know how he makes jumps."

Hood looked at his watch. "Time to make the rounds."

Outside the main gate the new tin roof on Hoa Hao Unlimited Ltd. glistened as if it were wet. Moonlight dripping off. The last rain had been two months ago. There were only a few feet of water left in the fields, and they were disappearing fast. Soon we would have to go. Emotionally, I wanted to stay. To keep on doing what I had been doing, with the same people, in the same time. But that was all changing. Realistically, we were no longer needed. I couldn't go back to the past, and the future here would not be the same. Not now. Perhaps after medical school, as a doctor, I could come back to these brave people.

235

"How are your classes going?" I asked Hood. He was teaching geography and history at the school downtown for an hour each day. Choi had bought a blackboard—the first in the district—books, and maps for the school. Choi was also starting work on a separate schoolhouse near the pool hall.

"Pretty fair. It can be frustrating, though. I have the feeling at times they aren't understanding anything I say. If you've never seen the ocean or even a picture of it, how can you really imagine it?"

"You mean like the old joke about the elderly woman who saw the ocean for the first time and said, 'I thought it would be bigger than that'?"

Hood chuckled.

"Still, it must be flattering to get so many new kids and adults coming in," I said. Santee said Hood's classes were always the biggest.

"In a way. I figure a lot come in because I'm a mixed. You've seen them pulling the hair on my arms and rubbing my skin."

God, if it isn't Top, it's Hood getting the crazies. "They pull the hair on my arms, too. It's simply because they don't have much hair."

"No. They know. People always know that sort of thing. You can't run away from it. The Army's really the best place for me. In spite of what you hear, a black man can get promoted in the Army. It ain't a bad life."

22

GRANNY's mains'l popped as a gust of wind from the southwest suddenly filled the canvas. Shielding my eyes from the sun, I squinted at that quilt of a sail and marveled that it held together. A patchwork of mending stitched together by a half dozen owners and captains during fifty years. Did she care that she now hauled Chinese mercenaries instead of oysters?

Teewee, myself, and the Nungs were taking a two-day patrol to Se Toi, north of Giap Phang and the only place in our area still harassed by the Viet Cong. The area was sparsely populated and remote. The few canals there had silted nearly full, and the only way in or out was miles of hard trucking through thick grasslands and forests.

I was laying up sorry under the boom, trying to catch some sleep before we arrived at Beo Con, our jumping-off point. Sandalwood incense drifted back from the Nungs' medicine man. The strong perfumes were no longer strange and foreign to me. Like Tiger Balm, they were part of this life. At home my father said grace before meals. And while God and I did not believe in one another, the blessing was, nevertheless, a proper and familiar part of our mealtimes. Now, as I smeared Tiger Balm under my nose to keep the evil spirits from entering, it was the same emotional process: a touch of the routine, a mental crossing of my fingers, a token to the god of luck. If life was absurd, as the Aristocrat believed, then Tiger Balm was equally absurd. Or equally meaningful.

"*Bac si?*" a voice interrupted.

"Yes, *an?*" I said. It was a Nung gunner who spoke some Vietnamese.

He complained about a stomach ache. It wasn't anything serious, most likely patrol jitters. I asked, "Have you ever had any children before?"

He stared at me a moment and said, "I don't understand."

"Have you ever been pregnant before?"

His eyes crinkled as he caught the joke. He broke into wild laughter, touched my arm, and repeated, "Pregnant before?" He raced off to a group of Nungs at the bow. With much elaboration and animation, he told the story to them. The Nungs laughed loudly. Several poked the man in the stomach, while others waved at me.

Shortly, the gentle rocking of the boat stole my consciousness. I dozed off. I was awakened two hours later when we arrived at Beo Con. From here we would go east-northeast to Se Toi and spend the night there. Tomorrow we would swing up to the border and return to Phu Duc to meet *Granny* tomorrow night. If all went well. *Granny* would spend the two days offering the wares of Hoa Hao Unlimited Ltd. to the villages around Phu Duc.

We ate a quick lunch in Beo Con and left. A dozen children trailed us for several hundred yards until their parents called them back. The land was untilled and, judging from the size of the trees and bushes, had lain fallow for ten or fifteen years. That could be explained by the fact that this area lay between the Hoa Hao and Cao Dai territories. Before they formed a loose alliance against the Viet Cong, the two religious sects had often been at war with each other.

The Cao Dai had about two million followers, who lived from here northeast to the Central Highlands and southwest to near Saigon. The proper name of the sect was Dai Dao Tam Ky Pho Do, or Third Amnesty of God. According to Cao Dai doctrine, God had already proclaimed two "amnesties": the first in the West through Moses and Jesus and the second in the Orient through Buddha and Lao-tzu. Thus, Cao Daism was a synthesis of Christianity, Buddhism, Taoism, Confucianism, and spirit worship. The religion began in 1919 when the Cao Dai (the supreme being) appeared before Ngo Van Chieu in a séance on Phu Quoc Island, off the southern coast of Vietnam. The island was now a giant POW camp, or, I should say, a captured enemy camp. Chieu quit his job as the island's administrator for the French and took his vision to the countryside.

Cao Daism spread rapidly during the 1930s under the leadership of Le Van Trung, a one-time colonial official. He laid the broad doctrinal foundations and established a priestly hierarchy modeled along the Roman Catholic lines. Except that he added female cardinals to the structure.

Once on a trip to Tay Ninh I saw a Cao Dai cathedral. The church towers were European in inspiration; the open sweep of the floor suggested a mosque, and the wall decorations of plaster cobras and dragons were similar to a Buddhist pagoda. Statues of Confucius, Jesus, Buddha, Lao-tzu, Brahma, Siva, and Vishnu were spaced around the walls. Dominating the huge nave was a single staring eye, "the eye of God," the supreme symbol of the Cao Dai religion.

Three of the major "spiritual fathers"—we would call them saints—of the sect were Sun Yat-sen, Trang Thinh, who was a Vietnamese diviner, and Victor Hugo, the French writer and poet. Like the Hoa Hao, the Cao Dai had raised and supported their own army until Diem double-crossed them in the late 1950s.

When you added up all the minorities in Vietnam, they almost became the majority. There were a million Hoa Hao, two million Cao Dai, a million refugees from North Vietnam, more than a million Chinese, between one and two million Montagnards, a half million Cambodians, and assorted smaller groups. Making a strong national cohesiveness even harder was the fact that these sects and nationalities still clung tenaciously to their separate culture and their own political view of the world.

Two hours out of Beo Con, the *tranh* grass appeared. The Nungs called it knife grass and the Vietnamese called it elephant grass. A dull green grass that grew ten to twelve feet tall, the blades were four inches wide at the base, tapering to a thin point. The first time I had grabbed a blade to push it back, I'd received a quick, deep cut across my palm. The edges of the blades were like razors. Now I knew better and used my carbine to push the grass aside. As if that weren't enough, it emitted a fine dustlike pollen that clogged your throat and lungs and crawled around on your skin like ants. We tied handkerchiefs across our noses and mouths. Because of the thickness of the grass, we moved in a long column, strung out like a picket fence for a quarter of a mile.

The first shot rang out at 1345 hours, and we were flat on the ground before the echo died away. It wasn't close—probably four or five hundred yards away. I crawled back to Wheaty and the Nung commander, Charles. His name was actually Hiung Tse Fsu, but he had adopted the name of Charles after Charles de Gaulle many years ago. After ten minutes of silence we decided the shot had been a warning or someone hunting supper. Earlier our point man had reported tiger tracks on the trail.

I was surprised at how few wild animals I had seen in Vietnam. Our country training had indicated that the jungles abounded with monkeys, wild oxen, deer, tigers, bears, leopards, elephants, panthers, and a host of snakes. Except for a few pet monkeys, a couple of water snakes, one small python, a glimpse of a racing deer, and the wild pig Cranston shot, I had seen only domesticated animals. The villagers confirmed that the wild life had been a major casualty of two decades of war.

We moved on. By the time the fifth shot came at 1700 hours, we didn't even break stride. They had been fired every forty-five minutes, and all came from points northwest of us and slightly to our rear. Obviously, they were signal shots, giving our location and speed to sentries on ahead. The method was old, cheap, and as effective as the quarter-million-dollar helicopters our army used. Even moonshiners back in the hills of North Carolina used the system to warn of approaching revenue agents. It would have been useless for us to chase them. And there was the possibility they were trying to lure us into a trap.

We reached Se Toi shortly before dark. It had been a frustrating day; we knew the Cong knew our exact location at all times, the number of troops we had, and how many guns we carried. A proper guerrilla war.

Se Toi guarded the intersection of two canals, both overgrown and silted. I wasn't really sure what it guarded the canals against. A hand-dug moat surrounded the outpost and gave it the appearance of being on a tiny island.

We crossed a plank bridge and were met by the camp commander, a middle-aged, tired lieutenant named Ha Si Phuc. He led us to his house, where preparations for supper were under way. We sat on the porch. Next to me was an ancient mantis shotgun. It was a steel tube, which looked to have been the top cross frame bar from a bicycle, fixed on a bipod. The tube was filled with gunpowder and glass and metal bits. Phuc said the gun had been here since the war with the French and was still used.

Soon Phuc's wife rolled out a large clay pot of what I suspected was rice wine. Vietnamese rice wine was delicious. The wine was light, with a round taste and a hint of American scuppernong. It was made by placing dried rice kernels in the bottom of a two- or three-foot urn. The fermenting agent, made of powdered roots and rice flour and resembling small, porous white cones, was added next. Then the pot was filled about one-third with water and covered. The wine would sit undisturbed for four or five days. The longer the better. When the wine had fermented, water was added to fill the pot. Although the potency varied from batch to batch, it was always strong enough to fill one's mind with rambling discourse, lecherous thoughts, and a sharply modified rational process. It wiped you out.

Phuc's wife poured water from a hundred-twenty-millimeter artillery shell into the urn. Lotus petals floated to the top, along with the rice kernels. The Hoa Hao often added lotus, chrysanthemums, and other flowers for flavoring. Sometimes they also added rats.

Phuc pushed a bamboo reed down through the floating kernels and flowers. He spit out the first mouthful as an offering to the spirits and to clear the reed and held it out for Teewee. Wheaty thanked him, took a long pull, and, following tradition, offered the reed back to Phuc. He declined, as was the custom. "Give it to the doctor who walks on water."

"Cam on, ong," I said, taking a drink. "Ah, *tot lam!"* Delicious, I said, and it was.

Phuc asked us about the patrol, and Teewee told him of the VC signal shots. Phuc said the Cong had been coming into the few nearby villages at night, taking rice, and forcing the people to listen to propaganda speeches. He thought they came from the direction of the Mekong. They might even be

Cao Dai, he theorized. That would explain why they hadn't gotten the word yet on the ban on operations.

We chatted about the VC and sipped rice wine for another hour. At one point Phuc asked, "How is Hoa Hao Unlimited Ltd. doing?"

"Pretty good," I said.

Phuc smiled broadly. He bent over toward me, and for a moment I thought he was bowing. He reached behind his head and held up the back of the shirt collar. The label read, "Ba Linh Hon." *Granny's Ghost*. He leaned back and rubbed the shirt between calloused fingers. "Good material. I like it. How is the stock doing?"

"It's nearly sold out," I said, scarcely believing that word of the stock offering had reached this far. "The price should be moving up soon."

He lowered his voice. "I have twenty shares of Hoa Hao Unlimited Ltd." From inside his shirt, he pulled out several stock certificates. "This is the first time I have ever owned anything like this. The shirts and the pants are made of good material and cheap. I bought them and perhaps everyone will buy them." His words were softly spoken but unmistakably proud.

A few minutes later his wife brought a small, live pig to the porch and Phuc placed joss sticks in the cracks on the bamboo floor. The pig, which had its feet tied together, probably weighed twenty-five pounds. We were about to see a sacrifice. In the mountains and in some parts of the delta, animal sacrifices to honor one's ancestors or to please other spirits were still common. Tradition demanded Teewee and I stay.

It wasn't pleasant. After lighting the incense and setting aside wine for ancestors, Phuc and the elders began sticking long, ice-pick-shaped knives into the pig. Its screams were awful, high-pitched wails filled with terror and death. The men seemed to be taking no particular delight or joy in it. The stabbings were quick and sure. Their attitude suggested that

243

this rite must be done and must be done correctly. I never did find out exactly what the occasion was. It could have been someone's death or a particular ritual for this village. After fifteen minutes that seemed like days, the pig shuddered and died. Its eyes were wide and staring. Phuc carefully slid a thin knife into the pig's heart. When the blood rushed out, it was captured in a small bowl. Later it would be placed in special areas around the camp as offerings to the spirits. Sacrifices were not sanctioned by the Hoa Hao religion but, rather, were tolerated as part of the animism that permeated all Vietnamese religions.

Only fifteen minutes before, Phuc and I had been discussing stock prices.

"God, that's terrible," muttered Teewee.

The pig was taken away to be cooked.

We were exhausted, and after a supper of rice, nuts, and pig entrails, Teewee and I strung our hammocks between two poles beside Phuc's hut. I had just made myself comfortable when Wheaty whispered, "Warren, you asleep?"

"No."

"Top figures we can leave in two or three weeks. What do you think about going back?"

"I don't really want to go. But what I want can't be. I'm not the type to settle down as a civilian," I said.

"That's not what I meant. What do you think the Army'll say?"

"They'll ask if our shot record is up to date. What can they say? The Army abandoned us. They got too wrapped up in their own paper work and their own systems and their own image to care about what happens to us mere soldiers," I said.

Wheaty said, "Hmmmm."

"In a way, it's the same situation that Choi and the Hoa Hao are in. They've been abandoned by the South Vietnamese government and the GVN army. For all practical purposes. Carry it a step further and say the people of South

Vietnam have been abandoned. The only time anyone cares about them is to move them to a strategic hamlet, to draft soldiers, or, in the case of the VC, to take their rice and bore them to death with political speeches."

Wheaty said, "A year ago, *bac si,* I would have argued with you. I've forgotten what the arguments were."

"Just as we were left out here with the lions to fend for ourselves, so have the Vietnamese been left stranded." I suddenly wondered why the phrase "out with the lions" was popular. There were no lions in South Vietnam. I went on, "You remember a week or so ago when the radio reported the government in Saigon was bragging about the fact that over a million leaflets had been dropped by airplanes to the South Vietnamese in the delta?"

"Yes. Hood had one. It was something about supporting the government and to be patriotic."

I said, "It strikes me as one hell of a note when the government has to communicate with its people by means of leaflets dropped from planes."

"I never thought about it that way."

I slapped at a mosquito that had found its way inside my netting.

A few minutes later Teewee said, "Still, I wonder what they'll say about us being gone so long. I could really get in trouble."

"We tried to get out. And once the floods started there was no way," I said, yawning.

Teewee fell asleep mumbling something about being a private detective in Norfolk, Virginia. God, of all places to be a private eye.

A few minutes later the sounds of a Nung singing softly and playing a gentle guitar drifted over. One of the young Chinese had been carrying a guitar on his rucksack. The music bespoke an awful loneliness and aloneness. It took me back to Methodist church camp as a teenager. Long evenings around a campfire. Soft air and dark woods. We spoke our sins into pine cones and threw them into the fire. Even then there had been the twisting hollow in my stomach. That awful aloneness. There are no Buddhas.

We left Se Toi the next morning at 0800 hours. Phuc wished us good luck and asked me to autograph a picture of me skiing. "Take care of our company," he said, patting the stock certificates bulging in his shirt.

We crossed the east-west canal and headed north to the Cambodian border. Today we might run into trouble. It would be obvious to the Cong we were heading back to Phu Duc. They had let us go yesterday to see where we were going.

The day was as hot as yesterday, if not hotter. More elephant grass and dust. The VC sentries didn't pick us up until 1100 hours. We had reached the border—the only demarcation was a wide canal—and turned west, when the first shot sounded. It was in Cambodia. Not only were the shots good military strategy; their psychological effect was all too clear. It was subtle torture: We waited for the next one. Hoping it wouldn't come, or, if it did, that it would be only a single shot. All the while knowing that eyes watched our every move.

We stopped at 1230 hours for lunch. The Chinese were tense. If the VC were going to attack, it would be soon. Before we got within mortar range of Phu Duc.

By 1315 hours we were moving again, along an old trail on the canal bank. The elephant grass was thinning and the afternoon wore on, hot and dusty and strained. We all expected the attack and perhaps for that reason no one, except Teewee, was hit when it came. My first clue came when handfuls of dirt began exploding in a moving row down the bank. Their guns were low. A fraction of a second later the noise of the shots reached us and we were already spilling down the bank to our left. It sounded like a full company. Rocks, dirt, and twigs sprayed over my head, and I detected

246

one machine gun sweeping back and forth along the bank over us.

To our backs was flat, open land. No trees, no bushes, nothing to hide in. The only good thing was the three-foot bank we were lying against. The Nungs were well tucked in, checking their guns and waiting for the first volley to die down.

In a minute it did. Carefully, I poked one eye over the bank. Across the canal was a large empty rice field. The firing came from a large grove of trees beyond the field, one hundred yards away. I could see only an occasional flash from the shadows.

The Nungs shouted commands to each other and assorted curses at the VC. The Chinese were quite vocal in combat. Frenchy was hollering, "Death to the Japanese!" Beside me, a machine gunner was jamming his tripod in the dirt. The man on the other side of him was quickly unwrapping ammo links from his neck, preparing to feed them in.

Suddenly I realized a message was being passed down the line. A Nung a dozen men away shouted, "The lieutenant wants you, *bac si*. He's hit."

I looped my medical bag over my neck, rose to a crouch, and ran. Our guns were beginning to return the fire, and the noise was deafening. Halfway to the front, something snatched at my back and I almost lost my balance. Probably a branch or a bullet. Finally I reached Teewee. He lay on his side, one hand behind his back and his face filled with pain.

"Where?" I asked.

"In the ass, of all places," he said, turning over on his stomach. His pants were red with blood.

"Unbuckle your pants. What happened?"

"That first volley. One caught my stock."

The stock of his gun was shattered. A dumdum round had smashed it and hurled dozens of wood splinters into Wheaty's ass. I hoped the bullet had been deflected or had spent itself.

I slid his shorts down. His right cheek was freckled with

punctures. Blood oozed out steadily, and I couldn't tell if there was a bullet wound. I didn't think so. As I unzipped my medical bag, I noticed a bullet hole, neat and clean and dead center on the canvas bag. Maybe tomorrow, Cong. I cleaned Wheaty's fanny with cotton and peroxide. There were wood splinters every half inch, but none serious.

I said, "Take this codeine. There's nothing I can do here. You've got a million splinters in your ass, and each will have to be pulled out. Don't sit down for a while."

"It really hurts," said Teewee, while we both pulled his pants up carefully.

"You may get your medal yet."

"That's right. Wounded in action. I hadn't thought about that," he said happily.

That would make him feel better. I sprawled on the bank and sighted my gun on a flash in the woods. The firing was still heavy. Charles, the Nung commander, lay a few feet to my right and was obviously having difficulties. He had tried to send a squad up the canal to see if there was a way we could cross. Their movement caused a hail of fire from the grove. If we tried to back off to the rear, we would be sitting ducks. There was no cover beyond this bank for a good three hundred yards. We were trapped.

"What's happening, Charles?" I shouted over the noise.

"*Beaucoup* problems. We may have to wait until dark, unless we can find some way across the canal," he said, never taking his eyes off the trees.

"What if they decide to come over?" I asked more out of curiosity than a fear that they actually would.

"We will fight."

"To the last man?"

He looked around fiercely. "We will fight to the last man because our contract runs until May eleventh."

That's one way of looking at it, I thought. Actually, we

248

Americans could say the same thing. Yes, we will fight bravely and with honor until our ETS, and then we will go home.

A couple bullets cracked overhead, reminding me I wasn't home yet. Up and down the line the Nungs were shouting obscenities to the Cong. Some reviled them in Vietnamese, some in Chinese. Their favorite was *"Do ma,"* which meant, "You fuck your mother." I guess most people think mother-fucking is gauche.

A message was suddenly being relayed from Nung to Nung. "Stop shooting."

I realized that gunfire from the Cong had also stopped. A Nung ran up to Charles and spoke with him briefly. Charles nodded, then stood up, leaving his gun on the ground. Wheaty and I both lunged for him, but he irritably waved his hands at us. The man's crazy, I thought.

He cupped his hands around his mouth and shouted a half dozen sentences in Chinese. A moment later one of the Cong answered, also in Chinese. Back and forth Charles and the man talked. The other Nungs were grinning and whispering to each other. Had the whole world gone mad?

A few minutes later Charles turned and spoke to the Nungs nearest us. Then he casually picked up his rifle and said, "We go now." And began walking.

"Wait a minute," said Teewee. "What the hell is going on?"

"It's all right, *thieu uy,* we do not fight any more today."

"What do you mean, 'We don't fight any more today'? What about the Cong?"

Charles said, "That was not Viet Cong. That was Nung. I know them. They know us. They said they were hired by the Viet Cong as soldiers, but since we were Nungs also, there was no need for us to fight. I agreed. We are all Nungs. We are all the same family."

"I'll be damned," I said, helping Wheaty to his feet. "Nungs fighting Nungs."

"We're lucky it wasn't Viet Cong," said Wheaty.

Across the canal in the woods, men were standing and waving at us. There were about seventy-five of them. Several conversations were being carried on across the border. Probably family gossip. How's old Aunt Ling doing? Still alive and mean as ever? Have you seen Cousin Lio lately?

I waved at the enemy and we began walking to Phu Duc. In front of me Teewee limped along, bloodstains on his ass.

23

"DO WE all understand what we are to do?" asked Major Choi.

Top asked, "What if the whole thing blows up in our face?"

Choi's jaw muscles flickered and he said, "My guards have their orders. There will be an unfortunate accident involving two generals. Are there any other questions? Good. That is it. We all will speak carefully today."

Choi stood up. The meeting was over and we walked back to our team room. It was 1305 hours, Thursday, April 29, two weeks after Teewee and I and the Nungs had run into the Viet Cong's Nungs. And I wished I were on patrol today. I'd take my chances there.

The chickens were coming home to roost. Only it was generals, and the roost was our heads. Within the hour Major General Truong Phat, chief intelligence officer for eastern Cambodia and the western half of the Vietnamese delta for the Army of the Democratic Republic of Vietnam (North Vietnam), and Brigadier General Richard "Feisty" Arlington, MAAG OIC for intelligence, IV Corps, would arrive here.

Both of them. At the same time. There had been no way around it. By a bizarre coincidence both generals had notified us they wanted to inspect our camp on April 29 and discuss our "secret operations."

Arlington had been scheduled to arrive at 1100 hours, and if he had, we could have shuffled him in and out before Phat arrived. But obviously he was going to be late. Phat was to arrive by boat at 1400 hours. Our soldiers up the river had orders not to interfere.

"I knew that damned Rand egghead crap would get us in deep shit," grumbled Top.

"You don't say no to a general," said Hood.

Top said, "Let's just remember what we talked about last night. There ain't going to be any killing of any American general."

We had agreed that, if our razzle-dazzle failed, we would surround Arlington and attempt to get him on his helicopter. After that? We didn't need to discuss it.

Wheaty said, "Twenty-three hours from now it'll all be over and part of us will be halfway to Can Tho."

"Uh, huh," said Santee. "Cutting out when the going gets rough. Leaving the shit here for me and Cranston to pick up."

"Shit, hell, Hogjaw. You're probably worth more right now than ninety-five per cent of the niggers back home," said Top.

The decision had finally been made, independent of the generals' visit here. We were going home. Home? Or away? I wasn't sure which was the correct word. Tomorrow Top, Teewee, Hood, and I would attempt a full-day sail to Can Tho on *Granny's Ghost*. Once we got there, we could get to Saigon. Word had come a week ago that our aluminum rolling machine was sitting in Can Tho and Choi was anxious to pick it up. At the same time the Viet Cong blockade of the Bassac had been broken and boats were passing freely now. The dry season, U.S. Navy Seabees, and twenty thousand more GIs in Saigon were relieving the pressure on the Bassac. We would be

252

taking four extra machine guns, three mortars, and a platoon of Nungs.

Santee and Cranston were staying here. We had agreed to report both had been lost on a patrol. Suspected captured. In a way, they had been. A couple nights ago on guard duty with Santee I'd asked him if he'd have stayed here if we'd been able to return to the States last September.

"I've thought about it, and I would have gone back with you all. Then I was just a jive soldier looking for a fast dollar. I used to think that money was what you could con somebody out of. That's not it. A dollar or a piaster is a symbol, a symbol representing your work. You are trading something of yours for a piece of paper, and you trade that for the results of someone else's labor. That piaster represents my skill, my work, my own talent."

Santee stopped, then continued, "There's more, too. Our company and our Vietnamese are working and trading their skills for a better way of life. It's the first time in my life I ever felt I was doing something more than carrying things." His voice changed to a point between resentment and anger. "And there ain't no way that will happen back in Augusta, Georgia, for me."

A quiet minute later he added, so softly I scarcely heard him, "I sleep good at night here. They accept me here. My people."

Today would be the big test for Santee and for the Rand plan. So far, the plan had worked beautifully. Operations by GVN, MAAG, and the Viet Cong were suddenly unheard of in our territory. After the absurd shoot-out with the Nungs, comparative peace was spreading like the floods of last fall. A few sniping incidents were reported around the fringes, but nothing of consequence. On medical patrols I had sensed a new feeling of hope and trust.

That was here. Elsewhere in Vietnam the reports only got worse. According to the radio, late last month the Cong had blown up the American Embassy in Saigon, killing fifteen officers. A week later a joint U.S.–GVN operation in Vinh-thuan wiped out a company of VC and moved the two thousand local inhabitants to a strategic hamlet about thirty miles away.

A distant rumble sharpened to a tight drum roll, and we knew the general was coming.

"Okay," said Top, "This is it. Hogjaw, Warren, let's go. The rest of you wait here on word from Phat. Fuck 'em if they can't take a joke."

I adjusted my black beret, made, of course, by Hoa Hao Unlimited Ltd. and checked my forty-five. We all wore pistols today. Santee, like the rest of us, wore no rank.

The drab-green chopper was dropping low over the dispensary as we joined Choi and two of his officers beside the machine-gun tower. A last-minute dab of Tiger Balm and I was ready. The helicopter settled roughly to the ground, and we turned away momentarily to let the dust blow by. Even while the rotors still turned, Brigadier General "Feisty" Arlington jumped out. He was tall, lean, and tough-looking. A jutting jaw, a first cousin of Santee's, underscored a drooping mouth. Sharp, beady eyes were set deep in a tanned face. On the form for becoming a general there must be a question, "Does the candidate look like a general?"

The pilot stayed in the helicopter.

We saluted, and it felt rusty. After making the introductions (Santee was introduced as "Mr. Leroy Santee of the Agency"), Choi said, "Come, General, let us show you around the camp."

"Yes, Major, that's what I'm here for," said Arlington in a voice that sounded much like Wheaty's when he was trying to sound like an officer. Except the general's didn't crack every few words.

"But first I'm afraid I need to take a little whiz."

"A what?" asked Choi.

"A whiz. You know, ah, uh," the general stuttered, then put his hands together in front of him, as if holding his root.

"Ah! Yes. A piss," said Choi brightly.

We led the general to the catfish latrine, while he commented on our defense system. "Looks good. Looks good. Nice fields of fire. Good terrain clearing." On our soldiers: "Serious-looking men. Healthy." And on our latrine: "Primitive, eh? Good for the fish, I suppose."

He hesitated only a moment before striding across the shaky narrow planks. While he waited, I remembered the time the Aristocrat and Jasmine were here and how the strikers had cheered her shit. Nobody cheered the general.

He finished and we began a tour of the wall.

"I've been very anxious to meet you, Mr. Santee. Your intelligence reports are always detailed and accurate. I want to hear more about your plan."

"Thank you, General," said Santee in a fine, slightly lofty voice. "But the credit for our idea must go to Washington and to the Agency." Santee glanced around, then said in a whisper, "This is for your ears only, General. Perhaps a dozen men in the world know of this plan. And one of them is in the highest place possible. Later on today Major Choi will give an over-all viewpoint of our entire operation here. Forgive me if I cannot answer all your questions. You must understand the international implications of it. By the way, in camp here I am incognito as a sergeant, so at the briefing and elsewhere consider me an ordinary enlisted man. I find it easier and freer to work in disguise."

Arlington snorted, "Certainly. Cloak-and-dagger business. You can depend on me, sir." He switched topics. "Tell me, Choi, have the Viet Cong ever hit your camp?"

"No, General. We have had a few probes now and then. But, sir, we always call the Viet Cong the 'enemy.' We feel that reinforces the spirit of the soldiers and is a more accurate word."

"Right. Good thinking, Choi."

We continued around the wall, with Santee filling in the details of our "plan to deceive the enemy." We had code-named the operation "Parthian Shot." Hood, who suggested the name, said he ran across the term while taking history courses at the Army's War College in Pennsylvania. Parthian soldiers would ride their horses at the enemy, stop, fire arrows, whirl their steeds as if retreating, then turn their horses back around and repeat the procedure. Hood said he was intrigued because it was such a simple development in warfare, from today's standpoint, to have such serious effects. Parthia was the only Mediterranean country to turn back the great Roman Empire.

At one point in our walk Arlington asked why we were all dressed in black. Santee answered, "We dress this way to look more like the enemy at all times."

"Dressing to look like the VC? That's an interesting concept."

"The 'enemy,' " Choi gently corrected.

"Yes, the enemy. I'm not sure about that. Soldiers need uniforms to boost their morale and increase fighting effectiveness. Somehow, fighting in black pajamas is not the proper way to run a war."

We said nothing, but I was thinking that a ragtag army dressed in black pajamas fought the French to a standstill.

"Anyway," Arlington continued, "I had suspected something was going on in this area. We had a top secret report, oh, seven months ago, about a half dozen Americans disguised as Viet Cong operating in this area. I tell you, I suspected the Agency then. Plus, this area is continuing to make improvements toward Level Five on our pacification maps. More and more secure."

One of Choi's lieutenant's ran up and whispered to him. Choi nodded and dismissed him.

"Please continue your inspection, General. I have received

word that our chief double agent has arrived and I must speak with him. You will meet him soon at the briefing." Choi saluted and left.

"Ah, hah!" said Arlington, cocking one eyebrow. "What's this about a double agent?"

As rehearsed, Top said, "We are in the process of infiltrating the enemy with an agent, carrying the rank of a lieutenant general."

"Good God, man! That's a breakthrough," said Arlington, never breaking his precise three-foot stride. "How did you accomplish that?"

"A little hocus-pocus involving the kidnaping of the real general who was newly assigned to this region and who was not known. We got him and substituted our own man. I should warn you, sir, that he plays his role quite seriously. If he says some unusual things, go right along with him. He is on his first visit to this camp and will also attend the briefing."

At that very moment Choi would be telling the Viet Cong general the same thing about Arlington. Each general would be told the other was a double agent. Not a great idea, but it was the best we could come up with. I wished we had a Rand projection on the success probability.

Santee glanced at his watch. Choi's twenty minutes were up. "Shall we go to the briefing now?" he asked.

"By all means. I am anxious to meet this VC 'general' of yours."

"Enemy," said Santee a trifle sharply.

"Enemy it is."

We walked to the team house and entered. Choi and a tall man with a crisp haircut turned around from the map they had been examining. The man seemed in his early forties and was perhaps an inch or two shorter than I. He had high, well-defined cheekbones and thick white teeth. Choi stepped quickly across the room, taking charge of introductions.

"General Arlington. General Phat."

The two made formal salutes to each other. Both said, at the same time, "I've been looking forward to meeting you, General." They both laughed—polite and serious laughs, as generals should laugh.

So Phat spoke English. That was bad. Arlington spoke no Vietnamese, and we had hoped Phat spoke no English. That would have made things much easier.

But right now they were getting worse.

Arlington was openly inspecting Phat's uniform. Phat wore the North Vietnamese pale-green fatigues with a plateful of tossed salad on his chest. Well-creased pants were tucked into black combat boots. His headgear was the simple fatigue cap with two silver stars pinned to the peak. He wore an ammo belt with a pistol. The butt identified it as a Walther, P-38.

At the same time, Phat was examining Arlington's heavily starched and pressed fatigues. The American general was dressed simply, with no decorations other than cloth Airborne wings sewn above the pocket. His lone star was also cloth, a faded green slightly lighter than the color of his cap. He was probably one of those officers that believed in dressing down to his men. His pants must have been bloused with garters—the roll was too round and even not to be. He, too, wore a pistol.

"Very impressive, General Arlington," said Phat.

"Thank you, General. And your uniform, also. Down to the last detail. Quite convincing," said Arlington.

"It should—" began Phat.

"Come, gentlemen, we can talk later," said Choi, showing them to their chairs. They sat down. On the left a brigadier general in the United States Army, and on the right a major general in the Army of North Vietnam. We and Choi's top three officers lined ourselves across the rear of the room. Sweat trickled down my back.

Choi appeared calm and collected. He would be; he hadn't survived the Japanese, the French, the Viet Minh, Ngo Dinh Diem, and twenty years of combat, political intrigue, and personal attack by panicking easily. He began, "Gentlemen, let us start by welcoming you to Camp Nan Phuc. First, I will outline the geography of our area and then I will discuss the population."

Choi turned to the map. "As you know, our region of responsibility . . ." He continued for fifteen minutes, describing the number of people, what they grew, how the fishing had been lately, and our work in dredging the canals. I decided it was all deliberately boring.

"And now we come to the military side of the picture. To be brief, approximately six months ago your intelligence arm began an experimental espionage and subversion plan for this area. The plan—named Parthian Shot—became operational three months ago, and so far it is exceeding expectations. A major part of the credit for the success of the plan should go to you." Choi's eye rested in the eighteen inches of space between the commanders.

The generals turned to each other and gave deprecating smiles of self-congratulation.

Choi flipped a clear, plastic overlay down on the map of our area. "Here we have a situations map as of a year ago." This was one of the tricky parts of the briefing. Choi and Santee had worked three hours on the maps and overlays to make them as confusing as possible. Some villages were marked in red, some in black, and others were crosshatched. The overlay looked like a Klee painting. Choi spoke rapidly, shifting his pointer from area to area in absolute disregard of his words or the truth. Then he flipped another overlay down.

"As you see, we are now in virtual control of the entire population of this area. Contact with the enemy is rare and we are not only defeating him on the battlefield of guns but on the battlefield of people. Defections from the enemy's ranks are up considerably," said Choi, moving to a chart on the wall. Labeled simply "defections," the chart showed, in truth, the number of (VC) soldiers who had turned themselves in each

259

month during the past year. The latest month, March, had the highest figure: thirty-one men defected.

"The reason for this great success is, of course, the plan from your intelligence branch. I cannot stress too strongly the importance of the total secrecy of this plan. Its success depends on this: We must allow the enemy to believe that we are cooperating fully with him. The enemy believes that he is winning us over to his side and that he is winning the war in this area. Since he believes he is winning, there is no need for combat operations and further destruction of our people. And, at the same time, we are undermining his strength in this area and winning the people over to our side."

Both generals nodded in agreement.

"The best evidence that the plan is working is the lack of enemy operations in our area," said the major. He pointed to another chart which showed a drastic drop in the number of contacts with the "enemy."

"In order to facilitate this plan, we have acquired certain military, ah, paraphernalia of the enemy, which you will notice around camp," said Choi, waving his arm in a half circle that took in the helicopter, our black pajamas, and the lack of any service identification on us.

Choi absent-mindedly had pulled the shrunken pig's teat from his pocket and was fondling it.

"We are exchanging intelligence information—cleverly and carefully written, of course—with the enemy. Thus, not only are we telling him what we want him to believe, but we are learning much about his intelligence and operations."

Arlington nodded slowly while stroking his chin. Phat sat with his arms crossed on his chest.

"All that I have outlined is what we call preliminary Phase I," said Choi. Generals loved phases. "We are about to embark on Phase II—the infiltration of the enemy with a high-ranking officer"—Choi gestured with his hand in the vague direction of the generals—"to further ensure the success of our plan."

The commanders turned to each other and smiled, each believing the other to be the object of that sentence.

"Phase III will be the total cessation of all enemy activities in our area, and Phase IV will be a return of power to our people, and Phase V is, naturally, peace. You may wonder what timetable we are working on. As you know, our enemy is devious, resourceful, and patient. It may take years. Like the enemy we must be even more devious, more resourceful, and more patient. That concludes the briefing. I will be glad to answer any questions. None? Good, let us—"

Phat interrupted, "What has been the reaction of the people to Parthian Shot?"

"Excellent," said Choi, probably referring to both the reaction of the people and the question. "All of our people are cooperating fully with us to drive the enemy out. The rice harvest this year was the best in the last ten years. People are no longer afraid to walk outside at night. We are preparing for the day war is forced from our land and we live in peace and for the brotherhood of man."

A little too elegant for my blood, but then generals preferred eloquence, even at the cost of clarity.

"If there are no further—" Choi started, but the rising of Arlington stopped him.

"Thank you, Major Choi. That was an excellent briefing. Before I head to Can Tho, I'd like to give a short briefing of my own. It never hurts for a general to stay in practice." He chuckled briefly and grinned at Phat, who grinned tolerantly back. Arlington walked to the front and turned around. Choi's eyes skimmed warily across us, and he stepped to the side.

The general placed both hands on the lectern. "Major Choi has given you an excellent briefing as far as the local situation. On the national level, we understand the number of American troops will be doubled within the next few months." This was going bad. We were all tense.

Arlington said, "Their role probably will be expanded offensive combat operations, particularly in I and II Corps." His eyes dropped to the lectern for a moment and caught on something there. He picked it up and I recognized Choi's pig teat. "As I was saying, ah—" Arlington held the object closer. His attention was taken by the leathery object in his hand. "Uh, this looks like a . . ." He turned to Choi.

"A pig's teat, General. A good-luck charm," said Choi, coughing to hide a blush.

"Yes. A pig's teat. Well, as I was saying the enemy is building up his forces in I and II Corps. We understand the bombing in North Vietnam will be stepped up considerably. At least that's what I heard—Johnson doesn't tell me everything." He smiled broadly at the little joke. The reference, however, sent Phat into gales of laughter. It released the tension. We all began laughing.

Arlington waited patiently until the hilarity subsided. "That's the big picture, Major Choi. We are doing an excellent job here, and I can assure you I will do everything in my role in Can Tho that I can to ensure the fulfillment of Parthian Shot. There must be peace for the Vietnamese people."

Only then did I realize my shirt was soaking wet.

As Arlington settled into his chair, Phat said to him, "That was very good."

"Thank you," said "Feisty."

Major Choi, visibly relieved, stepped back to the rostrum and retrieved his teat. "Thank you, General Arlington. And now let—"

This time he was interrupted by General Phat, who stood up and walked to the front.

"It is only fair that I give a briefing also, after the fine briefing by General Arlington. I want to speak briefly about other plans we have under way in other districts in the delta. We are intensifying our efforts of self-help medical and sanitation programs in the villages. We are also increasing emphasis on more involvement with village affairs, and we have even begun a pilot program in self-government. These are part of our over-all effort to win the hearts and minds of the peasants. On the military side, every day that goes by brings thousands of, ah, enemy troops into Vietnam. As noted by Arlington, we intend to step up the pace of the war and attempt to lure the enemy into confrontations where he may be convincingly defeated. Only if we win on the battlefield can we hold the upper hand at any negotiations. Peace for the people from foreign aggression. Major Choi, you have my full cooperation with our ingenious plan, Parthian Shot. Thank you." Phat bowed his head curtly and sat down.

"Thank you," said Choi. "The briefings were excellent." In a moment of relief and courage, he added, "I can see that you will have no trouble convincing the enemy of your genuineness."

The generals smiled at each other.

"For many years," said Choi, "our brave people have struggled against all odds. Time and time again, foreign invaders have tried to take over, not merely our physical possessions—our land and our rice—but the minds of our people. The spirits of our children. And time and time again we have survived. With the cooperation of such men as you, we will survive yet. I think it was an ancient Greek philosopher who said, 'In peacetime children bury their parents. In war parents bury their children.' Let us work for the success of our plan. Let these children live to bury their parents."

"Hear, hear," said Arlington.

"*Tot, tot*," said Phat.

"Fine. Come," said Choi. "Allow me to introduce my staff." He led the generals to us. We pulled to stiff attention. My shirt stuck clammily to my sides.

Choi gave each of our names, plus a brief description of our duties.

Phat was exuberant. "Yes. Yes. It is good to meet such brave and courageous men. Not everyone would do what you men are doing."

"That is so true," said Arlington. "I wish we had more men like you."

Suddenly Phat stopped, stepped back a pace, and said, "I didn't know we had any Negroes working for us."

He was looking at Santee, but Hood answered. "Believe me, General, the color of my skin makes no difference. My heart is with the people."

Phat stared at Hood. "No, no. Actually, I was speaking about . . ." He waved a hand at Santee.

Arlington, frowning, looked from Phat to Hood to Santee and back again.

Santee broke into a string of rapid-fire Vietnamese. I caught an occasional word: ". . . general . . . Southerners . . . Chinese . . . Bering Straits . . . the Cherokee Indians . . . interbreeding . . . true Orientals."

At the end of the explanation, Phat looked puzzled, as if he wanted to say something more. But then he shook his head, slowly and to himself. He simply said in Vietnamese, "You speak our language very well, comrade."

Meanwhile I noted that Arlington was steadily giving me the fish eye.

Finally he asked, "See here, don't I know you from somewhere?"

24

I TRIED to focus on the Hoa Hao flag at the far end of the room, but it kept blurring. Don't let me blow it all now, dear God. The faint odor of Tiger Balm drifted by my nose.

"Here in camp, sir," I said in a voice that sounded like someone else's.

"Take your beret off."

I did, knowing that my bald head would be covered with sweat.

"I knew it," Arlington said, snapping his fingers. "You're the one they call 'the doctor who walks on water.' Right?"

"Yes, yes! He is!" broke in Phat. "I've heard a great deal about you, Doctor." He shook my wet hand. *"Than thanh bac si dao bao!"*

"Cam on, trung tuong," I mumbled, feeling rivulets of sweat catch in my eyebrows. Recalling the several weeks I had accidentally studied a North Vietnamese dictionary, I added a sentence about it being a pleasure to meet the *trung tuong,* in

what I hoped was the right accent. It must have been. The general beamed.

Choi coughed as he herded the generals toward the door. "Come, come. I would like to show you around our little people's enterprise we have here, called Hoa Hao Unlimited Ltd." We followed them out the door, exchanging looks of relief.

Which faded instantly. Phat was pointing at the helicopter. "I meant to mention it before. How have you managed to get a helicopter?"

Arlington prefaced his answer with a short laugh. "Then you've heard how hard it is to get one. Actually, I found that, as a general, I can get one nearly all the time, if it's available. This particular one is assigned to IV Corps headquarters. I simply assigned it to myself for the day."

"Amazing," said Phat thoughtfully. "I've always wondered what it would be like riding in one. Do you think, perhaps . . . ?"

"Certainly. I would've thought . . . never mind. When we finish this tour, I'll have my pilot take you up."

"Very good," said Phat, beaming.

As rehearsed, we worked our way in between the two generals, separating them into two groups. I ended up with Phat and Choi, who kept up a rapid-fire conversation of camp defenses, our medical program, and how bad the rains were this year. Ten yards ahead of us were Arlington and his group.

As we passed through the camp gate, Phat stopped and put his hand on Choi's shoulder. He spoke in Vietnamese. "I must tell you something, Major. I had doubts about the authenticity of the reports I heard about the Con Mat operating in this area. Frankly, I thought they would notify me of any special operations in my area. But then I received word of how the brave Hoa Hao sank part of the Sou— I mean, part of the enemy's navy at Chau An. Masterful!" With his arm still around Choi's shoulder, Phat turned and then continued walking. "Tell me again, Choi, how many boats did we sink? One? Two? Beautiful!"

Choi fed him the highlights of the infamous Hoa Hao battle with the Navy, skipping the fact that the fight had started as a barroom brawl over a girl.

In front of us an elderly Hoa Hao woman shooed away a flock of skinny chickens. No children were visible on the streets today. The village was clean, quiet, and tense. The only movement was the Hoa Hao flag curling around itself over the headquarters of Hoa Hao Unlimited Ltd.

Choi finished the story as we entered the building. Arlington was halfway through the assembly line. It took me a moment to realize that the room seemed strange because there was not the usual chatter and gossip. Only steady *clink-clink-clinks* from the treadles of the Singers. Every head was bowed intently over its machine; every foot moved in a steady, controlled rhythm, lest a mistake call unwanted attention to its owner.

Santee, who was with our group, unrolled his "Let me tell you all about Hoa Hao Unlimited Ltd." speech. Phat listened intently, and more intently when Santee got to the bra paragraph. Phat picked up a 32C from a nearby table and felt it.

"Very interesting," he chuckled, nudging Choi in the side. Choi smiled weakly.

Santee ignored the comments. "Our distribution to the people is picking up considerably. We are now producing more than seventy-five brassieres a day. . . ."

He continued talking as he led the general from machine to machine. The women were back to making bras individually. We had tried the Aristocrat's idea about assembly-line bras, but the women said it was too repetitive and boring. Plus, each woman had a stronger feeling of accomplishment when she sewed a bra from beginning to end by herself.

The reasons for our rapid increase in sales were Santee's

training program for salesmen and our new junk, christened the *Harvest Wind*. She was back in the water and today was selling clothes and bras along the Xuyen Song Doa canal. In the more remote areas the salesmen went in on foot with sample kits, took orders, and carried the goods back themselves. It was not a strict cash program. We accepted goods for payment and even extended credit until the next harvest season. Our PT boat, named *Dragon's Tooth*, was not fully operable yet. She was in a hidden berth behind Tan Dao. We had to keep some secrets.

". . . and an aluminum rolling machine, which should be here soon," said Santee, winding up his speech.

Phat said, "Hmmm. All of this stuff sounds rather capitalistic."

"Ah, hah!" said Choi. "That is the best part. This factory belongs to more than twenty thousand people—and more every day. In fact, we've gone a step further than socialism and actually given people a piece of paper, certifying their part ownership in the company. All this"—he waved his arm around—"was built and paid for by the people themselves. And the people get the profits."

Choi lowered his voice slightly. "Are you familiar with the term 'Common stock,' General?"

"Common stock? No."

"Then let me tell you how the people make money. You see, in return for a small contribution to the company (which is in turn used to buy new machinery and create more jobs), we give each person a common stock certificate, representing one share. If the people's company should make excess income, beyond costs and expansion, it is given back to the people in the form of dividends. These are paid . . ."

Choi explained to Phat the intricacies of being a stockholder, while I, thirsting for a drink to replace the pints I had lost sweating today, found a warm sassy in the corner. Nearby, a sewing machine operator looked at me with a question on her face. I winked and whispered, "Okay."

She smiled, showing betel-nut-stained teeth, and went back to pushing the treadle.

I had no doubt that, in the other group, Teewee and Top were enthusiastically extolling Hoa Hao Unlimited Ltd. as a fine example of capitalism at its best. Whatever we called it, it remained impressive that nine months ago this factory had not existed and these people had been sitting at home minding the kids. Sipping and waiting.

By the time I caught up with Choi and Phat, they were entering one of the rooms at the far end.

"And in here we have our flag-making section," said Choi, handing Phat one of the battalion-size Viet Cong flags, neatly pressed and folded.

Phat said, "Yes. I have seen some of your work. I believe several of our companies now order their flags from you. Fine work. I shall recommend your company to my officers. Tell me, does the enemy know that our company makes flags for the Vietnam People's Army?"

"Yes, but as mementos for GIs. They buy quite a few from us as souvenirs to take home."

"Our flags? Souvenirs? Crazy Americans."

"Enemy," said Choi.

"Enemy."

Choi, throwing out a steady fog of conversation, bypassed the room across the way in which the fake AK-47s and GI dog tags were being made. Arlington, of course, was shown that room, with the story that we were an independent subcontractor for a Philippine company in Saigon.

As we left the building, Phat put his arm around Choi and said in a near whisper, "Look here, Choi, I happen to have a few piasters saved, and I wonder if—" I couldn't hear the rest of the conversation.

Near the front of the building, I spotted Arlington and Teewee and walked to them.

Arlington was saying, "Excellent initiative you've shown. Did you say you were interested in being a meatcutter?"

"Yes," said Wheaty, replying in a shaky bass. "I've completed the La Frume Correspondence Course in Advanced Meat Cutting. I'm also studying their new course in private investigating. Of course, those things are only if I decide someday to get out of the Army."

"Something to fall back on, eh? You should think twice about leaving the Army, young man. Great career potential for bright young men. Especially with a war like this one going on. With the combat experience and the work you're doing for the Agency, there's no telling where you'll end up. Although don't get me wrong, meat cutting is a good profession to have in reserve should worse come to the worst."

A few minutes of small talk later, we were joined by Choi and Phat, who reminded Arlington of his promised helicopter ride.

"Sure," said Arlington. "I'll have my pilot give you a spin around the area."

As we started toward camp, Phat said, "Between us, Arlington, how soon do you think we can defeat them?"

My heart stopped.

Arlington said, "To be honest, Phat, I don't know. We can win, but the enemy is tough. And persistent. They're a lot tougher than we figured."

"You're right there. Our original timetable to win this war was five years. We never thought they would commit as many men and supplies as they have."

And just as I felt blood being circulated again, Arlington asked Phat, "Have you heard any reports of the enemy using tanks?"

Phat said, "Yes, a few. But mostly in II Corps and around Saigon."

"Yes, I've heard of the ones around Saigon, also. Tch. Tch."

We reached the chopper and helped Phat in. I wasn't

worried about the pilot accidentally blowing the game—the noise in a Huey foiled any conversation.

"Good luck," shouted Choi as the helicopter lifted.

A half hour later Phat was back, and we were all saying good-byes. He had been thrilled and exhilarated by the ride, but it was late afternoon and both generals wanted to move before dark.

Arlington left first. "A very enlightening afternoon, Major Choi. With men like you and General Phat, the Vietnamese people can look forward to a brighter future. Take care of my little investment. General Phat, a real pleasure meeting you. Good luck in your assignment in Cambodia."

Phat said, "Thank you, General. But the good luck should go with you to Can Tho. You are embarking on an exciting and valuable mission for us all."

"Ah, well, yes. Thank you." We saluted and less than a minute later the chopper was airborne.

Phat shaded his eyes and watched the helicopter bank to the left and aim southward. "A fine machine. That's what I need. But *c'est la vie.*"

A few minutes later Phat left, carrying a green-and-white lawn chair Choi had given him.

"Whooeee! Goddamn!" shouted Top. "It worked!" We were all grinning like idiots and shaking hands and slapping each other on the back.

"Gentlemen," said Choi, raising a hand, "I would like to announce that General Phat bought one hundred shares of Hoa Hao Unlimited Ltd. and General Arlington bought one hundred and seventy-five shares. I would also like to announce that beer is now"—he clapped his hands—"being served."

Two strikers carried out a case of beer, covered with ice.

"I'll have to eat my words," said Top, punching holes in the first can. "We pulled it off."

"There were some close moments," said Cranston.

"The middle path," Choi said softly. "It was amazing that it worked so well. But if you don't use the words 'Viet Cong' or 'American' or 'South Vietnamese,' it all pretty much sounds the same. By eliminating their flags, those two generals, sworn enemies, sounded the same."

We ate supper that night with Choi and his staff—a celebration over the success of Parthian Shot and a going-away party for us. In spite of the Ba Muoi Bas and the rice wine, there was an undercurrent of sadness. For the four of us who were leaving, Nan Phuc had become more than a home; it had been a testing ground and a proving ground. We had risked our asses, in Teewee's case literally, for certain things and certain people. And the risk had been worth it. Perhaps not in the grand sense of winning the war or the hearts and minds of the people. If the truth were known, they had won our hearts and minds. But in the smaller, more personal sense of getting our corner of it straight. Of Top and his hybrid seeds. Of Hood and his geography lessons. Of me and my patients. Of even Wheaty and his bookkeeping for the company. As for the two of us who were staying, they would be on their own now. A new life and the playing of the game to its end. A big gamble with big stakes. For the first time in a year Santee spent an entire meal without talking about one of his many plans to get rich.

It wasn't until much later that night, about 2030 hours, to be exact, that I found out Top wasn't going with us tomorrow. We had the first shift of guard duty together. Somehow it was fitting that my last night at Nan Phuc I would be on guard.

"What?" I said.

"You heard me, *bac si*. I'll catch up with you all later. Phat put the word on Choi today. A group of American prisoners is being held in a temporary camp near Banam. It's on the Mekong about sixty miles inside Cambodia. I'm leaving tomorrow with Frenchy. With luck, we can be there in three or four days. There's a chance part of the old team will be there," Top said.

I ejected the clip from my carbine and checked the bullets. There was nothing I could say.

"By the way, Top, I'll be hand-carrying your X-rays and medical records with me to the group surgeon. You might lose them here. Just drop in there when you get to Danang."

I could make out Top's crooked grin in the dark. "You're catching on, *bac si*. You might make a good medic yet."

The night was chilly and cloudy. We spoke little. There were too many thoughts and feelings to narrow any down to words.

I asked, "You have what? Seventeen, eighteen years in?"

"Seventeen. And I feel every one of them."

"You going to retire at twenty?"

"I don't know. It depends on what they offer to stay on." He laughed harshly.

"What'll you do if you get out?"

He leaned back. "That's hard to say. I don't know a damn thing except the Army, and there ain't much use for old tankers. I thought about going down to the Everglades and seeing if they'd let me be a highway patrolman. Or maybe an ABC officer. Chase down bootleggers. You ever see old Army sergeants after they retire? If they don't die an alcoholic, they become a cop. Or both." He stopped and laughed strangely. "Killing people is all I know. It's all I've ever been trained for." His voice held bitterness and sadness. The explanation was somewhere between a reason and an excuse.

"What about going back home?"

"Shit, no! There's a few good people there, and there's a lot of crooks. The cops are as rotten as the politicians. I'm a prejudiced motherfucker and I guess I always will be. I'm just not cut out to be one of those liberal do-gooders. But there's a difference between being prejudiced and being crooked."

I saw what Top was saying. The pattern was too deep. The identity was too fixed.

He asked, "Did I ever tell you about the first moonshine I ever sold?"

"No."

"I was thirteen, and the first pint of shine I sold was on a Sunday morning to the sheriff, who was dressed in civilian clothes. In fact, he became a steady customer of mine," Top said, chuckling at the memory. "Sure like to take a little moon with me into Cambodia. I figure me and Frenchy can catch a ride over the Mekong and borrow or steal a sampan . . ." Top talked on about his trip the next morning.

It looked like, as Top would say, every swinging dick in Nan Phuc had come down to see us off. My duffel bags were already aboard *Granny*. Choi was not going with us—the first stockholder's meeting of Hoa Hao Unlimited Ltd. was coming up tomorrow—but he was here shaking hands with us all. The excitement had gotten to me. In spite of guard duty last night, I had been awakened by the mad drummer of Nan Phuc at 0500 hours this morning. Over the months I had grown inured to his predawn pounding.

I spotted Phu in the crowd and went to him. In the six weeks I had been training him, he had grown into a medic I was proud to turn the dispensary over to. Choi had promoted him to sergeant, and Lon had him writing and reading Vietnamese like a high-school graduate. He was still a little shaky on sterile technique, but he would do. He understood the theory of medication and could handle minor surgery better than I.

"Phu, I want to wish you good luck with the dispensary. Remember, do no harm. And I have something for you." I gave him a small package wrapped in a towel in lieu of wrapping paper.

He opened it and his face lit up. It was my personal Special

Forces emergency medical kit, which was given to each graduate of dog lab back at Bragg. It might not sound like much to someone who's not a medic, but it held forceps, scissors, scalpels, and all sorts of other shiny instruments. Phu grabbed and hugged me.

As I turned to go, he handed me a new bottle of Tiger Balm. Someone shouted from *Granny*, "Let's go. Get aboard."

Cranston and Lao were there. I held them both close and wished them long lives, happiness, and many children. I imagined I could see a little protrusion from Lao's stomach. Lovely Lao even kissed me on the lips. She smelled of lotus blossoms.

"Far out, man," said Cranston, mocking his own slang. "Seriously, take care of your life and be good to people." As we shook hands good-bye, I felt him slide something into my palm. I glanced down. It was a finely rolled joint. He whispered, "I know you don't smoke. But take this one anyway. The first crop of aristograss came in. It's very pleasant."

I shook hands with Santee, who in black pants, white shirt, and sunglasses looked for all the world like a black Vietnamese businessman. Wednesday I had sold back to him all my stock in the company. He'd bought the shares at one hundred and forty piasters each. "The price is already going up," he had said. "It's like the over-the-counter market, and I'm the only market maker around so far. We're quoting one thirty-five bid, one forty asked now. We've had inquiries all the way from Can Tho about buying stock."

But this morning he was subdued, even a hint of melancholy in his eyes.

"Good luck, Leroy," I said.

"I found my home, Phil. It's already been good luck."

Top, dressed for his patrol and carrying his knapsack, was saying good-bye to each of us, in his own way.

"Wheaty, be a good officer. Think once in a while and for

God's sake quit trying to sound like a damn cow. Talk normally," said O'Hara.

Teewee, who was proudly wearing a Vietnamese purple heart (WIA or "wounded in the ass," as we all quickly pointed out), blushed and said, "Thanks, Top," in a tenor.

"Hood, I still think you're yellow for leaving. But I knew you'd try anything to make sergeant major before me."

Hood shook hands with Top, taking Top's hand in both of his. "*You* be careful, you goddamned crazy fool. Your ass better be down in Saigon in a week, or I'm coming out here after you."

To me, Top said, "And, Warren, shithead, let me give you some advice. Don't try and kill any rats with a knife. Of course, anybody crazy enough to be dating a colonel's daughter couldn't have much sense anyway. Though I don't see what she wants in a bald-headed medic."

"Good-bye, Top. I hope you find them."

"The way I figure, either I'll find them . . . or . . . I won't."

We went aboard, and as we were pulling anchor, I heard Santee talking to Choi about a holding company with a subsidiary franchising out Hoa Hao rice stands.

Minutes later we were in midstream, turning to the south and unfurling *Granny*'s quilted sails. On shore several hundred people were waving good-byes. I waved until I couldn't see the town any more.

Along the banks early morning fog was rising slowly. It would be a long sail to Can Tho. We had a good wind, and the motors were not running. I rubbed Tiger Balm under my nose to keep the evil spirits away. In the distance someone was singing. Hmmm. It sounded familiar. I cocked my head. Yes, it was familiar. A man's voice, singing high and pure and in Hebrew. It was the "Hava N'gila."

Yes, it would be a long time going home again.

25

THAT WAS all a few years ago. And that was how I had planned to end my book.

Until I received a newspaper clipping in the mail from Top. There was no letter, and the return address on the envelope was "Sgt. Maj. Wiley O'Hara, Womack Army Hospital, Fort Bragg, North Carolina."

The story read:

Military Reports
Worst Bombing
Accident to Date

SAIGON—(UPI)—The U. S. Military Command yesterday reported American jets accidentally killed 85 South Vietnamese civilians and soldiers when the planes mistakenly bombed a small village a week ago.

Another 121 civilians and soldiers were wounded. It was the worst such incident of the war thus far.

Lt. Col. Harold Petram, MAAG briefing officer, said Air Force jets dropped more than 15 tons of high explosives last Thursday on Nan Phuc, a small village near the Cambodian border in the South Vietnamese delta. The incident was not revealed until yesterday, Petram said, because of a preliminary investigation.

The area had been one of the most secure in all South Vietnam.

Among those killed were a Maj. Lam Than Choi, the commander of a government outpost there, two unidentified Americans, and a number of women and children. A small textile factory was also demolished.